Sunset

A Novel

Ry C. A.

Printed in the United States of America

First Printing, 2021

ISBN: 978-0-578-92605-6 (Paperback)

Dedication

To my wife, my perfect partner.
To my sons, my inspiration.
To my family and the community that raised me.
I can't imagine a better childhood.

CHAPTER 1

Prologue

Most people would be terrified to be out at sea. To be buried under a dark moonless night far enough away from shore where stars have escaped the lights of Los Angeles, with nothing to hold onto, nothing to stand upon, and God knows what, filling the depths below.

Underneath a great black canvas, Jack floats at the surface above the leagues of water that lay below. He feels his open wound and calculates all that has poured through it, everything that he has already lost, and the feeling of fading away overwhelms him.

Jack is out in the channel, a fissure on the ocean floor, an underwater canyon created by divergent tectonic plates. One plate flees west toward open water, while the other is slowly crushed under by another coming to takes its place. Out here, in deep water, is where monsters patrol.

The ocean laps over his shoulders, climbing his neck, and splashes unto his ears. Jack is exhausted, with not much more left in him. He raises his chin and breathes through his nose as he lowers further into the black sea surrounding him. He opens his mouth and lets the water pour in, and tastes the salt. Salt is everywhere. In every drop, and every drop has gathered to form a great ocean. The largest and deepest ocean. One named after peace.

The salt gives the water its buoyancy. Salt is lift. Salt is carry. One can let the salt pick them up, hold them, and keep them. Likewise, one can choose to slip under, to sink below, and let the salt drown them. To bury themselves not only under the night sky but under the night's inky black water as well. And lay themselves to rest in the rift on the ocean floor created from being torn apart.

The water climbs over Jack's ears, and he can so clearly hear his beating heart. His breath escapes into the night in a thunderous hush, and the following inhale is quiet in comparison and feels so short of what his body needs. The hairline above his forehead dips below the surface as he floats on his back, with only his face, eyes, chin, and mouth, out of the water.

He looks up at the brightest star to cut through. Its pulsating light is ancient. The star producing it is at an unfathomable distance, and even as fast as light travels, Jack sees the light it created before the dawn of man. Still, it has arrived at that moment to shine that down onto the water that night. A message from the past only now come home. He makes a wish. He can feel the depth below and space above. He isn't scared or worried. He's finally free. Free to make his own decision. And right now, he is only thinking of where he should let the salt take him tonight.

CHAPTER 2

September 2, 2007

How often does someone find a bullet? Perhaps, like most things, it depends on the circumstances, where it's discovered, and by whom. Suppose the place it's found is somewhere considered an unlikely location for a bullet to be. And that the person who found it can be classified as someone who was never intended to come across something like it in the first place.

Aside from power lines that hang too close to homes, it is a beautiful street with mature palm trees that line the sidewalk. On sunny days the trees cast shade down the block, and the shade leaks onto the neighbor's front yards. Today is an odd day, though. The weather is wrong. Wrong for early Autumn. Today the palm fronds drape languidly against a lead sky full of moisture and heat.

Jack felt it, climbing the black railed stairs to his apartment. His clothes stick to his skin. It's the weather for another part of the country, for another time of year. But it has found him all the same. It only took a stride or two to get from the staircase to the thin worn welcome mat that sits in front of his screened-in door. He almost didn't notice it at first. Really such a small thing. And who would be looking for it? This isn't a bad part of Los Angeles, not compared to other places. It is adjacent to the town Jack grew up in, an affluent beach town, and there is value in it that other areas don't have. There are gangs. There is graffiti. But here, neighbors move their cars for weekly street cleaning and keep their lawns trimmed.

Still, stray fire is inherently random, so for Jack to come across a bullet, it's not out of accordance with probability no matter how unlikely it is supposed to be.

A misfired bullet lodges into wood, or plastic, or even thin metal. Or they flatten on impact against concrete or steel. The exterior to Jack's apartment is an inexpensive and easy to maintain soft stucco, which a bullet might sink deeply into, having missed its intended target. The apartment's finish is rough and uneven and would easily obscure a bullet's entry. The building's railings are steel painted black, paint-chipped in several places, and the stairways and walkways are made of cheap large grain concrete. Either of the railing and concrete would pancake a bullet if it fell from the sky. But that's what makes this so strange, and in part, has Jack asking himself questions. This bullet isn't embedded in a wall, and it isn't flattened on the ground. It sits perfectly upright and factory forged, with its firing casing completely intact.

Jack looks toward the street. Cars pass in volume on the road that runs parallel to the city block. Their engines grumble on as people inside commence with their morning commute. The power lines hum in harmony. He peers over the railing toward his neighbor's screened doors and their own thin green welcome mats that all come with the lease. There are three other apartments in the complex, each filled with a neighbor he has never met. He doesn't know if they own guns. It's possible that the bullet is one of theirs. It's possible then that this just an accident. A shell spilled from a box of ammo and left behind. Even at 18, Jack already knows all about accidents, oversights, and mishaps. Yes, it's possible it's a neighbor's bullet, in the sense that most simple events are possible. Possible, but unlikely, and that's because of the apartment buildings' black railing staircases. There are two apartments on the ground floor and two above. Each second-floor apartment has its own staircase leading to its own screened-in front door, and Jack has never in three years seen any of his neighbors walk up to his.

The bullet is black and small. Tiny for something so powerful, and yet Jack feels a tremendous weight as he holds it between his thumb and index finger. He holds it up to the overcast sky for further inspection. Moisture clings to his skin. Cars drone in the near distance. Power lines buzz in protest.

Behind him, a large palm peers over his shoulder, and the fronds wilt and swoon in the heat. The sky is wrong, wrong for early Autumn.

The bullet is wrong. Jack was never intended to find a bullet like this, but identities are true until they're not, until enough things fall into life to break them. Now the bullet is right.

He looks down at his father's watch, having to twist the face around to see it. The band is two links too big, and he has given up on the fact that he will ever fill it. The watch's abalone face shows that it's too early to find a thing like this after work dragged him through a long night.

Yes, Jack is thinking of all the potential outcomes and possibilities of coming across something like this, but he isn't asking himself why a bullet sits at his front door. The truth is he already knows the answer to why. Why it's there waiting for him. What he has done to come home to such a thing. Instead, he thinks about random accidents and mistakes and asks himself how often someone finds a bullet? How many can fall into a lifetime?

CHAPTER 3

February '01

"You have to accept some things in a story as true." It's Jack's turn to hold the flashlight, and he didn't have a chance to make a hand shadow puppet before Bree stopped him, telling him that his story didn't make sense.

She counters, "What if it's wrong? Do I have to accept them then?"

"You don't know that yet! The story is just beginning. You need to trust the storyteller a little." He defends himself, though truthfully, he hasn't figured out how the tale would go.

"Maybe I just don't trust you." They both laugh. They sit Indian style, with their legs crossed, on the floor of her bedroom, well past when her parents told them that they had to be asleep.

With a giggle in his throat, he continues, "You can poke holes in every story ever told. Characters don't behave like you would, or should. The story needs someone to turn left when they could have easily turned right, so the whole thing is just dumb luck. Or the bad thing that happens is really not that bad, at least not as bad as the characters act like it is. Or it's the solution. It's too unbelievable. Goes against everything that has happened up until that point. Or, it could be that the solution is too easy. Why didn't they just figure it out right away?"

She smiles, "Okay. Tell me an example."

Jack thinks for a bit and grips the flashlight. The flashlight is made of cheap light plastic, and the battery inside makes it completely unbalanced, with the weight entirely toward the bulb and battery upfront. As he tries to narrow down choices from the practically limitless options of stories to choose from, he bounces the unbalanced flashlight in hand. Hoping to come up with an answer that will help his dearest friend in need. Then he sees her bookshelf, "How about this?" He asks as he picks up Charlotte's Web.

"It's a kids' book and totally make-believe." She giggles.

"So?" He is adamant. "It's a good story. And there are so-called adult books that are just as made up and unbelievable." She smiles at him. He continues. "So in this book animals talk with each other. And have a good idea about what happens on a farm and what humans do to them. I'd say that's a stretch. Sure, the bad thing is that the main character is going to be slaughtered, so that isn't an overreaction." He laughs.

"Maybe not, huh?" She jokes.

"But, the solution is that the spider can write?"

"Hey! Spoiler alert!" They laugh.

"Okay, spoiler alert, the spider can write. You've read the book and know, but hey, just in case anyone else is listening. The point is, yes, it's a kid's story, so anything can happen, but even in a world where all of these things can happen, does it make sense? Why would anyone give the pig credit for what happens on a spider's web? To me, that's a stretch. Like, wouldn't they credit the spider first?"

"Yeah... it's a kid's story!"

"Well, you're still a kid, at least, last I checked." He continues. "But my point is that it doesn't matter. As long as the story makes you think or feel, then it has done its job. We can stop thinking about what would or should happen if it does either one. And we'll consider it a good story if that happens."

"You know Jack, you're too smart for 12. Has anyone ever told you that?" With that, she kisses him on the mouth. It is so quick that he doesn't have the time to purse his lips. This is his first kiss, and he knows for sure that this is hers as well. Warmth pours over his face and washes down his body. He wants to kiss her back, but he missed the chance. "Okay, go on." She permits.

He is too focused on the kiss coursing through his blood and pooling in his cheeks to begin. "Well?" She adds as if nothing happened at all.

Jack knows that he needs to tell her a story that will make her feel better. It will have to be a little sad to acknowledge her pain and sadness because when you don't talk about loss or pain, it stays within you. It doesn't just go away on its own. It grows silently inside of you and becomes a weight that drags on you, pulling you down from whatever your life was supposed to be. So yes, given her recent loss, there will have to be a fair amount of sadness, but mostly it will have to be uplifting, even when it doesn't seem like there will be a happy ending. There will have to be some mystery and drama. Some suspense and danger to keep her interested. Some childish, even rude humor to lighten the mood. And, of course, romance, but that could be just what he wants.

But that stuff isn't nearly as important as the message, the one that will cheer her up. That will make her feel better when she needs it. And Jack hopes so dearly that he can do that for her. To help her when something terrible has happened that she can barely talk about it. A tragedy only a week old, and he is the only friend that has been over since. It is his letter that she taped to the wall next to her bed when he knows for a fact that every child in her sixth-grade class wrote one.

They are best friends. And he hopes much more. He can be there for Bree, in the same way Jack's mother says that his father was there for her. During what she calls her dark days. Days that his mother never explains other than to say, "Your father saved me from the hard time I was going through. And then I was given a little angel from God as a gift for following his path." Then she always kisses and hugs Jack so tight that there is no doubt about the angel in her life, the gift from God.

Jack is sure he can do the same for Bree. But he can't be obvious about any of it. Because pointing it out will defeat the very purpose of the exercise. Which is to let Bree forget about her troubles for a moment. That's why he is there. To allow Bree to be something other than a little sister who lost her older brother, Adam. It's just like the shadow puppets that he'll cast on the wall of her bedroom. Neither will look at his hand; they will only see its imprint on the light, it's negative.

12

Similarly, his message will only be an imprint on the story told. The truth is something that cannot be said and cannot be seen. It can only be interpreted by the shadows it casts. And that meaning only comes through the story. With the cheap plastic flashlight in hand, while the rest of the house is mournfully dark and silent, Jack begins to tell her his story.

CHAPTER 4

September 2, 2007

His apartment bedroom is sunk in the shadow cast from the blinds of his window, blocking the streetlamp outside. More dim than dark.

Smashely asks, "Have you told him yet?"

"No," Jack responds. He found the bullet earlier that day and moved on with himself as if it didn't matter. Day drinking at the beach with his friends, playing a volleyball game where you have to pound a beer if you let the ball hit the ground without getting at least a finger on it.

And when he had drunk enough, he answered her phone call, and despite his friend's protests, he met her back at his apartment, and they moved immediately to the bedroom.

"Ugh. Are you going to?"

"Maybe." He lies to her just as he has tried to lie to himself that morning. Pretending that the message placed on his mat didn't apply to him and wouldn't change anything. And when he did, the sorrow of what he has become, and the anger at everything and everyone that made him that way, thinned into something he could ignore.

But she isn't talking to him about the bullet. He hasn't told anyone about it. Certainly not her. And will probably never mention it to anyone. None of them would understand anyway.

They lay next to each other, he on his side, she on her back. Her arm rests above her head. Sheets gather diagonally across her chest. It does little to hide the rise and fall of her long, slender body, its nooks, and round forms.

She reaches over and runs her hand along his back. Jack feels the weight shift in the mattress. Fingertips drag along his skin. He faces away from her toward the wall. She is reaching out to him, reaching for something inside of him, something that remains out of her grasp. He closes his eyes in the dark and thinks thoughts that go unshared.

"I shouldn't have come over," Smashley says with a disapproving sigh like he's let her down. Her leg stretches over to his side of the bed.

"It's okay." Jack lies again. He is on the farthest edge of his side. The old mattress has broken down, and the middle of it dips, and if Jack isn't careful and moves only a little, he will fall back toward her.

"Now, I'm completely missing out," she huffs.

He exhales and says without any sympathy, "Sorry." Jack keeps his balance on the small plateau near the edge, a place no one slept on enough to wear out. It is old, so its breaking down is not unexpected. His parents bought it before he was born. To help his mother during her lone pregnancy, which was full of sore hips and a tight lower back. At least, that is what his mom told him when he was young and would climb into bed with her on sleepy weekends. "You were such a big baby", she said, "I had to waddle from the bed to the bathroom, and back to bed cause I could hardly move." Jack spent those mornings in her arms, with her stroking his hair before his dad came back from surfing to make a pancake breakfast. "I'll bet you an ice cream cone after dinner I can flip this one five times," his dad made sure to drop the pancake and lose the bet. That was back when Jack wasn't old enough to join his father in the water.

Smashley challenges him. "You always say that. But you don't mean it."

"What do you mean, I don't mean it?" He feigns.

"You'd be nicer to me if you did."

"When I say something, I mean it," he lies again.

"Why am I here with you?" She asks while taking up so much of the space of the king-size bed that used to be his parent's and given to him when it became pretty evident that he is the only one left to use it.

"I'm sorry. I don't know," Now, Jack isn't lying. Her hand continues to stroke his back.

At least she has fought for him. Which is more than he can say than just about anyone else. Like Senior year prom when Smashley made Jack's date cry in the party bus on the way to the hotel. Smashely started telling rumors about Jack's date the week leading up to the dance. Smashley had that type of influence where she could spread something quickly, and the kids would feel obligated to repeat to her.

Smashley and her friends laughed loudly around the girl after whispering to each other secrets. And they stared in Jack's date's general direction to make sure the girl understood at whom they were laughing.

When they boarded the bus, Smashley and her friends became even more direct, yelling in the darkness all the things they had been keeping to themselves. The words are not owned by a single source, unclaimed by any person, the barking of distant chimps, raining down on Jack's date from the treetops. Jack's poor date broke down with sobs she kept to herself and tears she wiped away at as quickly as they came.

That's when Smashley left anonymity behind and stood over the girl and gave all those horrible things a face and a mouth to say them.

As tall as she is, just shy of six feet, Smashley uses her height to glower down at people. Most girls shrink under her, and Jack's date was no exception. His date ran past the line drawn on the floor that demarcates the no past point to the bus' door, standing on steps leading down to the exit, despite the driver's yelling to move back and forcing the bus to pull over in a hurry.

Jack should have known better and just gone with Smashley instead, but they were fighting at the time, which is more often than not, the status of their relationship. But they always seem to get back together. Just like they did prom night. After his date bailed in tears. When Smashley put a hand on Jack's shoulder to prevent him from standing as his first impulse, and the ensuing commotion of the driver yelling, and everyone else yelling, and Jack freezing and ultimately doing nothing despite an instinct to the contrary. The poor girl didn't stand a chance. It was Jack's fault to even put her in that position.

Smashley is a bully, but it isn't that she will only pick on younger girls. She has also fought with college girls, back from school, visiting their hometown. And girls from elsewhere who attended some school nearby.

And now she is college-aged, at least technically by a month to be specific. But Jack is now thinking of all the women that she has fought off over the last year. She is fearless in a way he admires. Though he has never told her. She has even taken on grown women, professional women, perhaps twice her age, and all for him. And yet, he can't find any words for her. He feels sorry for Smashley, and he has told her as much, just not why.

A drowning man will cling to anything and pull it down with them, and Jack is no exception. So when he says that he doesn't know why they're together, it's because Jack knows they shouldn't be, not because he doesn't understand the reason why.

They're together because he has little else to hold on to, and she keeps fighting for him, even though she shouldn't, and he shouldn't allow her. It's more than flattery. Its devotion, ugly, toxic, and misguided, but devotion nonetheless. When someone is abandoned, as Jack has been, the persistence of another by itself can feel like enough.

Simultaneously she can't lose. She can't let herself be defeated. Jack has a good guess why that is, why she'll never quit, but that has nothing to do with Jack. Still, he gets to be wanted. And not in the way most women want him. He has enough people who desire him. Smashley wants to possess him, and deep down, Jack needs someone to want ownership of him.

They find a way to satisfy adjacent needs in each other, the pieces broken inside of them, that does nothing to mend the damage. In fact, their very actions create more significant strains than existed before. Smashley, who has always gotten the men she wants, has picked him as a prize that has to be won again and again. In this dynamic, she must feel more defeat than victory. And he gets to be something worth winning but not worth keeping.

If she finally realized that it's harmful and stopped playing games for him, maybe they could find people who actually make them happy, perhaps even making themselves whole. He knows this, and she doesn't. That's why he feels sorry for her. But anytime he loosens his grip, tries letting go, the lack of another handhold serves as a reminder that he has nothing else to which he can grasp. And so he must keep her at arms distance.

"It's only… you still haven't set your clock? How long is that going to take?" She exclaims indignantly, pulling her hand away from him. A red blinking clock flashes on the darkened nightstand. She brought it over months ago. The clock's light is caught on the glass top at an oblique angle so that it is warped and blurred in its reflection. He has never set it, so the clock set itself and flashes as a reminder that time passes incorrectly.

"I'll get to it." It's gotten to a point where he can lie without thought.

"You've only been saying that for two months." She shifts her weight on the mattress and picks up her phone. "It's only 11! I should be out at our kappa sigma chi mixer. Instead, I'm stuck here with you." She blames him even though she was the one who asked to come over. "Really, you should come up and visit me and be my date."

Jack thinks for a bit. "I don't know. The French are assholes." He wonders if she knows he's quoting a movie. It might be better if she doesn't know that. Maybe the confusion it would cause would kill the conversation.

"I just want to show you off to my new friends. Come on, be my arm candy for a night."

This starts a fight that they had several times over the summer. She knows Jack doesn't feel comfortable with the idea of going to college functions simply because he'll eventually be asked if he goes to that school, and then when Jack says no, they'll ask what school he does go to, and Jack can't think of a good answer to that question. Even though he's imagined this particular scenario over and over again so that he can prepare the best possible responses to any situation, he can't come up with anything that he'll feel good saying.

"What are you going to tell people when you and The Tard move in together?" She sounds angry, but she is busy playing with her new phone, which doesn't have any buttons.

"That's different. You're talking about a school thing. House parties will be easier." His tone is combative, even if he doesn't mean to sound like that. He takes a breath and tries again, "I'll feel out of place at your thing."

"You're just coming up with excuses as to why you don't want to hang out with me. I don't even know why we're together. You don't even have a driver's license. What kind of person doesn't have a driver's license?" She always likes to point out the things he lacks.

He retaliates, "We're not together. We broke up. Remember?"

"This again?" The light from her phone turns off. He can feel her body roll toward his. Her hand is back on him again.

"Yes." He lets his eyes roll towards her but otherwise stays still, safely tucked on his plateau.

"Why haven't you told him yet?" She asks.

"Because…" He stops and remembers he doesn't owe her an explanation. He is the wronged person, the one who was betrayed.

She starts to protest before he can finish. Listing all the reasons why they belong together, including their looks, height, popularity, and athleticism. Jack looks at the clock's flashing light like a caution sign. "People are drawn to us." She finishes.

He doesn't correct her on any of it, but she must note his silence as disagreement because she starts to list her accolades. "Captain of a volleyball team that finished top ten in the country. Enrolled at USC. The first girl to receive a bid from Kappa. And voted Most Beautiful girl in high school." It's impressive how she rattles them off so fast. As if it were practiced. She stops stroking his skin, and instead, she cusps his shoulder.

"Yeah, you're awesome," he says sarcastically. His hand pantomimes in the dim light though neither one can see.

"And I hardly ever talk about any of it because you don't really have anything going for you! And I feel bad bringing any of it up because I don't want to make you feel like a loser." It's a speech he has heard too many times to believe she doesn't like bringing it up.

"Yeah, Smashley, you're really good about that." He pushes back, knowing full well where using her nickname will take the conversation. He just can't help it anymore.

"You know I hate when you call me that. Some fucking stupid name you and your dumb fucking friends made up." She pulls her hand away, and it claps against the comforter as it comes down to her side. "I can't believe you haven't said anything to him."

"Why would I?" But he thinks for a second. Maybe he should get in front of it. Let his friend know that it's not a big deal. Not that he would tell her even that he did broach the subject with his buddy.

"You're such a fucking pussy." She laughs louder than necessary, a derisive cackle.

"Does it fucking matter?" He rolls on his back. Looking up to the bars of light that have slipped through blinds cast on the ceiling. He knows it doesn't. Not to him, but he has moved off his plateau and closer to her.

"Yes, it fucking matters! Don't you care at all?" She props up on her elbows.

"Do I care? Do you?" Finally, he looks at her. Her delicate features glow in the low light.

"Well, you're the one that broke things off!" She defends herself.

"Yeah. This time I did. This time, and maybe a couple of times before that. But you've dumped me a dozen or so times over the last year. You're the one who hooked up with one of my friends the moment we broke up. I never touched any of yours. And why should it matter? We aren't together. We shouldn't be. The fact that we are talking about this is a giant red siren blaring in our faces! We're not good for each other."

"I only did it to get your attention. I did it for you."

Her voice seamlessly drops a decibel, and her tone raises an octave. She is changing into the victim, which would make Jack the perpetrator.

"You did it for me?" He laughs sarcastically.

"You know it would be nice if you cared at all. About me. About anything."

"Maybe I just can't." His words slip through unguarded. She won't pick up on the genuine fear in his voice, though, because she isn't interested in talking about him if it doesn't concern her. Still, it's better if he doesn't let it happen again.

"You're such a fucking loser. I already have so many guys at school lining up to take me on a date. Something you've never done." Her body crashes back onto the mattress in a thud.

"Great. Bring back leftovers if the food's any good," Jack says coolly. He's regained himself.

"Ugh. How many of your friends do I have to fuck before you get mad?"

Jack bathes in her anger and calmly replies, "hmmm... A million."

She kicks him under the covers. "Fuck you!"

Jack feels the springs of his mattress release. The comforter slides quickly toward her side, pulling away from his torso. The bedroom door opens, Jack hears a voice from the television in the living room, and then she closes the door quickly. He stares at the clock. It blinks slowly back at him, laboriously, reminding him just how wrong it is. The sound of the power lines outside his window fills the room. Two digits turn on the clock before the bedroom door opens again. The mattress springs compress. Pillows make light sounds as they are adjusted.

"That was fast. A million just isn't as big a number as it used to be." He's still composed and without any noticeable emotion.

"You're such a dick." She says without emotion either.

"I know." He is honest again. "Tell me again why you think we're perfect together?"

She runs down the same list given has before and adds, "For whatever reason people want us around. They want to hear what we have to say. And then there are our fathers."

Jack does everything he can to stop screaming into his pillow. "Your dad just remarried. He lives in Ventura. You get Christmas and birthday gifts."

"So that's okay then? I'm not allowed to be fucking sad about my dad leaving my mom and me for some other family just because I get presents and cards? But I never get to see him, but that's okay." She has a point that Jack has to concede.

"You're right. I'm sorry." He feels bad for how it came out. It's his best guess as to why she wants Jack. She seems to constantly need to prove that her father was wrong, that he made a mistake, and that she is a person worth keeping. Any perceived loss that she suffers justifies his leaving, and so stakes are always higher for her than anyone else. And when Jack is honest with himself, like when a flashing clock reminds him that he wastes his time, he'll admit that he too needs to prove that he is worth keeping, and then it makes even more sense why they are together. They're both hurt in similar ways.

Jack continues, "I didn't mean to sound like that. Just the circumstances are different. That's all I'm saying. Look, your mom remarried, and you like your stepdad, right? Now, look at me. You think it's the same thing?"

"I'm sorry too. It doesn't matter anyway." The only time she says anything worthwhile is when she isn't trying.

Jack rolls back over to the edge of the mattress, and they resume their previous positions, including her leg stretching far over toward his side. He asks earnestly toward the wall, "Why do we do this again?"

"It's nothing. Just stupid fights." She reassures him, and Jack can feel her pull the covers over to her. At least she has fought for him, which is more than he can say about anyone else. Finally, her hand reaches back again. Reaching for something inside of Jack that remains out of her grasp. She is beautiful, and so is he. He feels sorry for her.

"When are you going to tell him that you know? You are going to confront him, right? If you don't, I will." She threatens in the softest, pillow tone.

Jack doesn't respond. He lays silently on the edge of the mattress in the dim room, making sure to keep his balance, watching the time pass in red, and imagines the numbers moving in reverse to unwind the person he has become.

All those unshared thoughts scream at him for hours, keeping him from sleep. Then without warning, his front door thuds as if it were being kicked. He goes to his closet for the guns.

CHAPTER 5

August '01

"Aren't they so cute together?" She asks. The breeze pushes off the water in a fit. Jack holds down his corner of the towel while Bree's hair whips his shoulders and neck. The rushing air is loud, so Jack's mother projects and her voice carries through. Jack eavesdrops.

He and Bree share a towel. Both are on their stomachs facing the ocean. Their parents sit on canvas folding beach chairs in a semi-circle, yards away.

The kids are slightly closer to the water, inside the high tide mark, but safely out of reach of low tide's push. Sandpipers scurry along the shoreline with their stick-like legs, hunting burrowing sand crabs. Jack watches them chase after the receding water with their beaks poking in the wet sand, digging for food, and pretends not to hear the parents through a gusty late summer afternoon, and he steals glances their way.

"I know what you mean. I think they're adorable," Bree's mother agrees. A closed rainbow-striped umbrella lies at her feet. The sun is four hands from the water. Ribbons of cirrus clouds occupy the high canopy of the sky.

"I can just picture the grandkids. They'd have Jack's curly hair and Bree's beautiful green eyes," Jack's mother continues loudly. He's grateful that the other block families have left and that no one else is close enough to hear.

The afternoon crowd is thin compared to the midday peak. When the beach is full of clusters of people, towels and chairs huddled around one or two umbrellas. The families trend toward the water while young adults remain closer to the strand. On a crowded day- and today was one of those days- people scattered across the wide strip of beach that pushes for miles in both directions. One group adjacent to the next dwindling as the day goes along.

"Hey, those were my eyes first," Bree's Father interrupts, his arm resting on a cooler. "Did you hear that? Your wife thinks I have beautiful eyes," he says in sarcastic confidence.

"Jack's smarts," her mother continues despite the interruption.

"You should hear what she says about your ass," Jack's father retorts, holding a beer in his hand, which they all do, except for Jack's mother. Another closed umbrella leans against the side of his chair.

"Yeah. Is it that it sits on my neck?" Bree's father cheerfully answers. Jack's father says something that Jack can't hear behind a particularly loud gust of wind, but the trailing laughter is audible.

The wind is typical for this time of day at this time of year. Southern swells begin at the end of July and last until November, bringing with them warm water. The rise in the ocean's temperature prevents the fog so prevalent in the early summer months when warm air meets cold water. The warm rising air over the land pulls with it the air from over the ocean. If that air is crisp because the water is cold, then it will create fog. Fog sits, it blocks, and the wind doesn't move. When that water is warm, the air pulled with it is not cold enough to create fog, and it runs from off the water to fill the void of the lifting inland sky until it too is heated and rises. And then the cycle continues.

Even now, as the sun approaches the ocean, the air is still warm, though mildly so compared to the earlier high. The breeze is pulling from over the sea, bringing with it a coolness that still feels refreshing, only if just in the memory of the waning heat. Once equilibrium is created, and the air temperature off the water and over the land is nearly the same, the air becomes still, and the ocean follows suit. This time of calm, usually just before the sun sets, is the evening glass.

"Oh, Bree's athleticism for sure," Jack's mother chimes in, ignoring her husband as well.

"Damn!" Jack's dad continues to laugh, "I think we might be hanging out too much."

Bree's mother boasts, "Let's be honest. If the kids get either of their looks, they will be doing just fine."

"Yeah, I know, man. I hate you too," Bree's dad sounds severe, but the trail of chuckles gives away the sarcasm.

His mom quips, "Hopefully, the sense of humor is passed down from the mother," but both men don't hear or just don't register the slight.

"The holiday dinners would be so fun," Her mom exclaims.

"We practically do every holiday together anyway," Jack's father protests.

"Do we? With Captain heavy hand here pouring drinks, I can never remember," her father teases. However, Jack, on several occasions, including many holiday parties, has heard him say as much.

"I would love it if they were high school sweethearts," His mother says. Jack side-eyes Bree. He wonders if she hears them as well. He hopes she does. Hopes that these romantic wishes push deep inside of her so that even if she can't listen to them, she'll one day make them come true without ever realizing someone else thought of it first. Bree doesn't respond in any way that Jack can tell. She's in her own space somewhere far away and utterly oblivious to the conversation. It would be embarrassing to tell her what their parents are saying about them, so he just lets his shoulder rest against her, hoping that the weight might pull her back from her stare far over the water. Though the truth is, if she never made it back, Jack would cross any ocean to be with her. He steals a smell of her hair so close to his face, and the sweet smell of mango closes his eyes with complete satisfaction.

"Come on, honey, they're not even teenagers yet." Jack's father contends. His shoulders rise well above the back of his chair, his neck is thick, and his Adam's apple protrudes distinctly.

"Well, they will be in a couple of months." His mom retorts.

"Do we really have to think about dating? They're still babies." Jack's dad sounds confused and a little disappointed.

"I guess you don't remember 13," his mother's voice cuts from under a wide-brimmed hat and dark sunglasses. She still wears a bikini while most other mothers opt for more concealing attire, but it fits her well.

Her father jokes, "Well, if Bree is like her mom, then she'll probably be boy crazy here in a minute. And she'll just about hate her mother and only tolerate me. You know what that means… I'm the new fav in the house."

"I don't know about Jack…. "His father pauses, clearly weighing his next words. "He is such a geek. I mean, I love it. I really do. The kid is super smart and does well at school. Most importantly he's kind and sweet. But he isn't street smart. He's naïve and trusting." his father continues. "Unless there is a dating manual for him to read, I doubt he stands a chance."

Bree's dad teases, "So he is his Daddy's son?"

"Well, he's really handsome, and I think before long, he'll be beating away the girls," says her mother. Jack thinks about nudging Bree more and puts his head against her shoulder.

"Just like his dad," his mom says. "I see so much of him in Jack."

"Remember how obsessed he was with geology? And before that paleontology," his father continues to make his case, "Now it's astronomy or physics, I can't really tell the difference the way he talks on and on about it. He always has some book in hand." Jack looks at the book he's reading closed on the sand next to his towel. It's fiction, which is better for the beach.

"He has been glued to the telescope we got him for Christmas," his mom notes to her mother.

"I remember when we were in Tahoe skiing a couple of winters ago, and we just had to go the state park with all the ahh… hmm, I'm blanking… um… dolphinish guy." Her father struggles.

"Dolphinish?" His father teases back. Jack silently answers the question, The Berlin-Ichthyosaur State Park in Nevada.

"Ichthyosaurs!" Her father exclaims triumphantly. "Yeah, the ichthyosaur fossil park."

Jack's mother interjects. "What do you mean, 'we'? You two got to ski all day while we," pointing to Bree's mom, "took the kids off the mountain and drove most of the day. And by the time we got back, you too were already drinking in the hot tub."

"Yeah. That was a great day." Her father grins back at the wives extra widely. The smirk both acknowledges and celebrates the uneven responsibility. He lets it simmer for a second like a playful poke in the ribs. "Really, though, so random.

Who leaves a perfectly good mountain, good snow, and two devilishly handsome husbands for the cold desert?"

"I think it was Adam's idea," Jack's father answers too quickly. "How he knew about the park, I have no idea." The conversation stops, and the wind moves through the silence, filling the vacancy. Jack looks at Bree and feels sad for her. "Yeah, it was Adam's idea for sure," He says with some regret in his voice. No one speaks. Jack's shoulder still rests against Bree, but now it feels like there is a different reason for it to do so.

Finally, after several heartbeats, Jack's mother says, "He was so good with the kids that day. He just watched them bounce around, and even though he wasn't into dinosaurs, he was just excited seeing how excited the kids were."

"See, honey. You had it easy. Adam basically watched the kids," Bree's father turns away from the others, takes a drink, and shifts in his seat. Her mother keeps her head down and moves her feet back and forth in the sand. No one else speaks, and the wind returns.

Jack still can't believe that Bree does not hear any of this. He wonders what is possibly keeping her attention. Two whales passed earlier. Really close to shore too. Just beyond the orange boat buoys that sit in front of every lifeguard tower, so every four blocks, and those are only three hundred yards out. Maybe she saw them again, just further out this time. After all she was the one who spotted them, and stood up excitedly, pointing out that they were Grey Whales, which she could tell but the shape of their spout. Now Jack has only yet to see again, but she is tracking them at a great distance.

In the foreground, kids his age and adults body surf the shore pound for short rides while the better body surfers tread water a dozen yards further out, waiting for a set to come through. Even farther are three sailboats at various distances, taking advantage of the conditions. The closest being in roughly the same spot in which they saw the whales. To Jack's left, which directionally would be South, the sand extends to the edge of his frame of vision beyond their parents, even past the distant brown pier. Its sister pier, concrete with a blue house and red tile roof at the end, sits over Jack's right shoulder only a half dozen or so blocks away and pushes far into the water.

Two miles separate the two piers. They are the markers for an annual open ocean swim and serve as the last leg of the thirty-two-mile Catalina paddle.

His father completed the paddle twice, and Jack heard others say that he had finished first in his class of board, "the classic," which has size limits. The other division, "the unlimited", uses larger, faster boards. Jack didn't know for sure if that was true because his father never mentioned winning. He only talked about throwing up at the PV turn and that he was trailed by a Great White for at least five miles. Jack can never tell if he is kidding about the shark or not.

They are in the water, the babies in close, and juveniles about four to five hundred yards out. Adult Greats, the real monster size sharks, would be in the channel and all-around Catalina. Still, the tone of Jack's father's voice makes Jack think he's kidding or at least embellishing what really happened.

The sharks don't scare Jack. In fact, this is the first year Jack will swim the "pier to pier," placing him right into the water with all those juvenile Greats. His father is going paddle next to him to help him stay on course, which also helps, and though Jack is young, he is a strong swimmer, mostly from surfing. He can already swim around those orange buoys at least a dozen times. His father has already taken him out on a couple of practice swims. Jack can hear him under the water yelling, "That's it, buddy. You're doing great. You're almost there. Don't give up. Keep pushing." His father doesn't know that Jack slows down when he hears his father yelling at him because Jack can't help but smile, causing him to swallow too much of the water.

"I am so happy they will be going to school together this year. Jack has talked about it all summer," Jack's mother declares seemingly out of nowhere.

"I'm happy we will no longer be paying for private school," his father slips in.

Bree's mom exclaims, a little too enthusiastically, "Another one for the carpool!"

"Plus no more mandatory Sunday mass," His dad celebrates

"Public school with the rest of us sinners," Her dad jokes.

"We are still going to mass," his mom chastises. "You know how important the church was for me. You know, when I was... lost."

"I know, honey. We will still go, but we don't need to go every Sunday.

Plus, Jack seems to have grown out of the church."

"You don't outgrow God, honey."

"You know what I mean. Jack had a hard time reconciling some discrepancies between science and church doctrine." The explanation is less for his wife and more for their friends.

"I don't know why anyone would let small details derail them from the larger truth."

"We'll still go, I promise. But you can find God everywhere. Just look here. Better than any church I have been to." The water dances from the edge of the sand through the horizon, a million shards of light glinting off broken water.

Her father asks, "Is Jack worried about the transition?"

"No. Not really. Jack already knows a lot of the kids, plus Bree will be there, and his other best friend is going to change too," his dad answers.

"Is that the kid who's as big as a freshman or the one who looks like he is in fourth grade?" Her mother asks.

Her father interjects, "A freshman on steroids."

"The big one, Timmy." His father confirms. Jack's other best friend is big. And when Jack was picked on, the year before, Timmy put an end to that quickly.

"First, middle school and then high school, all in a flash. Hey! They can go to prom together!" His mom recaptures the earlier theme. Jack smiles to himself, dimple on one side of his face but not the other, his lips uneven, and he hopes the wind doesn't interrupt them.

"Dresses, tuxes, boutonnieres, and corsages?" Her mom nearly sings in response. "Sign me up."

"Maybe we can chaperone?" His mom asks.

"No!" Both dads object simultaneously and chuckle at the fact.

His mom responds, "You two keep throwing water on this, but just watch it happen." Jack silently roots for his mom to win the argument, and his feet nervously tap against the sand.

"I really don't know why we let them hang out with us?" Bree's mother says to his mom.

"Yeah. The kids are going to be high school sweethearts. They are going to prom together. And they are going to lose their virginities to each other!" Jack's mom smirks just as her father did, letting it linger for longer than it naturally would. Jack blushes and turns from Bree. She doesn't move at all. Lost somewhere on the horizon.

"Whoa. Whoa, Nope, too far," Bree's father objects.

Jack's dad repeats himself, somewhat comically, "Wow! Wow!"

"Is she serious right now?" Her father asks His dad.

"What? You realize at some point in their lives, they will have sex. Wouldn't it be great if it was between the two of them? Inseparable since they were babies. So much history." His mother argues.

"They probably see themselves more as brother and sister, I bet." His dad says, and Jack worries at least half of that is true. That is how she sees him. Jack, more than worries. He is pretty sure. His feet continue to tap.

Bree's father declares, "She is going to be locked in her bedroom for all of high school. No dates. No boys. Only extra layers of clothes, as many, as she can wear."

"I don't know." Her mother lingers on the question for a beat. "I mean, I understand that, but I sometimes wonder if Adam ever had that experience. He did have a serious girlfriend for a while, but he was only 16, right?" There is a pause for several seconds, and no one says anything. "At the time, I was worried about him having sex. Is the door to his room open? Whose house are they at? Are her parents really home? How late can he stay with her? Will they use protection if they do? Like every parent, right? He was just too young for something so adult. But now... I don't know. Did he? It would be weird if I asked his girlfriend. But I am curious. On the one hand, I would like to think he got to have that kind of joy, to be able to experience that essential human rite of passage," she continues. "But on the other, at that time, I would have said he was too young, and he was. Anyway, I think about all the stuff I don't know. And how I have no one to ask."

Jack can't help but look at them. To see the loss that continues to haunt them. Bree's father reaches over and lays a hand on her leg. He says something below the wind that Jack can't hear. Her leg retreats. They are skinny and muscular from running, and her whole body has thinned dramatically. Her husband, on the other hand, has thickened in his midsection. He calls the portion of his stomach that pours over the front and side of his shorts his muffin top.

Someone else says something, and the whole conversation dips below the audible bellow of the breeze.

Jack draws in the sand but erases it before Bree can see, even if she isn't looking. He has drawn thousands of times in that sand. Often with Bree or someone else. Each child has. Every doodle is erased or just slips back into the sand on its own. The sand knows, though. It is the collective consciousness of all of those who come. It knows every movement of every person who visits the beach. It knows that Jack and Bree threw a frisbee by the water, that the families played each other in volleyball, and that they chased after the broken waves like sandpipers. Jack loving the freedom of running barefoot, the sand gripped in his toes, a connection that shoes don't afford. Only their time in the water, body surfing with their parents, both inside and out in the larger surf, is not seen by the sand, but it knows they walked in and when they walked out an hour later.

From the single-story bungalows that sit on a ridge higher than the beach. And the green ice plant which separates slope of sand that rises to meet them, some 90 yards or so from the water, footprints leave pockmarks dotting every inch of the beach. It's the culmination of the day's comings and goings. An account of unseen activity written in sand. Authored by those still there and those who have already left, a collection of the footfalls of ghosts.

Jack wants to comfort Bree to go with her somewhere out there on the water. To protect her. To console her. Jack sets himself to do just that. He pictures himself getting off the towel.

He imagines walking to the surf as the sand crabs burrow, and the sandpipers peel away as he approaches. He hurdles over the small wave coming up on the shore where children play. She is far, but he can get to her. The adults continue to talk, and he can still hear them. He runs up the face of the waves before they can break where the more experienced swimmers body surf.

The distance is far, but he has covered much in a short time. He passes the buoys and the closet boat and can hear the water slapping its hull, and in no time, he has run out of earshot of its beat. But he can still hear the parents.

"We just have to push forward. We are so lucky to have the time we had with him. And we still have an amazing daughter. We don't want to mourn through her childhood. That would just mean we lost both of them," her father says.

"It's impossible not to be sad. I want to be sad. But like you said, I have a beautiful daughter, and nothing makes me happier, and somehow I appreciate her even more. So I am constantly happy and forlorn, both at the same time. And then I feel like nothing. Like they cancel each other out. Two extremes that when they meet, they sum each other out, and I can't feel anything. And now this… right? Like what else can go wrong?"

Jack races even faster over the rough water. He wants nothing more than to be next to her. To feel her. To unburden her of any sadness. To save her and be her strength.

He has found footholds in the water to run upon. Each glint of light is like a stepping stone. He moves faster on them. Sure-footed on each sparkle of the sun, the water has captured. They twinkle on the surface, flash, and disappear. The stone he sees may not be there when he completes his step. He stays on his toes and is moving as he arrives. To lose his footing would mean a fall-through. To be in open water miles offshore. Each step is a leap of faith. The wind is stronger, but he is so close to the horizon.

"Don't worry about me," his father says.

Jack pauses.

"Have you told Jack yet?" Her dad asks.

The wind pushes harder than before knocking him off balance and slowing his charge. And what is wind but the atmosphere throwing itself at you, the elements that find you? The stepping stones disappear faster. He no longer moves forward. Instead, he seeks any step available. To the right, he'll leap if an opportunity appears. Backward if there is anything to hold him up. To the side again. Sometimes forward, but not enough to make any progress. Unease in every step.

"I'm not worried," his mother says sweetly, "God knows I need him too much for anyone to take him away." The words pour over the ocean like a slick.

"I am going to talk to him today, actually. I just don't know how to start the conversation." Jack hears his father say.

"I know I don't need to say this, but we're here for you—anything you need," Bree's father pledges.

Jack falls through. The hue of water darkens as he sinks. Light green and blue to dark. Blue to black. He cannot see his hands or feet. His arms and legs disappear. He is underneath. Silent, unseen, and alone. Deep below, far from everyone. He cannot see. He cannot hear. He sways in a current he cannot escape. There is no footfall beneath—nothing to push against. No legs to drive with, no arms to swim with, and his breath has stopped. The rise and fall of his chest have been replaced with the oceans back and forth.

"Jack, can you move? My shoulder is falling asleep," Bree says in a soft hush, suddenly back on their towel.

"Sorry." Stunned, he moves.

"It's okay, you can put it back in a bit. Just let me adjust my arm first." She stretches her arm outward. "Hey, you might be lucky." She still looks forward toward the water.

"Uh," Jack is lost.

"Could be a swell on the way. See those clouds. Adam's pointed them to me before. They often show up before a storm. Which would ruin my upcoming dive. But you might see some surf out of it."

Jack lets his head fall against her shoulder again. Her hair covers his face. He should be next to her, the only place he has ever wanted to be, but instead, he is no longer on the beach.

CHAPTER 6

September 2, 2007

The thud of the door snaps inside of his ears. The quiet humming of the electrical lines outside disappears. Again the bang at the door resonates throughout the black room bouncing off of the thin plasterboard walls. Jack leaps out of bed and dashes to his closet. Sheets cling to his naked body. He sees the bullet on his doorstep in the darkness of the room, feels its weight on his back. He needs to move faster. He begins to pull clothes off of hangers, shoveling them onto the floor. The guns lay tucked away in a dark corner somewhere, a revolver and pump-action shotgun with scattershot ammo, best used for bird hunting. Jack needs to hurry.

"Fuck, is that the cops?" Smashley doesn't yell but speaks forcefully, fearfully. "Am I really going to be here the night you get arrested?" She has a point. Whoever left the bullet wouldn't knock, but the police would. Is someone forcefully knocking on the door or trying to kick it down? Does he meet the police with a drawn gun or go empty-handed at the people who left the bullet on his welcome mat? Quickly, Jack grabs the revolver and shoves it in the waistband of the jeans he threw on.

He rips open his bedroom door. The metal bolt does not completely clear the strike plate, causing the doorknob to pop in his hand. The bedroom door flies wide open, and the handle hits the wall inside his room, leaving a divot in the drywall. The mini-blinds clang against the windows due to the quick change in room pressure, and that same pressure shoots Jack through the doorway, closer to danger, and the pressure follows out of the room.

He sees the front door bounce back and forth in the door jamb. The thudding is coming from the lower half of the front door as if someone is kicking it. He places his hand on the handle of the gun. His thumb on the cock. The door continues to bang loudly.

His other hand comes up defensively in front of his chest as he slowly approaches the thudding door. As if it would stop a bullet. Stop the kicking. Stop anything. Someone continues to pound on the door. Jack's feet away now, holding a gun in one hand, and touches the bouncing door with the other. The vibrations pulse from his hand through his shoulder. He has run out of room to move forward. There is nothing left for him to do but confront whatever or whoever is banging on his apartment. He takes a deep breath and squeezes the handle of the gun. "Who is it?" He speaks deeper than usual and quickly, so it comes out as a single word like "who's't?" The thudding stops. Are the police going to announce themselves? Is someone going to shoot back through the door? Should Jack shoot first?

"Open the door." Comes a reply less urgent than the sound of the preceding kicks.

Jack presses his eye to the door. Inside the peephole stands a man who leans against the rail guard. His head is far bigger than his body, and the warped glass makes the railing outside appear v-shaped. Jack lays his head against the door and lets out an audible exhale, and opens his door.

"Fuck, man! What took so long?" His eyes don't focus, and his skin is white, translucent, and ashen. It reminds Jack of plexiglass. He wears a beautiful leather jacket and jeans despite the unseasonal heat. In total, his outfit costs as much as Jack's rent.

"Shut up. Get the fuck in here."

"Sorry, I called and messaged, but you weren't responding." Plexiglas is someone Jack knows two or three times removed. He is a friend of a friend, or more accurately, an acquaintance of an acquaintance.

Jack stares out onto the street. No one is there. He closes the door and turns the deadbolt.

"That's cool, man. No worries." He manages to forgive Jack. "I need a couple of grams. Actually, just make it an eighth," he slurs most of his words.

"Stay here." Jack does most of his business away from the apartment, but when clients come over, he never lets them past the living room. They never see the money or the supply. He never mentions a gun. These are some of the simple rules he was taught. Discretion is on that list too, and it has just been crossed off.

The best thing to do is to get rid of Plexiglas as fast as possible. Jack sets himself to do just that and heads back to his bedroom.

"Who the fuck is it?" She asks, still lying in the dark. The light from the open door drapes across the lower part of the bed.

"A customer."

"It's two in the fucking morning! What a loser."

"A loser with cash."

"I wasn't talking about him," Smashley rolls away from the light pulling the covers to her head. Jack responds by turning on the overhead lamp. She mumbles something under her breath.

Plexiglas stands in front of the TV, switching channel after channel.

"Here you go."

"Thanks, bro." He turns off the television and puts down the remote. From his pocket, he pulls out a roll of twenties and hands it to Jack. Plexiglas then gives Jack a high-five hug and leaves.

Jack locks the door, turns off the lights in the living room, and turns the television back on before returning to the bedroom. She keeps silent, a welcomed punishment.

Jack sits on top of the comforter with his jeans still on. He leans back against the pillows, and the gun pushes against his lower back, reminding him that it's still there. After removing the revolver, Jack lets his head lay against the bedroom wall, with his back propped against his pillows and keeps the gun in hand. He cocks the pistol and lays it on his chest. Jack takes several deep breaths with his finger on the trigger guard before decocking it. Then he pulls the hammer back again, takes several more breaths, and pushes it back in. He cocks and decocks the gun again and again and again. Then he places it on the glass nightstand and stares at it as it catches and reflects the light of the flashing clock. His index finger flexes, closing and opening, he imagines the recoil push from his wrist up through his elbow, maybe all the way to his shoulder, before realizing that there is a better chance that he would never feel anything, not even the trigger give way.

Then Jack finally falls asleep.

CHAPTER 7

September 3, '07

Jack left that morning before Smashley woke before she could demand again that Jack confront his friend about her. Or demand that he visit her at college. He surfed by himself, even though the waves were terrible, and he stayed in the water for as long as he thought it would take Smashley to get up and leave his apartment. Then for good measure, he stayed down by the beach longer to make sure he wouldn't run into her again.

He used the outdoor showers on Eighth Street to rinse off and changed back into his clothes. He carefully laid his surfboard on the other side of the bike path. The tip of it resting on a trashcan, so the sand doesn't get in the wax. And its tail in the sand, so its thin glass doesn't scratch or crack on the concrete. It's how his father taught him to lay down his board.

Jack picks up his phone. He knows the number by heart even though he hasn't dialed it in years. Not saved in his contacts, but quickly entered, his thumb hovers over the call button. He sits on the concrete wall that divides the pedestrian portion of the strand from the bike lanes. His feet avoid the rose bushes that have replaced the ice plant.

It's the same spot he and his father sat when they checked the surf in the morning. His father pointing out the sand bars and riptides and swell direction, or any other detail to select the best break in view. "Look Jack, we can use that rip tide to paddle out faster and the water will push us south into the break on second." While his father spoke, Jack used to float his feet over the tips of the ice plant, letting them tickle the bottom of his feet, and listened intently to wisdom his father had to pass down.

He is at the bottom of his street. His old street. The one on which he grew up. There is an iconic home a couple of blocks down. The house was once used for a show about young people. The program showed the home's exterior and the surrounding beach repeatedly, even though they hardly ever shot scenes there. The show was about another Los Angeles town, more famous than Jack's hometown, but one that didn't have a beach even though the show claimed otherwise. Still, years later, people stop and take pictures of the beach house that is somehow misplaced only because a show made them believe it was so.

This town often showed up in television shows and movies, particularly the pier, the sand, and the water. It's the nicest town in the South Bay, a stretch of beach communities south of LAX and north of Long Beach. It's the southern bookend to Santa Monica Bay, with Malibu as its counterpart to the north. Those shows never mentioned this town by name and always tried passing it off as some other town or part of the city. It has the widest beach in L A, the finest sand, and the cleanest water. And now it has that name recognition other, more famous towns in Los Angeles owned to themselves. Jack can still remember the Los Angeles Times article announcing its coming, "Beverly Hills By The Beach" was the headline. He was so proud then for it to be recognized even if he had already moved into his apartment.

This is where he grew up. This is where he's from. It's how he defines himself, "a beach kid" and a "waterman." Sitting on the wall, Jack can see his mom holding his hand or carrying him across the hottest stretches of beach. Before Jack learned to dig his feet into the sand below, which was still cool and hidden from the sun. Jack can see his father doing pull ups on the lifeguard tower before they went into the water.

This is the stretch of beach where he and all the kids on his street spent their summer days. Every child on Jack's block adored his dad. He used to play tag with them, red light, green light, and all the other games kids loved. Ten children lived on the walk street Jack grew up on, including Bree, and

Jack's dad found ways to play with them all.

Even with the other kids Jack and Bree were inseparable, building sandcastles together, digging for crabs, and racing on the soft sand. Bree's mother stopped bringing a towel down to the beach for her because she always ended up sharing Jack's. Even if she napped while he read, there was more than enough room for them to lie together, day after day, summer after summer.

She was the creative one. The one who always came up with games to play like Tron style races in the sand, using the footprints to build walls around the other. She was the one who always egged on Jack to "hookiebob" a lifeguard truck. It was a trick they saw her brother pull off several times. Grab onto the back of a lifeguard truck as it pulls away and let it drag you through the sand. After her brother passed she was the one who wanted to do it, and Jack went along too, even if he was scared to get caught. "Don't be a sissy," she goaded him, "what's the lifeguard going to do but yell at us to let go?" That was the way things went with her for a good year after Adam died. She was often looking for trouble, looking for a boundary to cross, to see if her parents noticed. But then later, she called Jack her, "brother." And most importantly she laid her head on his back and said, "I love you."

Jack looks at the number he entered into his phone. It's Brees number. He can't make himself place the call. He doesn't know what he would say to her. He could walk up to her house, it isn't far, but he won't. They haven't spoken in two years. Even while walking by each other in school, she ignored him. He still managed to keep tabs on her. He knew when she broke up with her high school sweetheart a year after he left for college and how she went traveling all last summer. He knew what college she got into, Hawaii, and under what major, marine biology. He wonders if she's kept tabs on him. Probably not. Then he deletes the numbers he's punched into his phone.

Jack doesn't belong to her anymore. There's no towel to share or sandcastles to build. There's no mom to carry him or dad to point out all potential considerations one should take while making a decision. The wisdom accrued through years of experience.

Jack doesn't live on this block anymore or even in this town. He doesn't even belong to any of them anymore. At some point, they have all left him behind. Now he's a man with a false identity, a misleading definition, and there is nowhere left that really feels like home.

He is as miscast as the house that convinced everyone that Beverly Hills has a beach. He is as misplaced as the camera shots attributed to other parts of LA. And there is ever-present turmoil, a feeling of sinking when someone is forever out of place. When they want to say this is who I am and know it to be true but are left uncertain of what is real and what is not.

Jack puts his phone away, he hopes Smashley left, and wonders just how long he has to wait to go home again.

CHAPTER 8

September 3, '07

The night sky cooled gray. The light turned red, and Jack closed his eyes. His friends stopped at the intersection, and he threw himself into oncoming traffic.

After surfing, he returned to his apartment, and Smashley was gone. He ate and then napped. Then he met his friends to pre-party for the night at Mutts house.

Mutt's parents were home, but they might as well not have been. None of his friend's parents ever checked in on the boys. They were free to come and go as they wished. They were all leaving for college soon, and the parents adopted an authoritative style as if they had already gone. But they had begun parenting like that almost two years earlier. So the fact that Jack and his friends were all doing coke and drinking in Mutt's bedroom didn't matter. His parents might as well have been miles away.

Jack borrowed a bike from Mutt, and he grabbed the one that had been stolen. It was spray-painted black and had all of its light reflectors removed so that it was no longer recognizable as the bike it had been. He chose this bike for a reason, to come across a changing light at the right time.

He waited for this light to change, timed it perfectly, knowing when it would happen. This light is the fastest to change in town. After only five flashes of the crosswalk's "don't walk" hand, the traffic light turns red. Jack started counting them at the top of the hill. He slowed down so that his friends moved in front of him, and then he built up speed. He timed it to pass them while they stopped at the light, and they waited to cross.

The bicycle he borrowed rolls. He keeps his eyes shut tight. The night air rushes over his face and legs and neck and beats against the thin long sleeve jacket he wears, covering his arms. His friends shout his name and cheer him on as they always do. As they always cheer each other on for these kinds of things. They have zeal toward misadventure, whether it's stealing beers from delivery trucks while the drivers are inside, drinking and driving, or streaking public events. They have their own overture toward unnecessary risk, even if Jack is the only one who will run red lights on a bike. It could be simply because their lives don't have any, other than the danger they invite in, and everyone needs something to conquer. It is like the fresh night air passing over Jack's face as he races toward oncoming cars. They all throw themselves against the wind just to see how it pushes back.

Under tire, the street turns from concrete to the tile that lines all the crosswalks in the area. Then quickly back to concrete. Jack's hair blows backward and tickles his forehead. Horns honk to his immediate left. His thin jacket whips in the rushing air, and he feels it shaking on his forearms. The wind of a car passes just in front of him, moving his front tire in its wash. He lets go of the handlebars and raises his hands into the air. Some tires screech in his path. Jack lets out an audible exhale. His friends continue to cheer from behind as he passes the sound of the car slamming its breaks. They call his name and laugh. There is another horn, but this time behind him and to his right. Held down longer as an act of protest. Jack takes his feet off of the pedals. Someone yells at him from very close. He passes them with their voice still in his ear. A crash could be imminent. Then he feels the tile of the far crosswalk under his tires, and he opens his eyes.

"There's a ground Monte, there's a ground," a friend yells in triumph quoting an old movie.

"My dear sweet brother Numsie!" Another joins in, offering a different line from the same character.

"Roberto!" They call out disjointedly.

Jack made it, as he has every time thus far. He slows down and pulls to the side of the street to let his friends catch up and relishes the fact it is he who they weren't able to keep up with.

While he waits for his friends to cross, Jack looks over at a store that used to be an ice cream parlor where his parents would take him after soccer and baseball games. If Bree was available, she would join them. She got the blue bubblegum while Jack had the rainbow sherbet, and his parents let the two kids sit at their own table as if they were adults. He can still hear his mom say, "Oh, look, honey, they're letting each other lick their ice cream."

His father replies, "I see, babe." Jack hated blue bubblegum but never mentioned it.

The light changes, and his friends cross, and they head to the bar.

They lock their bikes together. They cross the street together. There is a wall of people in front waiting to get in. It looks like an hour's wait.

On the other side of the street, Jack finds a concrete seam between blocks of tiles and walks across it like a highwire. Altogether they move toward the back where the line mushrooms a bit. They bypass the wait and head toward the back door. The bouncers won't let them in the front. They're too young to be in the bar. But that doesn't stop them. Someone will let them in through the dark back door. Trees are lit from below and cast shadows on the red obscured windows. The door opens, and the music smashes against them.

"Aye! Get the fuck in here!" League screams at the boys from inside the bar. Warmth and darkness pour over the boys as they squeeze through the crowded dance floor. Music plays at a deafening volume, so loud it pushes down on the room, as if they were on a distant planet, with stronger gravity, where you would be crushed by your own weight.

Colored strobe lights poke holes through the black back room in an irregular pattern. Jack keeps his hand on the back of the friend in front of him as they march single file through elbows, shoulders, backs, and hips.

In the darkness, someone grabs him. She wears her hair in a way that is odd and unflattering and demurely smiles at him. Her body slides toward his. He smiles and nods. It is the same smile he has worked on for years, accentuating the dimples in his cheeks while eliminating the slight deviation, the crookedness, naturally present.

The smile is not fake, though. It sits white, with square teeth, right in the middle of Jack's face. The authenticity of the cause is another matter. The smile speaks of feelings that just don't exist, so the smile is only insincere. The girl who smiles back doesn't know all of that, so to her, it says something much more straightforward, something everyone wants to hear. In that way, his smile speaks most appropriately about him. He quickly turns toward the bar and his friends.

Just as they had bypassed the line outside, all of the boys walk through those waiting for a drink. League has led the way and pushes up against the bar top, reaching over to grab a bottle. Smashley calls, but Jack sends her to voicemail. League lines up the shot glasses. A bartender walks by, shaking his head. If League notices, he didn't seem to care.

"John Wayne, these bitches," He says as he hands out the drinks of some terrible cheap liquor. Jack holds the shot to his nose but can't smell the alcohol that's poured high on the glasses' thin rim. His sinuses are swollen shut. Quickly the drink disappears. The thud of thick glass bottom slamming soundly against the bar top follows. He barely tastes the shot as it goes down his numb mouth and throat. This is drinking made easy. He looks around at his friends' faces keeping his eyes steady and, most importantly, his lips even and flat. Most of them wore the same expression, complete indifference.

It isn't tough. The boys had snorted lines for hours, and the shot barely registers behind the deep numb burning through Jack's mouth and throat. Only Smoker reacts. His eyes narrow, his lips cringe, and he opens his mouth slightly, showing off the wide gap between his two front teeth.

"Pussy," League says as he hits Smoker in the chest.

Around the bar, faces have already been softened by alcohol. The ceilings and walls sweat with the thick air, and dew collects on the windows, and it appears as if the glass is melting.

Mutt yells, "Crackie!" and hands Jack a beer. "Drink to this line for personality," Mutt points to the bottom of the label. It's a line he says way too often and mainly at Jack's expense. Jack laughs anyway like he always does.

"Hey, did you guys hear what happened to me?" League throws out like a baited line. He is six foot six, and his height alone easily commands the boys' attention.

"No," says The Tard.

"Since spring quarter, I've been flooded with random dick pics. Sometimes mother fuckers call and just breathe super hard. No fucking clue why. So I'm out with this moustie ….."

League always has a story to tell, and to Jack's best guess, it's why so many people like him. Jack enjoys hearing the one about the time League, then their sophomore year club volleyball coach left their hotel, where they were staying for a tournament, for a blowjob at a massage parlor. When he got back, all the parents were awake and scolding the kids on the team for stealing alcohol from the hotel bar. League snuck past the lobby, where the team had lined up against a wall, taking on lectures. Made his way up one flight of stairs and then took the elevator down. He pretended that he had just woken up and admonished the team about playing at a "big league" level. That was when they started derisively calling him League.

He always manages to have some detail he saves in his stories, making the story even funnier, like a callback. So when he is done telling how the team won the tournament, an important one at that, and that Jack and Smoker were named co-MVP's, he'll smugly and jokingly take most of the credit as a great coach. "Really, it's all because of my training techniques," he'll say. Then League reveals the fact that Jack and Smoker went with him to the massage parlor. "That's why we won," he'll add, "my advanced focus and relaxation strategies. And of course the talented mouths of those South East Asian beauties." He pauses to laugh. "The best part is the parents couldn't have been any happier with me afterward, the said 'keep doing whatever it is you're doing.'" Which was true. Jack was there by himself, but all the other parents seemed to quickly move past the hotel bar incident. The results were hard to argue with. But the results were always good with them, with school and sports. What could a parent say when they were excelling? After all, it was the parent's motto, "Work hard, play hard." Of course, League's story isn't entirely accurate, they only got hand jobs instead, but that doesn't sound as good.

League raises his voice. "All over campus must have been there for weeks. Now I'm just praying she doesn't see them."

Jack checks his phone to see if Smashley sent a message, the worst possible one being that she told has his friend that Jack knows about the sex, but she hasn't sent anything. There are several messages from numbers he hasn't bothered to save but contain previous texts. Some from girls, some from clients. He has a message from Montana, asking where he is, asking Jack to meet up with him to talk shop. The second message of its kind in two days from him. He isn't someone Jack can ignore for much longer.

Jack types that he is still at Mutt's house, promising to update when they go out. Jack surveys the bar to make sure Montana isn't there before pressing send. Jack can't be caught in a lie with Montana.

"... It's even worse. That same guy comes back with one of those flyers. Picture of me naked as can be, holding a beer with my phone number at the top, and I have no choice but to show my date."

"Oh, shit, all that work to keep her from seeing them for nothing!"

"Here's the best part." He always says 'best' or 'funniest' when he comes to the end of his stories. "She reads out loud the 'For A Good Time Call Me' title, pauses, looks at the picture, and says 'you know I really do like a good time,' and we go back to my place."

"Bullshit."

League holds his hands and arms up and out, "Swear to God, bro."

"Who put all those fliers up on campus, and where did they get a picture of you naked?"

"Couple of guys on the team getting me back for rat fucking them. All good. Pic was probably from some sweat party we had at the house. Who knows. There are so many pics of my junk in the world, who cares about another one."

"Fuckin' League," Luggy laughs, and open palm pushes League in the shoulder. His reaction greater than warranted, like some kind of equation where x stands for a variable of unspoken worship. No one knew how to make friends with all the right people better than Luggy.

"I call bullshit. Your date sees that flier and asks if it was a cold night."

The Tard jokes and leans against League, and the gangly ex-coach takes two steps to his right to regain his balance. They are the same height, but The Tard is wide and thick, and when he is drunk, he walks through people with a bowling ball's concern, with Jack often following in the wake. He is Jack's oldest friend and the reason why he has all his other friends.

League quickly responds, "Thank God cameras add ten pounds."

When League finishes, Jack moves away from the bar. He heads back past the dance floor, where the surrounding bench thumps in unison as men jump up and down with their shirts off. Past the broken emergency exit, Jack and his friends came through and out onto a small, restricted patio. He opens the door to the back office. "Sorry, I'm late."

"Yeah, no worries, we love sitting around holding our dicks." The owner of the bar is thick with sarcasm as he gestures to everyone in the back office. Jack apologizes again for being thirty minutes late.

"Any time your ready, kid," The Owner answers. He sits at his wood desk, which occupies the majority of the room. A bartender sits in a plastic leather chair on the other side. Everyone else, three women Jack doesn't know, and one of League's good friends who they call Mumbles, sit on filing cabinets. It takes a second, but Jack recognizes the woman next to the owner as the girl on the dance floor with the weird haircut. The other two women lean against plantation shutters that are nailed shut, with slats that open and close to show no window behind them. The room is warm, and Jack feels the pores on his back and chest open and glistens underneath his light jacket.

He takes his queue and reaches into his thin jacket pocket, which he wore solely for this reason, and pulls out a brick of cocaine and lays it on the desk. Jack walks over to Mumbles and daps him. He daps the bartender too. He eyes the girls he doesn't know, the ones who shouldn't be in the room if the owner had any sense, and Weird Haircut smiles at Jack like they know each other.

The owner opens the contents and drops some on a large mirror before he tries the product. He is Jack's best client who buys every weekend, and the routine is almost always the same: try it, break it up, and package it to distribute.

The bartenders sell grams of coke in the front of the house. Jack just handed over a half-pound, so he gave the bar 228 'matchboxes.' That's how the customers order. They have to ask specially to "buy a matchbox," And that is what they get. A small matchbox that carries a gram of coke or "party" as it's being called this summer.

The operation works because matchboxes are ubiquitous. If someone asks for a match, they'll get a match. If someone asks for a matchbox without asking to purchase one, they'll get the same box with 20 or so matches in it.

It was Jack's idea. He knew the owner sold out of his office. Which was much more conspicuous and limited his sales to about ten grams a night. There are just only so many people you really want coming back forth on the patio. Jack came up with the system, and he took over the supply from his partner, Montana, who still made more this way than he did when he owned the account. For the owner, it's free 'party,' some cash, though not near his alcohol sales, and most importantly, longer lines than most of the bars in the area.

The Owner turns to Weird Haircut, "This mother fucker and his friends have been sneaking into my bar for the last year. I kicked his buddy out three times at least the first two months. The balls on these kids." Weird Haircut uncrosses her knees, shifts toward Jack so that the corner of the cabinet is between her thighs, and crosses her legs at her ankles. Then she pulls the longer section of her hair behind her ear, exposing her neck to Jack. The owner continues, "Still going through the back, right?"

"Yep. Bouncers won't let us through the front." Jack replies, smiling. She laughs out loud.

"Good. Who wants to wait in that line anyway? I get it. A hot bar full of good-looking people, 'party' everywhere, but I'd never wait two hours."

"Is that how long the wait is? My God." She sounds impressed and surprised. The surprise makes sense. If anyone hears something that doesn't seem realistic, they would say the same. It's the other part of her response that seems out of place. Jack doubts if she really believes him. No one should confuse that line for a two-hour wait. After all, she is sitting in the back office, and there is nothing special about this room.

It is too small for this many people to comfortably spend an evening stuck there. There are no windows, and on a hot night like this one, you could break a sweat by having to share the space with just one other person.

The only thing interesting about that room is what Jack delivered. It is the reason she and everyone else are back there. Jack looks down at the brick he brought and knows that sometimes people have to make concessions and the lengths people will go and the lies that they are willing to tell themselves, just to hold on to what they think they want. He silently sighs underneath the conversation that continues on about the line.

"Yeah. Every weekend. But don't worry, I'll get through line anytime you and your friends want." He looks at the other girls while he speaks to emphasize the point. They are busy in their own conversation with Mumbles and the bartender.

The Owner quickly stripes out two lines for everyone in the room, taking the first for himself. "Nice!" He hands a straw to the bartender. "I hear you're going solo, leaving Montana?" The comment catches Jack off guard. Everyone is looking toward him.

"No, no, not all," Jack stammers, and then he smiles and laughs as if it were a ridiculous statement. It's entirely untrue that Jack would leave Montana, but he could. He has grown out his share of the house at a rate his partner can't keep up with. People know too, which worries Jack. To some, it could be logical that he go on his own, and if people started to share that line of reasoning, then those rumors could reach Montana, and that scares the shit of him.

Jack feels the warmth of the room and sweat gathering on his temples and under his arms. These transactions are usually fast and end before Jack runs out of things to say. He is ready to collect a payment, and his share will be a month's worth of rent.

"I like your watch. Is it pearl?" Weird Haircut asks.

"Abalone," Jack corrects her.

Then she reaches over, grabs Jack's wrist, and moves the watch around, catching the office light on its iridescent face. Her hand lingers too long and drags along his forearm as she pulls it away.

Jack notices. So does the Owner, who sits back in his chair and narrows his eyes at the girl. She seems absolutely oblivious to his reaction.

They've done this transaction so much in the last months that it usually proceeds autonomously. And this is the point at which the owner should reach into his desk drawer and pull out a money roll wrapped in rubber bands, hand it to Jack and make some comment about how much it costs him, but it doesn't happen. The Owners hands fold on the desk. Jack stares at the Owners hands and narrows his eyes too.

The bartender reaches over with the straw toward Weird Haircut, who hasn't yet taken a line, but the Owner motions it the other way. The bartender passes the straw back toward everyone else, who already had a turn.

"He's a good-looking kid, huh?" He asks the girl to whom he has been paying attention. Jack's hand runs down the length of his abdomen and quickly bounces back to the bottle he is holding. He puts the bottle to his mouth and takes a long drink.

"Well… Yeah." She's confused. "I guess he's good-looking." She says without looking at Jack.

"Easy slut." He laughs after those sharp words. "He's too young for you." She challenges him, "How old do you think I am?"

The Owner, still laughing, "More than ten years too old." She looks back at him, uncertain. "Kid's only 18," The Owner clarifies.

She addresses Jack. "What? You're only 18!" She seems betrayed. "And you're in a bar?" Perspiration collects on the back of Jack's neck, and his mouth dries. There are just too many people there for a room that small.

"Dummy, why do you think he goes through the back? Can't have kids walking through the front door. It's too obvious." He condescends to her. Mumbles hands the straw to the owner after everyone else took both of theirs.

She is defensive. "I thought it was because of the coke. He doesn't look 18. You shouldn't be in a bar," she says to Jack.

"Really?" The Owner laughs loudly, "That's what you're thinking about? That he's underage and in a bar?" The Owners laughter is directed at the girl. "Is that crazier than the fact he just brought us a big fucking mound of 'party'?"

She shouldn't be back there. The other girls shouldn't be either. But every weekend, there are a couple of people in the room who have no business being there. How many of them have said something to the wrong person? What consequences can that bring? The Owners indiscretion and the girl's unaccountability can easily be the reason why a bullet would land at Jack's door.

She starts to defend herself and then stops and gives up. "Yeah, I don't know what I was thinking," she acquiesces.

"That's fine. I'll do that for the both of us." He says, holding the straw out in front of him. "Funny story about Crackie here," the Owner begins to tell her, "is that the first night he came in, he pissed himself, right on the dance floor."

She laughs, and the Owner hands her the straw. Before she takes her line, she rhetorically asks, "On the dance floor?"

"Yeah, but he wouldn't leave." The Owner continues as the girl lowers her head to the mirror. "And none of the bouncers would touch him cause he was soaking wet!"

Jack stays quiet and inert, although they are both staring and laughing in his direction. You couldn't tell that by looking at him. He's too busy calculating the likely hood of events worse than this.

Anyway, it was Luggy who pissed himself that night. When anyone at the bar pointed it out, he denied the fact and said that he was just wearing two-tone jeans. They called him Two Tone for a while after that. Before someone complained about carrying him through another night. That's when they started calling him Luggage.

Jack doesn't mention any of this. He doesn't correct the Owner or the girl, who are both still chuckling at the story. Jack doesn't say that the girls shouldn't be back there for the transaction or that the wait to get in is an hour max, and that the room is too small and hot. Instead, he smiles at them and has another drink to keep his mouth busy, to stop from saying something he shouldn't.

He watches the owner's hands. Waiting for them to move. To reach into the desk drawer, grab the money, and say something along the lines of having to double the cover to afford it. Jack has sold to him enough that he shouldn't have to worry about payment. Still, usually, by now, it is visible if not already tendered. The job is easy. Two parts. Give them what they want and collect money in return. Jack's only halfway there.

The girl and owner exchange a couple more laughs which are primarily at her expense now, and when there is a pause, the Owner asks Jack, "Want one?" There is one waiting for him. Set aside for him. It's not unusual for a client to offer. In fact, in a setting like this, it would be rude not to offer one. But this feels different because it usually follows payment. The Owner is withholding and is going to use Jack to prove a point.

The air in the room is stifling. If Jack took off his jacket, there'd be visual wet marks under his arms. He'll have to keep it on unless he stays in the darker parts of the bar. Jack can't help but think about how inviting the patio must feel and just how fast he can get to it, but the Owner is keeping it from him, keeping Jack uncomfortably warm and cramped. "Take it." The Owner insists as Jack is thinking of the heat and his sweat and isn't quick with a response.

The Owner is establishing his power over Jack in front of the girl. Jack's been used like this, as a strawman to be torn down or an effigy to be lit. Usually, it's by older guys whose date has taken too much interest in Jack. And they make fun of Jack or try to intimidate him. Jack finishes his beer and strangles the empty bottle. "Sure, can't think a reason not to?" Jack lies, and then he takes his bump. He feels it in his septum, in his sinus, and down the back of his throat. Jack swallows hard. His throat is dry and scratchy, and he slightly gags on the 'party' that moves down it.

The owner goes back to pulling out lines. Everyone talks. Still no money. Jack is going to have to bring it up. He shouldn't have to. He shouldn't have to ask like it's some favor he is requesting. This is money now owed. Jack isn't some delivery boy. He's the reason the bar has a line, why everyone is in the backroom, why this account has grown more than any other account Montana ever had.

The Owner would never try it with Montana. It would take all the bouncers to stop him. Jack would love to push the owner's head into the desk and maybe lean a thumb into his eye the same way he pictures Montana handling this situation. Demanding the money and respect be given. But Jack isn't Montana, and the owner is Jack's best client, and sometimes people have to make concessions, regardless of right and wrong, to get what they think they want.

"Hey, I need to go back to the bar. Any chance you can pay me out?" Jack asks.

"Huh?" The owner looks at Weird Haircut with a smirk. Then back to Jack for a pause. Jack can feel his veneer waning. The bubble that he hides in is drawing precariously thin under this heat and might burst before Jack can leave. "Ha! I'm Just fucking with you. Here you go. I should come work for you with how much this costs." He doesn't hand Jack the money. Instead, he tosses it on the desk toward the side opposite from where Jack stands. Jack reaches over to pick up the money, feels Weird Haircuts foot slide up his calve, and puts the roll in his jacket pocket.

"Aren't you going to count it?" Weird Haircut asks.

"No," Jack smiles, "I trust him."

The Owner declares to the room, "This is why when you bail Montana, I'm sticking with you." Jack can't think of a response. He is eyeing the door to the patio.

Sweat runs down his neck from his hairline, and he can feel beads of it on his nose. The potential consequences, justified consequences, of betraying Montana soak his shirt. Thankfully he gets to leave just as he has run out of things to say.

The Owner gets the bartender's attention and points at Jack, "Make sure he drinks for free."

Jack walks out of the room, takes several breaths, wipes his forehead, and counts the money. He pulls out his phone to see Montana has sent him a '?' and Smashley has asked, "Have you told him yet?" Which thankfully means she hasn't.

Jack pockets the phone and opens the door back into the club. He gets to the bar quickly, where his friends haven't moved much, just integrated with all the other friends standing around it. Someone hands Jack a beer, and he takes half of it to his neck in one gulp. Someone else hands him a shot. A large group of friends hold shot glasses and surround the bar, Jack's age, Leagues age, and older. They yell and scream together. Others in the bar look on with excitement and curiosity. They're all dressed like they just came off the beach. And some of them might have.

"Go!" Someone yells.

Jack takes his shot just as everyone else does. Then immediately, the chant begins. 20 or so yelling, "Hoist. Feast. Stab." It repeats several times over, drowning any other conversations in the bar.

They raise their arms and change the shape of their hands and move to each word. "Hoist. Feast. Stab." Even others join in, and you can tell who they are because they continue on after all of Jack's friends stop. They quickly realize, and it all fades into laughter and new conversations.

His friends have circled with some others. Jack could push his way in, but that would be strange to nudge himself into such a tight circle that has no room for him. To his left are a couple of guys Jack knows who he can easily step to, but he doesn't know them that well. There aren't enough inside jokes Jack has with them or shared stories that can be brought up to reminisce and laugh over. Not before too long, he'll run out of things to say to them. Not with another friend next to him that Jack can use to help carry the load. All he'll have left to talk about are the things going on in his life.

Other people come over and close that circle, so it's not even an option anymore. Jack is between several groups of friends who talk to each other, but he isn't included in any of them. He grabs his phone again so that no one realizes that he is just standing by himself, lurking around everyone else with nothing to say.

There is another message from Montana "yeah?" It's the last thing he wants to see, so he pockets his phone and moves away from the bar. Away from the people who he should be able to speak to but can't. Apart from the crowd that pushes against him and yells through the back of his head for a drink.

He stands alone and absorbs the wet heat and the underlying bass of the music. The clucking chatter of conversations surrounding him blends indecipherably into distant white noise. The bar feels like a womb.

"Crackie, let's go." Luggy grabs his shoulder and pulls Jack along with him toward League. Jack is relieved. All together, they walk into the bathroom. Jack's feet slide as he steps onto the red tile. Paper towels overflow the trash bin, and a mixture of urine and alcohol makes the floor shine.

"I hear you're leaving Montana?" League asks as the bathroom door closes and the sound of music and bar chatter turns down.

Luggy speaks up quickly. "My boy's fuckin killin it. He doesn't need Montana."

Jack glances at Luggy before turning back to League. "No, what the fuck? Is that going around or something?" Then he laughs and smiles again as it were all ridiculous. Meanwhile, out of his pocket, Jack pulls a plastic bullet the size of a skipping stone and hands it to League. League says he heard the news from a couple of people, and Luggy doesn't help by again stating that Jack doesn't need Montana.

"Just be careful, he's that guy" then League tilts it upside down and puts the bullet to his nose. Luggy starts to tell the story of when Montana choked out his own friend for talking to his chick. The light in the bathroom is bright. Jack keeps his head toward the ground. He can see the reflected shapes of the threesome in the sheen, League standing above both Luggage and Jack, working the bullet.

The plastic bullet holds cocaine in its belly. It releases some into a chamber at the narrow end when held upside down, where it is extracted through a small hole.

Jack wonders to himself if the rumors have already reached Montana. Luggy and League laugh at something Jack to which isn't paying attention. Could Montana have left the bullet? Is that why he is messaging him? That's the important topic that they need to discuss? To talk about the punishment Jack is going to receive.

Leagues' reflection reaches out toward Jack's, the image segmented on the red tile by the black seams on the floor. Jack takes the bullet and puts the hollow point in his right nostril, and snorts. The second bullet he has stared down in as many days, and he just now realizes the connection between them. He chuckles, Luggage and League echo a laugh. Theirs are detached, reflexive, and end abruptly. Jack assumes they laugh in anticipation. Expecting a joke. Unfortunately, Jack can't share the punchline.

Again he works the bullet. Cocaine slides down the back of his throat, condensing into balls that are hard to swallow. Another snort and then another, and the smell of urine disappears, replaced with nothing. Jack feels his septum burn as his sinus begins to reclog. Taste and feeling are buried in his mouth. For good measure, he takes another to remove himself even further.

Luggage has his turn and hands back the bullet, which Jack pockets. He hangs his head, sees his own reflection on the wet red tile. A thin transparent image drowned in the shallowest of water.

He walks into the black-painted toilet stall that encloses in close quarters. Jack wonders if death is just a deep black in such close proximity you could not see through. A darkness that neither thought nor feeling can penetrate, but you're left to observe this void through the end of time. There would be no stopping Montana if he chose to put Jack deep into the black. And very little chance of convincing him not to, once he has made up his mind.

Jack stares at the bowl holding his shrunken penis, and flushes the toilet to cover the lack of piss hitting the water. Jack hears Luggage say, "The waters cold." League answered back, "And deep."

Jack realizes he hadn't spoken in a long time, but he can't remember what old movie they're quoting. He lets them leave the bathroom before coming out of the stall and heads toward the front door.

"Crackie! What the fuck?" Jack hears Montana's voice before he sees him. Jack turns, keeping his eyes steady, and most importantly, his lips even and flat. He feels the wind in his face again. Jack is an effigy ready to burn.

CHAPTER 9

March '02

The curb he is about to step upon is painted red. The paint bleeds over the line that separates the curb from the stone grey tile sidewalk. The same tile lines the sidewalk on the other side of the street and will soon line all sidewalks and crosswalks in the area. Traffic is stopped for the work to be completed. So Jack freely skated down the hill without any concern for the cars that are usually present. The change in the tile has been made in part to force Jack into the street. To push all skateboarders into the street, even when the cars return. The new sidewalks are slick compared to the old concrete ones who had tiny grooves in their finish. The new tile has a smooth and even texture, and Jack's polyurethane wheels slide uncontrollably on them. And each sidewalk begins and ends with miny tile speed-bumps that stop the smaller wheels at impact.

So Jack goes where he is pushed, and that is in the middle of the street aimlessly turning back and forth on an empty road. Where no one can see the red in his eye. The mucus on the rim of his nose. And the streaks of tears running down his face. He has gone up and down the boulevard several times already. It runs right through the heart of downtown and ends at the pier. The pier is next. At least that's the rumor. Next to be refashioned. But these things take time and who knows when they will get around to it. When he was younger, a piece of it fell on a jogger paralyzing him. The city moved quickly to secure its integrity, but that is different, and this new phase is just an idea for now. The general beautification of the whole downtown.

It's hard to imagine that the tile will finish so quickly. Work only started weeks ago. But the days have come and gone at different paces. It's like Jack going up and down the hill. Time quickly passes as it rolls under the wheels, and it moves slowly as it gets trampled underfoot. It's more appropriate to think about the moments, the ones that impact, the ones that matter. Today is one of those days. A moment that Jack won't forget. One, he knows that will stay with him. And when he looks back on his life, he will think of these types of moments.

They will piece together to form his whole life but won't include his entire life. The monotony and drudgery will be filtered out, leaving only memories and moments that define him. Snippets of importance parceled together, and the collateral memories that they pull along. Not whole, a collection of fragments that fit together to form a picture of a person, like a mosaic.

The tile will be just that. A boundary in time when everything changed. And in this part of the world, one without real seasons, a place where a summers' day can show up in winter, these demarcations help sort the order of things. The tile is only weeks old but somehow tied to the moment when his father told him that he was ill. It's hard to imagine that the tile will finish so quickly, but it is just as hard to think that it has already been six months since that day on the beach when he first heard the news. Or that several hours have passed since he began to skate in the street. And he has gone up and down that hill a dozen times already. And again, he's at the bottom of the road, staring at the pier, ready to go at least one more time on this dark day. A day that doesn't belong in any season.

The bum who his friends call John Doe is at the front of the pier, pulling out recyclables from the trash. Jack picks up two of the cans that didn't make it in John's basket, and Jack puts them in for John while he has his head in the trash can. Further out, fishermen walk toward the end of the pier with their poles. Couples hold hands and chat and pause at various spots, stare down into the water, out into the horizon, and back at the town. Jack turns back up the hill. Walking up the newly tiled sidewalk.

His mom doesn't like letting him skate through downtown because of the traffic, even the foot traffic. She prefers for him to stay on the walk streets, the less busy alleys by their house, and on the strand. If he has to go across town to a friend's house, then she'll either drive him or make him ride a bike. His best friend lives the farthest away, in the northern part of the city, but they are both reasonably close to the water, and so Jack can skate along the strand the whole way. Another friend, on the other hand, has a home in the furthest eastern part of the city, across a couple significant intersections. Jack has to bike there. He's already a teenager, but his mother is still somewhat protective of him. More so than his friends' moms, who let their children come and go. But she hasn't been able to keep tabs on him as much anymore. She is so often at the hospital that Jack really only sees her there. That is where he has come from. Bree's mom drove him. And when he got back home, he couldn't go inside. Couldn't go to Bree's as her mom had invited him to. Instead, he ran to his skateboard and took off without saying goodbye. He had enough goodbyes already and who couldn't bear another. Bree chased him down the block, yelling his name, but she couldn't keep up with the skateboard.

As it turns out, his father's friends were right. His father had won the Catalina paddle. All these years, he had seen his dad wearing his diving watch. Jack had never looked at the back of it. Never picked it up off of a nightstand and read the engraving on the back. It has his father's name written on it. The year. And that he finished first in the Classic Division. Maybe his dad was more proud than he let on. He wore that watch everywhere, from surfing to more formal events like weddings and funerals. Jack stops walking up the hill at the thought. He grips the band even tighter in his hand. Jack would put it on, but it's too loose to wear. He'll have to grow into it. For now, he holds it tightly in his hand and carries his skateboard in the other.

Jack has grown so much in the last year and is now a head taller than his mom, soon to catch Bree's father, but he never thought he'd ever be as tall as his dad. And maybe he won't, perhaps he'll never fill the band of the watch. But his dad felt small today. As white and thin as the sheets on his hospital bed. Tubes and cords from machines looked like they had woven into his skin. He couldn't do much other than hand Jack his watch. Place it in Jack's palm and help close Jack's fingers around it. Then he closed his eyes and placed his hairless head on his pillow. Jack hugged him. His body was smaller and lighter in his arms than he ever thought possible. What stood out was his neck, how thin it had become, how the clavicles had protruded through his skin. Jack could barely look at him. Couldn't look him in the eye. Instead, he stared at his father's neck and listened to the blur and beeping the machines made as they dug further and further into his father's body. His Mom cried again. She's been crying every day since the summer ended. Then Jack left the room. Bree's Mom drove him home in silence.

Jack reaches the top of the hill. He stands on his board and lets the wheels carry him down the boulevard. Jack holds his father's watch in his hand. He does everything he can to not think of his dad and how he looked. Now all he can see is the tile. Mostly grey with a blue border. Both have flecks of black sprinkled throughout. And in Jack's head, the black specks grow and grow until they displace the rest of the colors. At least moving, no one can see him cry.

CHAPTER 10

September 3, '07

"Jack! What the fuck! Jack turns to see Montana as he enters through the front door of the bar. "You fuckin idiot!" Montana moves closer and raises his hands. Darkness moves with him. Jack holds his expression of indifference even as a fire burns in his chest. Montana throws his arms forward and lightly shoves Jack in the chest. "Dumbass forgot to text me." He laughs.

A half-smile pops on Jack's face and disappears quickly, and only a ripple of bravado remains. "Oh, right. Fuck dude. Sorry. I just got here not long ago…"

"Don't worry, bro. I'm not your fucking dad. You don't have to explain."

"I'm out." Jack blurts. "Just my personal left."

Montana looks concerned, and when his eyes narrow, the flat and misshapen bridge of his nose grows more pronounced. That and his bumpy cauliflower ears serve as warning signs to anyone he comes across. Montana continues, "Let's talk." He turns toward the corner. Jack follows. The safest place to stand with a guy like Montana is actually behind him and moving in the same direction. "Thanks for dropping off that cash the other day. It's already got a place to fall."

"No worries. Sorry I didn't get it to you sooner." Jack circles Montana, so each has a back to a wall in the corner of the bar. They speak to each other, shoulder to shoulder, with neither having to look at each other. Montana is not the biggest guy, but Jack has seen him fight before, and in that regard, he may have been the biggest guy Jack knows. Jack had a front-row seat when Montana beat up three guys by himself. He hit one with his right hand and another with his left before either could lift a hand to defend themselves. Neither one stood up after. The third had enough time to protect himself, but he was dragged outside of the party and choked out.

"No worries, bruh. You always pay. I don't worry about that. It's crazy how much you're moving lately. Honestly, I'm pissed at myself that I can't keep you fully stocked. Seen a lot of growth in the last year. That's good."

Growth sounds wrong. Then Jack hears his mother say it, her voice dropping from an expected volume into a hushed tone as if it were a secret. That's how his parents referred to his dad's cancer whenever Jack was around.

His dad puts down the phone after getting back test results. "What did the doctor say about," She pauses and looks at Jack and lowers her voice, "your growth?" "That it has spread." Jack fathers tell his mother. "And there isn't much time left." His mom starts to say something but it sticks in her throat and she leaves the room quickly wiping her fingers at her eyes. And then, for some reason, when Montana says growth, it sounds appropriate. Some unwanted thing inexorably embedded in Jack's life that almost on its own expands despite the fact it never should have been in the first place.

"Yeah... stoked." Jack lies.

"Anyway, I wanted to hang out tonight cause I have great news. Come with me on a ride." Montana's assertiveness borders demanding. "We've got a new friend. A new connection. Moving up in this world. We aren't going to have to worry about empty cupboards again."

He uses the term metaphorically, but Jack can see them. Real empty cupboards, a fleur de Lis with a carnation. They're the reason why he is being congratulated on growth. Jack nods and takes a drink. The carbonation swirls around his mouth, bouncing against his gums and teeth. He needs another bump or three. Montana continues and puts a hand on Jack's shoulder and, in a different, more serious tone, "But we've got to take care of something first. Tomorrow. I'll pick you up. Bring your gun." Jack looks away toward the door and nods his head. "Good?" Montana asks again. Jack nods again.

"In the meantime, if you need to, you can sell out of my shares, and I'll give you 20% of the take."

"That's fine. I'm flush right now. Call it paid vacation."

"Right? Let's celebrate with a couple shots."

Once they take their drinks and Montana turns toward someone else and starts talking to them, Jack slips away. He heads for the front door but sees 'Weird Haircut,' she smiles at him. He turns toward the door to the rooftop patio.

A quarter moon stands above the horizon, illuminating the rooftops of houses. Pale orange lights that line the streets leak listlessly into the night. Only a handful of the brightest stars cut through. Looking up at the sky, there is no way to know how many have been muted by the city lights, outshined by a fractional brilliance. The stars aren't out, but they aren't missing. They have just been replaced.

The thick ocean night mist dampens Jack's face freshly burnt numb. It has crawled across the beach and climbed up the hill to kiss him. Jack walks over to the side of the patio where his friends stand. His phone buzzes, and he sends Smashley to voice mail again.

"Well yeah, dumbass, look, they're still working on the pier this late. I'd say they're behind." Says the Tard. Most people would recognize the pier if they saw it, even if they didn't know the name of the town it is in. It's often used in local montages that networks use for sporting events to show off the city of Los Angeles. More than any other, this pier is shown more than Santa Monica, usually with the Griffith Park Observatory and the Hollywood sign. It is the prettiest pier on the west coast.

"You don't fucking know that. You don't know if this was on the schedule the whole time." Mutt argues. He liked disagreeing with people. For what reason, Jack didn't understand.

"Yeah, people make plans that include lots of overtime," Smoker sarcastically responds. He flicks the gap in his front teeth, which he does while Smoker thinks and argues and any time he is nervous. Smoker will engage in any conversation to prove that he is right. Even ones that aren't worth having, regardless of victory.

"A 100 bucks says they finish before next week." Mutt often dies on these hills that are so trivial and so clearly wrong, which suits Smoker very well. The money isn't an issue to Mutt anyway. He doesn't have a job. He just asks for it when he needs to. Jack grabs the drink out of Mutt's hand.

"Dumb ass. You got it." They shake.

"Hey Luggy, where's League?" Smoker asks in an overly sarcastic tone and then laughs.

Luggy rolls his eyes. He knows the shit he's about to get.

Mutt laughs too, "Surprised he's not within arms reach. How are you going to be able to powder his nuts from this far away?" Jack pulls out a cigarette and a matchbox with matches in it. As he slides open the box, he gets lost in thought for a second. Where is Montana taking him, and why does Jack need a gun? He knows, though, that it doesn't matter 'why' he needs to bring a gun. It's going to happen regardless. 'Why' is only a question for those with the luxury of a choice. Otherwise, it's entirely useless. Jack lights his cigarette and moves on.

Tard smiles, "Mutt, the only reason you don't powder his nuts is cause you're too short to reach 'em." Height jokes are Tard's go-to rip on Mutt. Mutt usually makes jokes about the Tard's intelligence, and they all have something they make fun of each other over. These same jokes have been said several times behind their backs but only after told to their face first, and then it's all fair game.

"Luggy, do you wash him up first before you start powdering?" Jack deadpans. "I mean, it would be pointless otherwise." He takes an exaggerated drag off his smoke to keep from smiling.

"Haven't you seen the heated towels he carries?" Smoker finishes off the joke.

"Poor League. Having to carry Luggage around all night." Mutt emphasizes the word luggage with disdain.

Luggy laughs and replies, "Mutt, people would complain about carrying your ass around, but you fit too easily into most peoples' pockets."

The joking continues while Jack reaches into his pocket when his phone vibrates. Smashley sent another text, "calling him now."

Jack reflexively looks at the friend she is referring to, who went behind Jack's back. His friend is busy saying something about Mutt. Jack watches his hands. One holds a beer, and the other is pointing as he laughs. It could easily slip into his pants pocket to grab his phone if it rings. And how far away is that? Two feet, maybe three? It's too close no matter what.

Jack texts Smashley back immediately. "don't! what do you want???"

Jack takes a long drag off his smoke as his friends go on. He tries his best not to stare at his friend's pants pocket while listening for a ring tone or the buzzing of it vibrating. His friend's hand dips past his waist, only inches away from his phone. Jack listens intently for a quiet ring tone or the buzzing of a phone vibrating. He takes a drag of his cigarette and holds onto his breath so that he can concentrate. But immediately, his friend's hands come up above his waistline to gesture again. Jack lets out a long exhale of smoke. This friend has a habit of putting his hand in someone's face during an argument or exchange. Jack follows every movement, fixated on every motion, watching the hands to see if they go to a pocket. Someone even says something about Jack, but he didn't hear the remark, so he takes another big inhale to free him from having to respond and only flicks the group off in return.

Smashley writes back, 'so your not going to ignore me or the rest of your life.'

Jack quickly, 'I guess not. dont. it ruin the last days we have' He's referring to his friends who are soon leaving for college.

Smashley 'glad you care more about him than me (angry face).'

Jack, 'he gone soon, you not. Please!!"

Smashley, 'Fineeeee. You can make it up to me another way.' She continues to compose another message, but Jack closes his phone before reading it, stares angrily at his friend before realizing it, and looks out over the water toward the pier.

"Speaking of luggage, where's Smashley tonight?" Smoker asks. Jack's right-hand balls into a fist and places it in his pocket, transferring both the drink and smoke to the other hand.

"How should I know?" Jack responds angrily. He accidentally lets his thoughts fall into his voice.

"Bitter." The Tard calls out mockingly. The Tard's girlfriend cheated on him last year. He cried about it to Jack. None of his other friends know. Jack feels guilty for thinking of it and immediately tries to push away the thought.

"Easy, sour," Luggy adds on.

"Fuckin catching lemons, mate." Mutt piles on.

"I'm not bitter, and I'm not sour. How should I know where Smashley is? She isn't my girlfriend." Jack tries his best not to stare only at her recent lover's face and body, more so than any of the other boys, but he does still sneak a glance at him to see if Jack can read him for any signs.

Mutt turns to The Tard, "Get ready to have two roommates, Crackie and his never girlfriend, who just happens to be around all the time." He laughs and puts his arm around Jack, then takes his drink back.

"Why one girl in college? When you can have all of them. Give me all the mousties." Smoker offers. "Moustie" is the newest word for girls. Jack made a note of it to say it more often. Comments like that were constantly popping up. They grew organically in conversations, sometimes an offshoot of other words, or sometimes sprouting seemingly out of nowhere. But they were still tied to the same topics, like girls, or partying, or whatever else young men talk about. So while they flowered in a varietal way, they always bore similar fruit. Only the initiated knew. Knew what they meant. And it changed so often that to miss anytime hearing them, speaking them, would mean being left out and left behind.

"Talking about more. Let's go take another fuckin shot." Luggy turns toward the stairs and screams, "Roberto!" Both Mutt and Smoker follow and yell at the sky, "Roberto!" as they walk down the staircase.

"Come on, Crackie." The Tard says to Jack.

They would have shots within three minutes. Jack's cigarette has a lifespan of four. "In a sec. I'll just finish my gritty first." Then he takes a slight conservative drag. "Remember, I need to talk to you about the apartment."

"Yeah." The Tard disappears down the stairs.

Jack smokes and stares out over the water. A portion of the pier remains dark. The workers have their own spotlights, and then there are the new lights that have been installed. There are the traditional lamp posts that burn brighter than the old ones. And they are also adding new lights that drape along the new railing of the pier dipping from its ties to form large consecutive "u" shapes. It looks like fireworks frozen in mid-burst, waiting to fall into an invisible ocean from far enough away.

About half the new railing and half of the lights have been put in. Jack knows because he surfed next to it that morning. They're working from out to in. So it is the end of the pier that has its lights in place.

First, they tore down the old building that housed the marine exhibit and bait shop. Adam, Bree's brother, used to take them there after school, where they had a tank to touch sand sharks and rays with two fingers. It was Adam who wanted to be a marine biologist first. Jack wonders if Bree has followed the path her brother set simply because it was left unfulfilled. Any anytime there's a vacant space, something comes along to fill it, and Jack was very much that to her, filling the space her brother's death left. Going to the marine exhibit together, the convenience store for candy, and putting on shows with stuffed animals. They were the last people they spoke to every night, and sometimes Jack fell asleep with the phone next to his ear. But he hadn't thought of that questions by then. By that time, they had stopped speaking to each other.

Once the old building was torn down, they moved the large cranes to the end of the pier to install the lights and railings. When those were in, they rebuilt the building to hold a high-end coffee shop. It's just wood now, but the facade will be as it was, sky blue paint and a red tile roof.

That doesn't mean it's not ready. It was built a long time ago, constructed on the belief that this town possesses something others either envy or lack. The distinction didn't matter. Jack made a similar pier within himself years ago, and it's about all he has left. The new lights show it. They sparkle over a black ocean and reflect in the water. Contrast against such a barren landscape, those lights appear magnificent. Likewise, in that emptiness, they are insignificant. Jack wonders which way people see it, and most importantly, what that says about them.

He smokes down to the filter and stokes the cigarette's cherry with a couple of short inhales. He stares at the glowing tip bringing it close to his eyes, then he lets it hover over his cheek and neck. Millimeters away, he can feel the fire on his skin. That's where Jack lets the truth go. All the words he can't say to anyone, he lets them burn at the tip of a cigarette. It's a bonfire for everything that remains unspoken. Then Jack pushes the glowing tinder against the flesh between his thumb and index finger, and all of those words disappear.

Around the edges, his skin rises in a grayish-white. Unfortunately, the fire goes out too quickly, and so does Jack's sense of relief. There was just no way to sustain the sensation with an ember so tiny. If anyone asks, he'll just say some drunk bumped into him.

Then he tosses it over the railing into the alley below. He walks back to the bar, hoping that he missed the round of shots.

The rest of the night replays like that a couple times. Shots, beers, and group bathroom visits. Different groups of friends congregate together, spinning one or two members to another circle like the cogs of a machine churning an assembly line. Jack careful of which landing spot to occupy and how much time he can spend there without running out of things to say. Conversations spill out that feel important but are not and are already forgotten. As the night wears on, the bar grows, the lights dim even further, and the music gets so loud it disappears. Finally, the lights come on. His friends move to get to the after-party. Jack follows them out of the bar. His leg stalls at the top of his stride over the tile of the sidewalk. He can't step on it, on the black flecks embedded in them. His friends move on, but Jack pauses. Everything else on the street continues otherwise. Brakes squeal as a taxi pulls in front of the bar trapping two cars behind it. A group of men laugh and yell as they walk away. Jack looks at the scene around him, and "pause" seems like an inappropriate word. A "pause" appears to be standing still while everything else moves along, so to pause is really only to be passed by. Jack thinks that sounds more likely. Then he hopes that there'll be some red lights on the way to wherever they're going.

CHAPTER 11

The next day Montana picked up Jack in the early afternoon. That morning he surfed with Mutt, and Smoker joined them for lunch.

Since Jack found the bullet, he hasn't left his apartment before peering through the lowered blinds and looking through the peephole. Then he steps through the doorway and locks the door behind him. Usually, he stares over the railing to the shared space below and descends the stairs listening intently for any strange noise that might send in back inside quickly. And he walks on the balls of his feet so that he can turn and flee at any moment. But when Jack sees Montana pull up in his ride, a dark muscle car with shiny rims and glossy black wheels, he walks straight out of the apartment and down the stairs as if there isn't any reason to do otherwise.

He doesn't let Montana see him peek out of every window or linger in front of his door. He even walks down the stairs without a glance over his shoulder at the blind spot underneath the staircase. All while moving at a slowly vulnerable pace. How can he not? What would Montana think about the trouble he might have caused him? How would he react to the danger that Jack may have inadvertently brought to Montana's business? He just has to pretend that everything is okay, and Jack is good at that, he hopes, at least he knows he is practiced.

They drive for 40 minutes in light traffic, with every inch of the eight-lane road occupied but moving near the speed limit. On the broadest streets in the larger area. Never too far from a freeway onramp, and knighted on each side by large commercial buildings and the strip malls that fill the space in-between. His mom used to drive him out this way to go see his grandparent's gravesites on his dad's side. "It's important to remember the past," she'd say when Jack complained, "how else will you know where you're going when you don't know from where you came. What fate has in store for you." Jack never heard her mention her parents. They didn't exist as far as he knew. She could have been an orphan, but it was one of those mysteries about her that answers were promised to be delivered at some point but never were. His father chose to be cremated over being buried and have his ashes spread in the ocean.

All of the block families and his close friends sat on their boards in a circle. They tossed the ashes in the air, letting them catch the breeze for a short time before falling into the water and sinking below. Some landed on Jack's hair and he made sure not to get it wet the rest of the day.

Jack's mom stayed onshore. She was inconsolable. It was the first time Jack could remember her having wine, and that was with breakfast.

Of course, who knows if that's true. Memories can be faulty. Like when Jack was young and driving to his grandparent's gravesite, he can't remember there being this many cars, this much traffic. Now even these wide streets barely contain the sheer volume of people headed this way and that, for whatever reason they had, the ones that put them on the same road as Jack and Montana. Jack still doesn't know why he has been asked to come along. What he needs to do. Jack thought that in the car, Montana might explain, but there is no conversation to have over the loud Punk rock coming through the stereo. Jack might have turned down the music and ask for an explanation but, he learned not to ask too many questions that can come off as being reluctant or downright subversive. He was only told that Montana needed his help and that included bringing his gun. Montana didn't say which one, but Jack figured he meant the revolver, which fit nicely in his pocket.

Jack watches the cars near them and the buildings that sail past, as they generally continue south by southeast. He catches his own reflection in the window and tries to stare resolve and courage into himself. If he could only switch places with the image staring back at him, the one trapped in the glass. It's inert and intangible, just light, free of pain and anguish. Much easier to become that than become brave.

The windows are pristine, and the interior carries the same high sheen as do the tires. The inside reeks of 'new car' air freshener, and Jack hopes that this means they're only trying to impress someone when they arrive at whatever destination Montana has set for them. With Jack and the gun in tow, they are more impressive together, and there will be nothing more for Jack to do than stand there as much an image as a person. He looks at his reflection in the window again and wishes he could just send that instead.

Montana turns down a nondescript side street and then into the parking lot of a commercial warehouse property. They pass five different warehouses—each one with slated metal doors. Then Montana pulls up in front of the only complex that has its door open and parks just beyond it, in front of a yellow-painted curb designating it as a loading-only zone.

"Loading zone," Jack warns and immediately realizes how stupid he must sound.

Montana responds laconically, "We won't be long." There's comfort in Montana's confidence.

Jack has been here before. It's a warehouse-turned venue for punk shows, with a stage built four feet off the ground and room for a hundred kids if it ever drew that big of a crowd. The area they live, particularly closer to the beach, has produced some of the most iconic bands of the genre, somehow a breeding ground for youthful angst and rebellious rage and resentment for always being told what to do and how to behave. Everyone who Jack has seen step on that tiny stage probably had dreams of making a similar impact, even as they play to crowds that only fill a quarter of the space allowed.

As Jack and Montana walk under the rolling metal door, Jack notes the simple steel staircase on his left. It leads up to the only office in the warehouse and serves as a 'back stage' for the performers. Someone's on stage with his back to the door tuning a bass guitar, standing by himself, in front of a drum set and two mic stands. Jack veers toward the office stairs but meanders back toward the stage, following Montana's lead.

Cans litter about on the concrete floors with cigarette butts. An open case of beer sits on the stage next to the bassist. He hits the instrument's strings and twists the knobs on the top of its neck while sound ascends in pitch in the smallest of increments, at a volume that seems entirely unnecessary for the audience at hand. Every step Jack takes toward the stage is accompanied by a twist of the knob, with the string stretched further and further and cries out higher and higher through the speaker. Jack can feel the gun in his pocket bounce against his thigh. He is glad Montana is now several strides in front of him as they walk toward the wailing screams that make Jacks swallow hard, and he too, feels stretched thin.

Montana climbs the steps onto the stage quickly, and the musician turns at the sound or possibly at the vibrations of the fast thuds Montana feet issue under the cheaply constructed set. As Jack takes the first stair and with Montana crossing the stage quickly, Jack recognizes the band member from his freckled skin, thick brow line, and most obviously the swastika tattoo on his chest, that his ribbed white undershirt, a 'wife-beater,' doesn't cover.

Taurus takes his hands off the bass. "Montana? Fuck you doing here?" He says, confused but not threatened. There is comfort in that as well that Taurus isn't concerned at all.

Taurus is a member of a local skinhead gang that touts itself more white pride than white supremacy. The gang sports a name of a street that is only a half-mile from the beach but not considered a nice neighborhood. Someone might call them surf nazi's because they are just as much beach as they are a gang.

They would show up to high school house parties from time to time even though they were already in their early twenties. They'd steal beer and booze and pick fights with kids much younger, and they'd all run to each other's call and swarm the other fighter. The Tard used to draw their attention and got into a couple of fights with them. The only time Jack got in a physical altercation was when he'd pull one of them off of The Tard, and it always ended with Jack getting punched, elbowed, or kicked. Jack never really helped enough other than occupying the violence that would have landed on his friend. But that stopped their junior year when The Tard became too big to mess with, and the first one of them who attacked Jack's friend would be hurt well before any call brought more of them to the fight.

Not much about them has changed over the years. They wear 15 hole steel toe boots and bomber jackets, surf t-shirts with 'wife beater's outlined underneath. You see them in the pit without shirt or jacket stripped down to the same ribbed undershirt that Taurus now wears, circling together and sieg heiling to the music at punk rock shows. Even afterward, they'll claim not to be white supremacists, just proud of their history and ancestors. Jack heard them talk enough over the years that the bullshit they spouted lined up more with Anarchists, but they still got Nazi tattoos having no idea how dramatically opposed those ideologies actually were. Any decent high school history class covered that in the world wars.

Montana is still moving quickly and doesn't slow down his stride right until he sits into his legs, raises his hands, winds and unwinds, and throws his fist through the location Taurus' head had just been. Taurus crumples, his bass bounces off his body and onto the plywood stage with the thumps of its strings jumping through the loudspeakers like some dystopian movie soundtrack until there's only screeching feedback.

Jack sees Montana land a few more punches as Taurus tries to stand up. But then Jack is down himself. He feels kicks in his ribs, head, and back. Some are sharper than others, and Jack balls himself with his knees and legs, protecting his stomach and his arms protect his face and neck. He can't see anything through his elbows but the thick tread black rubber souls of the heavy boots they wear. His frame of vision bounces with each blow to the head. Back and down, back and down. He tries to gather a coherent thought, a plan, but any idea is knocked free from his head by those steel toe boots, and he is on the floor reeling and dizzy from the commotion. Meanwhile, the kicks continue to compress his ribs, batter his shoulders and arms, and force air from his lungs. He's beaten and at their mercy.

Then, suddenly, one of the assailants falls on the ground next to him, and the kicking stops. Someone stands over him, and Jack stays tucked into his tight ball, but then quickly realizes that the person over him is busy squaring up with Montana. Jack knows who it is too. They call him Road Dog. He's in the band as well, so is Ringo, who's down next to Jack, and another Jack doesn't know who is helping Taurus stand.

Montana lands a heavy punch, and Jack hears the wind leave Road Dog's body. Jack stands and gets his bearings. They must of all come down from the office. There is nowhere else to hide in there. Jack thinks of running up the stairs himself, but his body won't move. He can't even take a step. He is stuck in place, pulsing like the feedback echoing through the empty space. Jack feels it inside of him, and he feels empty as well.

Montana has engaged again. Jack sees Taurus running toward them but at an angle that would have him pass in front of Jack and land at Montana's back. Only a second until Taurus arrives, and right before that mark, Jack sees his own arm raise, landing a punch with the wrong knuckles and bending his wrist on impact painfully. At least Taurus falls off the stage while Jack grabs his own arm and winces. Montana kicks the fourth person in the chest, caving him to the stage, and then he slinks off the platform with the rest of them.

"Gun!" Montana demands from Jack. Jack reaches into his pocket with his throbbing hand and gives Montana what he wants.

Everyone freezes as Montana cocks the revolver. All the band members start slowly toward Taurus and center on him, their collective heads below Jack and Montana, knee-high and wearing confused and angry masks.

Taurus still doesn't seem scared, but that no longer reassures Jack. "What the fuck you going to do with that?" Taurus yells over the cacophony of feedback raging through the speakers.

"Get my point across," Montana answers loudly.

"Yeah, and what the fucks the point? You going to go against them? Huh, better think about it, really fuckin think about it."

"This isn't about me. I got my marching orders."

"Really?" And then Taurus does seem afraid. And confused "For what?" And then he gathers some resolve, "If they wanted us dead, they would have sent someone else."

"Yeah, is that so?"

"Yeah, it's so. You ain't one of em. No way they let some stupid white boy see that through. Anyway this is a big mistake. A big fucking mistake. I'll clear up."

"You better. Cause like you said, they won't be sending me again." Montana starts toward the stairs, moving laterally like a crab.

Taurus sounds embolden now, almost victorious, "Oh, this shit, not going to be forgotten. Bet on it. Count it. All business aside, sucker punches are personal. We'll see you off hours." Jack thinks of all the places they could cross paths, the most obvious ones being at the beach or a house party.

"Just stay in your yard" Montana lowers his gun to the ground and walks down the stairs.

Taurus barks back, "Fuck you, we never strayed! You think we're stupid or something? And where are you right now? Doesn't look like your patio, huh? This your neighborhood?"

"Come on, Crackie, let's go." Jack follows Montana by leaping off the stage, bypassing the stairs, the most direct route to the door, and an exit.

"We'll see you both. Eyes up." Road Dog threatens.

Ringo laughs, "We're goin Fuck you up."

The guy Jack doesn't know yells, 'fuck out of here, Pussies!" as Montana and Jack walk out through the door.

Montana wipes blood off his hands in the car, and Jack can't remember seeing it anywhere. He hands Jack the gun and admonishes him, carrying the volume of his argument with him in the car. "Fuck, next time, have this out! We didn't bring it to keep in our ass. And watch our back. Should have seen those mother fuckers coming!"

Jack musters an apology and asks, "What was that?" His voice sounds far away from himself. His ears ring from the noise.

"Just guys who can't follow the rules, and till their own soil. And an opportunity to prove we can."

Jack doesn't know, but he hopes that somehow this is the end of the bullet. At least he can try to convince himself that's it, which is something for which he is also well-practiced.

He places the gun back in his pocket with his sore hand. The car pulls away from the yellow curb. Jack catches another glimpse of himself and lingers, staring back at himself. It is so much easier to become inert.

The distortion buzzes from the feedback in his ears as they drive away and a high pitched cry, a scream from being pulled to thin echoes in his chest, and Jack keeps his mouth shut so that it doesn't escape his lips.

CHAPTER 12

January '03

Jack wakes to the subtle grind of the patio screen door sliding open. He lifts his head off of the pillow on the floor of his room and props on his elbows. He is lying on the guest room comforter on the ground next to his bed.

"I heard your mom come in around three," Bree says. The sky behind her is light in color and awash with thick ocean dew. Birds chirp in stereo.

Jack nods in response. Looks over to his bed to see it made. "You didn't have to make the bed. I can do that. I can take care of it."

"She was only gone for a couple of days this time," her tone is positive. "Maybe it is a good sign?" Bree pulls on a thin purple hoodie to guard against the slight chill in the air.

The cold morning awakens the skin on his now exposed arms, chest, and neck. They slept with the sliding glass door open. It leads out to the patio, and that, in turn, leads out to his walk street. He tastes the sweet smell of jasmine on the back of his tongue. He is the one who waters and maintains them and has done so since they let go of the gardeners two months earlier.

He was with his mom when she bought them. "You'll love how these smell," she promised him. She was always taking him to plant nurseries, then letting him walk the grounds on his own, pretending he was in some prehistoric jungle stalking his prey, and then he would jump out at his mom and growl. She pretended to be surprised and to be scared. The jasmine was the last one of those trips they took together.

Jack answers Bree. "Yeah... maybe it is," Jack closes his eyes and rubs them, cleaning the sleep that collected in the corners through the night.

"Do you have the pills?"

She produces a prescription bottle, transparent orange with a white cap, in response, and shakes for effect. The dull rattle of plastic reminds the two that there are not many pills left. Jack feels that rattle within him, the new realities that have hardened and embedded in his life. Small but growing automatons are bouncing through him, tearing through him, tearing organs, tearing open his heart. Leaving a hole in which everything he loves is lost through.

"I can't tell if it is funny or sad that we kept getting rid of the same bottle without realizing it," she says lightly.

"Is it sad or funny that she kept going through the trash to pull it out?" He forces a smile.

With victory in her voice, "Well, unless she is willing to go through the neighbor's trash, she won't get this one back." She says reassuringly, playfully. Jack knows she says it that way for him. He is grateful for her, but this is not how it is supposed to be. He is supposed to be the strong one. Just as his father was for his mother. He thinks he is letting her down. It's been 2 years since she lost her brother. Has she even finished grieving for him yet? Is Jack selfishly focusing on his dad despite her own loss? Does anyone ever get over something like this?

"You think with all the shit she has been throwing out, his clothes, pictures, and God knows what else, that it would be impossible to find those small pill bottles."

She smiles softly. Jack can see the care she has for him but worries there's also pity. But he and his crumbling life are exposed. She knows so much about it, and he is embarrassed by it. But he needs her so much, more than ever before.

"I think she is just getting rid of all the things that remind her of your dad. Maybe it's good for her to move on?"

"She always said that she sees him in me. Do you think she'll get rid of me?"

She tries to hide it, but Jack can read it on her face even if it only briefly flashes in the green of her eyes. Only momentarily rests on downturned lips. It looks like pity. She feels sorry for him, and that isn't at all how it is supposed to be.

"Can you hear the surf?" She asks—the sound of the waves breaking behind her. On a quiet morning like this one, the surf echoes from the beach up the walk streets only a couple of blocks away. The sound is louder than usual which means the waves break bigger than normal. "If you want, I can get my mom to make us breakfast? Pretty convenient for you, seeing how I only live a couple of houses down?" She jokes.

He lowers his head and his voice. "His birthday's next week." He won't let himself cry in front of her. He can't allow it to happen. Why did he even mention this? He silently curses himself.

"I know. You should come over for dinner. My mom would love to have you. And my parents won't fight if you're there. We can all remember him together. I'm finally at the point where when I think of Adam it makes me happy."

"I miss him." He refers to his father. He can't help himself.

"So do I." She eventually smiles, drops her gaze to her feet, and closes the sliding screen door behind her. Jack watches her hop the low stucco patio wall as she makes her way onto the sidewalk back to her house. He wishes he had gone with her but he can't. He has to be stronger. It is only fair to her. How could she ever fall in with him as broken as he is? He'll just have to fix himself without her first.

Jack puts his head back down and stares at the ceiling. He can hear wave after wave break. Only to be dragged under the sand, in a loud sucking sound, out to the ocean to be broken again. Then he hears his mom open up the gate to trash bins and feels a rattle in his chest.

CHAPTER 13

September 4, '07

Jack had enough time to shower and change after the fight. To exam the purple bruises on his body and consider the potential for another altercation with Taurus and crew soon, one where Montana won't be present. Then he tucked it all away before Smashley picked him and drove them both to her sorority house for a date party.

The living room is large and communal, as one would expect a Sorority House's living room to be, with hardwood floors that creak and give way underfoot and glossy white beadboard and crown molding. It is full of people whom Jack doesn't know, save for Smashley.

"So, you're from the same town as Ash?" She asks.

"Yes, he is." Smashley answers for Jack.

The girl says, "It's my favorite part of LA. After college, that's where I'm moving." Jack still hasn't heard her name mentioned yet. Or he missed it and is expected to know it, but only if he addresses her. Which he probably won't.

"I can totally see you there. We'll get a place together." Smashley's voice is different than when it is just her and Jack. It's more bubbly, more interested in what other people have to say, and softer and invites further conversation.

"It has to be by the beach because it gets ghetto around there pretty quickly." The nameless girl states as if she really knew the area at all.

Jack wears a long-sleeve button-down to hide the bruises on his arms, which aren't nearly as plentiful as those on his back. It hurts to stand so much more than to sit, so despite Smashley's protest and without any explanation, he found an anchor point at the party. He sits on a chair inside the large living room next to a fireplace filled with lit candles. It is brick and built long before gas fireplaces. Older, as is the house, the fireplace has a large hearth and metal screens that have been pushed wide open. It is as clean as you would ever see a wood-burning fireplace, probably because it is only used for candles and never for wood.

"Where are you going this fall?" The girl asks Jack.

"He's taking a gap year," Smashley answers for him again.

"Oh! I'm so jealous. My friend is going to Greece and Italy for three months and going to school for the spring semester. I almost joined her, but I wanted to rush right away. I just couldn't wait!" The girl squeals enthusiastically and squeezes her hands into fists with her elbows at her side.

Smashley mirrors her energy, "I know what you mean; I had no hesitation. I knew this is the house I would join before I even got excepted."

The girl smiles, "Of course you knew you were getting in, star athlete and all. I can't believe you aren't going to play here, though. One of the best players on the best team in high school, the coaches here must be going crazy." Smashley was a captain on her high school team, and that team probably was the best in the country or close to it, but her captainship had nothing to do with her ability. The coaches loved her. She voiced a no excuses, winning is everything mantra that the program pursued. She helped build up the resolve of the girls who stayed on the team all the way through and weed out the girls who couldn't handle the pressure or just lacked the necessary skills to contribute and would have just dragged everyone else down. She was an example even the boy's team heard about from their coaches, at least while Jack was on it, and he also listened to the complaints from the girls who couldn't last, but no one ever mentioned them.

But she isn't a great player herself. She is taller but not tall for volleyball. And her slender body looks just like those women who model athletic wear, but her legs are too lean, her back is too slim, and her arms too narrow. She lacks the explosive power thicker muscles provide.

"They've approached me a couple of times, but it is so much time, and energy and I really want to enjoy this." Smashley motions her hand to her side to indicate that "this" is everyone and everything in the large living room.

The girl nods as she takes in the spectacle of the party before asking Jack, "Where are you going on your trip?"

"I have no idea," Jack speaks up first.

Smashley clarifies for him. "He's thinking Europe but will probably go on a surf trip through Bali, the Mentawais, and New Zealand."

"That would be fun, wouldn't it?" Jack asks.

"That would be amazing. I think surfers are so hot. That's why I wanted to go to school in So Cal instead of the Bay."

Jack thinks of all the famous Northern California surf spots with much better waves than he has at home. And how far USC is from the beach. He doesn't bother explaining, though. So much easier to let her continue.

"Jack's a really good surfer. He could be a pro."

Jack tilts his drink and stares into it, and doesn't bother to correct them again. It's some kind of punch that has a blend of different types of alcohol that you can't taste.

"Are you in any ads? I bet you look really good with your shirt off. You have that clothes hanger body. Really wide shoulders, muscular, but thin."

Smashley immediately puts her hand on his shoulder, one she doesn't realize is bruised, and Jack hides his wince. Smashely speaks to the girl. "Hey, do you think this party needs something?"

"Like what?"

"A jolt? A little pick me up?"

"I don't know... What are you thinking?"

"Go ask, sister Betsy."

"Okay!" She leaves toward the kitchen.

"Oh my God. She sucks. But do you know who her father is?"

Jack puts his drink on the side table next to the chair. "You know what? I can't wait to go to the Mentawais. Glad it's this year because they might be underwater in ten."

"Well, what did you want me to say? Believe me, no one wants to hear about your life." Jack is always surprised at Smashley's knack for capturing reality in throwaway statements. The only time she says anything worthwhile is when she isn't trying.

Smashley continues, "She's annoying though, right? Anyway, I know these girls like "party," but I haven't seen any in the house. If that's forbidden, then she'll be the weirdo who didn't know better. If she gets the green light, I'll be the one who made it snow, and they'll all love me for it."

Jack squints his eyes and tilts his head unnecessarily, "You have coke?"

"What? No, I don't. You have it. You're the drug dealer, remember?"

"I don't."

"What do you mean you don't? You don't remember, or you don't have coke?" She raises her voice above the level of the murmur of the room and lowers herself into a hiss when she realizes how loudly she spoke.

He smirks and doesn't clarify. "I don't."

"You didn't bring any, you idiot? I want these people to like me. Why didn't you bring some party favors?"

"I'm out. Sold out. Won't get any for a couple of days at least." He smiles. It's always the best when that last bit disappears, and he gets to pretend that he isn't who he has become.

"How does a dealer not have drugs? What does that make them? A nothing?"

"That's okay cause I am a pro surfer now."

"Don't forget our deal. You play nice while I rush, and I don't tell your friend that you know he fucked your girlfriend."

"I have a girlfriend? Is she here?" Jack doesn't even care about the tryst, doesn't care about her. And he can quickly look past his friend's misstep if his friend would not care either. But the news alone carries with it potentially much more considerable damage than the act itself. With only so many days left with them, how many moments would he lose if everyone wanted to avoid them? He's just lost so many people he can't lose another.

"If you didn't like it, you wouldn't be here," Smashley hisses again. The other girl, whose father is someone Jack should know, comes back.

"Okay, I talked to sister Betsy, and she totally agrees."

Smashley puts her hand on him and lets her elbow hit Jack in the ear. So subtle in movement but with enough force to sting

"Now I have a ton of Ritalin, and so does Maddi, and Tory, and... shoot, I forget her name?"

"Sounds like fun. I wish we had 'party' though" Again, Smashley strikes Jack in the head with her elbow. He moves his head to the far side of the chair by leaning further back in his seat, shifting through echoes of pain in his ribs.

The famous father's daughter questions, "Party?"

Smashely explains, "You know, coke."

"Oh," she laughs, "You're so clever. I like that. Yes, I wish we had 'party.'"

Smashley moves her arm again but can't reach Jack. She continues, "we also have some Percocet and Hydrocodone if we really want to mix things up."

Jack can see the names on his mother's prescription bottles. The ones he and Bree would throw out. The worst was the oxy, though. That's when she turned off.

"I think that would be fun. Can you get us one of each? A Rits and a Vike. Actually, bring the bottles over. You can hand out one, and I'll hand out the other like candy stripers."

"Great idea. We're so going to be best friends."

Jack waits until the girl is out of earshot. "Oh, shoot, your best friend left." He coughs a little, and his ribs break in pain.

"Shut up. I don't know why you're even here?" She keeps her voice low as another couple walks over to the mantle where the man puts his drink and kisses the girl. She is good at inflicting damage in subtle low tones where no one realizes it.

Once the other girl comes back, Jack swallows his pills, both the stimulant and depressant. He could sell them. His clients ask for them from time to time. Jack is sure Montana can get them. Probably a better mark up in price for them. But he won't, he doesn't like even taking them, they've cost him too much.

Jack watches Smashley parade around the room handing out the pills. Over laughing at people's jokes, enthusiastically moving her body. He can tell when she shows off her cleavage to her friends' dates and how she kisses all the girls in the same spot on their cheek as if they were unique. They all seem to love her, and that makes sense. She is a bully, first and foremost. They just see someone willing to push themselves into their life. A life that may not have as many touchpoints as they let on. In that way, Jack is just like them, pretending to have more than he does. Smashley acts, too, and is better than most. Smashley is as fake as her spray tan, as legitimate as her bleached blonde hair, and as timeless as the fashion trends she worships. Jack can see the planning in action, how she greets them, what to say, and who she needs to focus on. How Smashley moves, the expression worn on her face, and the sweet tone in her voice. She is calculating and untouchable. Quickly sizing up the value each person has to offer her and how to best use them. But no one can see that except for Jack.

Watching her count her moves off in her head, one tick at a time, and being able to hide that from everyone else, Jack understands why they had been attracted to each other in the first place. They are alike in ways that he doesn't care to admit.

She is looking for herself in the faces of all the other people. In their anticipatory raise of the brow in how excited they are to see her. Or the bend growing in the cheek just before a smile. The parting of lips just before a laugh or compliment. And better still, the desire pushing open an expanding pupil. To live in the small nuances written on other people's faces and have nothing more than that for yourself is something with which Jack is all too familiar.

Jack turns to watch the candles burn. He allows himself to caress his side and openly grimace, and he stares into the fireplace. The wax pours over the rims candles and drips onto the ground below.

He feels them melt away as they burn through themselves. He can feel the heat of the candle on fire, destroying the very element that allows the wick to stand up and fulfill its purpose.

Then he waits for the pills to kick in and watches the candles self-destruct. Eventually, all the lies we tell ourselves do not withstand. And as hard as he tries, he can't help see a swastika burning in the fire.

CHAPTER 14

September 5, '07

The waist-high cement wall with a round top separates the boys from everyone else. Green ivy blankets the wall, its roots buried in gold pots placed around the patio. White lattice carrying a flower that Jack doesn't know pushes up against the home. The landscaping does little to minimize the small, square, and boring layout of the patio. There is no need. The proximity to the beach and the sand makes the cheap white plastic deck chairs thrones, and all the boys who sit on them, royalty.

Sitting in a line, they stare out onto the strand. A never-ending parade of people flows back and forth, and everyone receives a look and a comment. It's not the people that they enjoy but the ridicule that festers when cool goes unheralded.

These are the days of nothing to be done, and nothing is all that matters. Summer idleness entertains in a way that leaves boredom close but inconsequential.

It took some convincing to get Jack there, one of the few places where he could run into Taurus or any of his gang. Really though Jack had no choice, all of his friends were there, and there is only so much time when that will be true. But that didn't stop him from vigilantly eyeing the horizon and taking measure of every passerby for their potential to harm.

Sand scrapes against the bottom of Jack's feet as he shuffles them back and forth. Each toe grips the concrete, and the heel drags them backward. He can hear the friction but can't feel the sand. He has his summer feet. Grown by going barefoot on and around the beach, he has built up calluses of thick skin that can withstand hot sand and hot concrete. They come up just short of being able to drag on asphalt to slow down his skateboard.

Out on the beach, a runner follows a lifeguard truck that passed by hours earlier. It's a trick that beach runners know. The tire tread compresses the deep sand making it easy on the runners' legs. Jack is not sure who it is, but he knows the runner grew up there.

Down the strand, to Jack's left, an elderly couple makes their way towards him. Their strides land the insoles of their lead foot no further than the toe line of the previous step. She bends over from the waist and shakes as the man supports her. Both have gray hair and dress for a much colder day. The man wears a cap and oversized black glasses, which hide most of his face.

They walk as a reminder to everyone else. No one can look at them and not think of death, of life's inherent weakness, and the fact that all things end.

Jack has found that people don't like to talk about death, to think about it. In his own life, the loss he dealt with made most people uneasy if they didn't know to expect it in a conversation if it wasn't known background information. It made them uncomfortable, as uncomfortable as staring at the overhead sun. So one day, he just stopped talking about it. He didn't let it go because that would imply coming to terms with the tragedy. No, that's not what happened. He simply ignored it. Jack concludes that is what the old couple bundles up against, why the man wears such dark glasses, to shield himself from deaths' ugly glare.

He feels sorry for them. He knows how it is when people feel uncomfortable with something embedded in another person, something out of their control. So he watches them for that reason.

"Fuckin Crackie strip and hop over," Luggy says, referring to the wall, "we need some bait." Jack is still wearing a t-shirt despite the clear blue sky and a full yellow sun and warmth it brings. He can feel the bruises underneath, the ones that feel like they push into bone, and they remind him to keep his shirt on.

It's not a matter of what Jack will say. He knows what he'll say. The question is whether or not they'll believe him.

Mutt declares, "I don't need Crack to get gash." Smoker laughs, and Luggy joins him. The Tard giggles too but seemingly more at the outburst than Mutts statement.

"Right." Luggy holds on to the vowel derisively.

"Come on, Crackie!" The Tard chimes in, "I want to chat up some older mit."

Jack tries to change the subject. "You guys hear about what's going on at the pier?" No one bites, and he grips the plastic chair in his hand.

Thankfully Smoker provokes Mutt. "Mutt, you've got no game." He raises his hand and points very closely to Mutt's face.

Mutt protests, "My dialogue is sick. Better than your vomit."

The Tard speaks up, "Luggy really has to best move out of all of us."

"Yup," Luggy agrees.

"Bullshit," Mutt disagrees.

"True," Luggy chirps.

Smoker goes in, "Have to agree, fuckin works."

Luggy smiles and says, "60% of the time, every time." It's a perfect use of a movie quote.

"He falls down. That's not a move!" Mutt argues.

Luggy, enjoying the attention, laughs. "Walk in the room and fall as clumsy possible, as big as possible, and everyone looks. Mousties too. And they're already laughing, so you got them smiling, you have their attention, and you got something to talk about."

The Tard shares, "I tried it. Fell too damn hard, I think people were worried."

Jack is quick to it, "probably broke the foundation," he says dryly. It garners a laugh, and Jack tries not to smile at his own joke and the fact he still has his shirt on. He lets go of his chair.

Jack's phone vibrates. It's Montana. Jack sends him to voicemail after yesterday he has earned a day off.

Smoker asks, "Is that Smashley?"

He pushes his tongue up to the gap in his teeth nervously. Jack knows why he asks, of course. Why he's asked about her every day, they have hung out over the last week. He's the one she fucked, and he is now waiting for the news to come out. Maybe even for Jack to confront him. Jack would like to think that to Smoker it isn't a big deal, after all, they were broken up at the time. But the fact Smoker hasn't joked about it as if it were hilarious only proves that he thinks he did something wrong, and that's damning. Jack pauses before he answers to torture Smoker a little bit longer. "No. Montana."

"Reloaded?" Luggy guesses.

"Nope."

Mutt jokingly hisses, "Boo. We need some fuckin chalk, bro." 'Chalk' is the new word the boys are using for cocaine. They were saying 'party' all school year but moved on when everyone started too as well.

"Almost," Jack smiles and winks at Mutt, "going with him up to SLO for some intro. So after that." Jack manages to sound upbeat.

Mutt doesn't share his enthusiasm, "Fuck bro, rough ride. Not sure if I can think of a time I'd prefer three hours of silence."

"Dudes gives me the sweats solo, always need a buffer," Luggy shares.

"Thank God Crackie's not a pussy like the rest of you," The Tard admonishes them, probably for Jack's sake. Jack is grateful but not surprised; he can always count on his closest friend.

"I'll go with you," Smoker says. "Mumbles is having a party up there before they start. He mentioned it to me the other night. Drop me off. You guys do whatever you need to and then meet up."

"Thanks, bro," Jack replies.

Smoker, no longer exploring his tooth gap, "No worries, I know you'd do the same for me." Whether it is guilt over Smashley or not, it's the very reason why Jack doesn't want her to say anything, and why Jack won't bring it up either, he needs him. He needs all of his friends. They're leaving soon enough. Let the news come out then when it won't matter as much.

The trip reminds Jack to bring up the apartment to The Tard again. They're supposed to move in together this spring, but if that happens sooner, then Jack could get away from the bullet, from Taurus, or whoever left it. Jack leans forward in his chair, about to get up and go over to The Tard, but before

Jack does anything, The Tard shouts, "I would!" Luggy is second and not too far behind.

Jack hasn't seen the object yet, but thunders, "I would."

"Of course I would," Mutt sounds off.

She walks by with a man in her arm. Striking and dressed for a day spent far away from the beach. She turns her head slightly toward the patio, but the dark sunglasses hide her eyes. Jack smiles, anyway. The man she is with pretends not to hear.

"Yeah, I guess I would throw her a bone," Smoker says charitably in jest. The boys laugh, and Jack's chuckle vibrates in his sore back.

"I wouldn't, but Mutt would. Several times actually." Luggy says quickly and in a lower voice. Jack understands when he sees the jogger approaching a block away.

Mutt fires back, "Oh, hey, the one chick Luggy hasn't taken advantage of."

Smoker coughs in a thin façade at Luggy's expense, "Manwhore."

"Guys! Crackie's right here. You know he can hear you, right?" Luggy feigns concern, redirecting the joke at Jack. Jack stays silent. Inert. It keeps any further attack at bay. They can make fun of each other for hours, and they do. It's the primary driver of all of their conversations. They constantly probe each other's defenses and wage attacks, leaving themselves exposed for rebuttals. It is a competition like anything else in their lives. The content doesn't matter. Their weapons are wit and ridicule, but most importantly, control. Don't let on to any wound, any weak spot that can be exposed. The more cutting the comment, the better for the recipient as it will prepare them for a future where they are not without flaws but live well to conceal them. To become excellent liars.

"Hey guys, how's it going?" She smiles and stops in front of the wall but keeps her legs moving.

"A.I." They respond enthusiastically

"A.I.," what are you doing?" Luggy asks.

"What does it look like?" Her breath is short.

"I didn't realize you ran." He responds. Jack can't tell if it is a subtle joke at her weight or not. She is short and round, and many have said that she looks as if she had once been hammered down from a normal height, ballooning outward like a mushroomed nail. She has always seemed like that, though. Jack has known her since kindergarten. He knows that she always fought her weight. Just another inherent issue that people can't control but for which they are held accountable. "What are you up to tonight?" Luggy sounds uninterested in the answer before she provides it.

"Jenny's parents are out of town, and she might have people over, but she's trying to keep mellow, so don't tell anyone."

"Welldubs, huh? Alright, sounds good. Have a good run."

A.I. takes her cue and heads north with her head down, running faster than when she approached. Jack sees her slow down a block away.

Smoker asks, "Mutt, how many times did you fuck her?"

"About half the number times you let her smoke you."

"You guys want to go to that?" Asks The Tard.

"Sounds lame," Mutts sighs.

"It doesn't have to be," says Smoker. He grabs his phone and starts texting. "Smoke signals," he laughs and garners a chuckle or two. Jack silently calculates the odds of ruining into Taurus. Yet, another reminder to talk to The Tard.

Jack moves off his chair and sits on the wall opposite The Tard. "You ready to move in yet?" He grabs the fabric of his boardshorts pulls it down his thighs as he shifts uncomfortably on the wall. They already hang low on his waist. That's because they weren't his shorts originally. They were The Tards until he outgrew them.

"I wish. Rehab sucks."

"You can't tell you even had surgery." Jack even sounds hopeful as he continues to adjust his clothes and how he sits. It's not that the clothes don't fit well enough. Jack has been wearing The Tards hand-me-downs since sophomore year, and even though he was embarrassed to do so, the clothes have always felt fine since he first dropped them off.

One day The Tard showed up at Jack's apartment with a bag of clothes and said, "My mom wants you to have these. They're taking up too much room, and they don't fit me anymore." Jack had gone through a growth spurt, and the majority of his clothes were too tight or too short, and obviously so because The Tard's little sister said so the week before. When the pants Jack wore were calf-high, and she asked him, "Are you wearing Capri pants?" No, it's not the clothes that are making Jack shift back and forth on a wall he's sat comfortably on for years. In fact, even though the shorts sit low on Jack's waist, it falls in line with what's fashionable, and all the kids have similarly low hanging shorts. And though Jack can now afford any new clothes he wants, he still wears the older board shorts because his best friend gave them to him.

"It feels fine, but you know the deal. Coach wants me to take off fall join the team halfway through the year, so I can concentrate on being 100% ready and healthy. Plus, with the scholarship system, if I join in the spring, they have more to offer in the fall. I don't really understand that, but somehow it helps them stack an incoming class."

"Yeah, I know. But the apartment isn't part of the scholly. Any chance your parents will let you move out early?" Jack tries hard not to let the desperation in his voice. That's why he's shifting on the wall uncomfortably; he's trying to get his friend to agree to move into their apartment early without divulging any valid reason why they do so. Jack is balancing desperation and fear with secrecy and shame and moves back and forth to not topple over and spill onto his friend the weights he carries.

The Tard must not hear it because he casually watches the crowd walk by and hasn't even looked at Jack yet. "I wish. Pops won't budge on the timeline of the apartment. Doesn't want me on my own without school or baseball. Especially with rehab. He thinks I won't do anything but drink. And he might be right. "The Tard takes a long pull off of his beer. "Why? What's up?"

"Nothing," Jack lies. He lets go of the board shorts. "Just stoked to get the new pad going." He moves back to his chair and slumps defeated into a throne he doesn't deserve. The bruises on his body ache to remind Jack that he can't escape. A minute passes, and a group of heavily tattooed boys, about Jack's age, pass on skateboards. They aren't part of Taurus' gang, but they are friendly with them, from the same part of that town. Jack lowers his eyes and slumps even further, and bends the plastic chair in his clenching fists. Unspoken pain pulses with each heartbeat and the bruises feel to have grown all over his body and wove themselves deep into Jack's flesh. He hears Mutt say it first.

"Shadow alert."

"Why won't he just find some friends?" Smoker complains.

"What do you mean, that's your boy?" Luggy jokes.

Smoker volleys back, "No, he's your boy."

"Remember when we were frying balls, and he chased us in his car, and we tried to ditch him down an alley?" Mutt unnecessarily retells the story that no one has forgotten. Jack pictures the narrow alleyway lined with tall wooden fences, telephone poles, and trash cans. Luggy speeding through drainage dips, and intersecting streets, which have no stop signs for opposing traffic, with The Shadow trailing closely.

"Fuck, if that wasn't a hint, I don't know what is?"

"I would never hang out with some guys that didn't want me there, you know, have some pride."

"Look, he's pretending like he doesn't know we're here."

"Good, then he can just keep on walking."

"What's up, fellas?" The Shadow forces with enthusiasm. The boy's oval shape resembles that of a punching bag. Without looking, Jack can picture his mouth. The two front teeth crossed each other, and the overlapped enamel had been stained brown. The bottom row grew in different directions. How unfortunate for him that they would always distract from the words he would say. Jack runs his tongue along the back of his perfectly straight teeth.

"What up?" Mutt answers back with no genuine regard to the recipient.

"Just cruising. What are you guys up to?"

"Hanging." Mutt does not give him much to with which to work.

"Would," Luggy says first loudly.

"Yes, sir" The Tard follows less enthusiastically.

"Would," says Smoker.

Mutt turns to those boys, laughs, and says something hard to hear. The Shadow looks around, confused. Still staring in the other direction, Jack pushes his back against the plastic chair, and his hands push down on its armrests, which bend against his weight.

He listens for The Shadow to ask what they were talking about, or worse, say, "would," he does neither, and Jack's arms relent, and the chair falls back into form.

"Did you guys see Timmy?" The Shadow inquiries.

"Who?" Luggy asks, and just before The Shadow answers, he continues with, "Cares?" Everyone chuckles.

The Shadow still sounds confused and cautiously says, "Timmy Miller."

This time Jack's armrests push out to the side. No one says anything.

The Shadow continues, "He is down by the pier practicing Falun Gong."

"Fall in My bong?" Smoker sarcastically cracks. Jack laughs reflexively, and pain follows along his ribs and sternum.

"No. It's some kinda Tai Chi."

Smoker continues, "Yeah, I heard Triller went to China in some big protest, got kicked out of the country... would!"

"No way. Wouldn't," Mutt says dismissively.

"That's a lie." Luggy laughs.

Jack squeezes the plastic armrest of the chair, waiting for The Shadow to say it when he isn't part of the game.

Mutt goes back to the protest, "Why would Triller give a shit about something on the other side of the world?"

"Fuckin drank the Koolaid," Smoker explains.

The Shadow seems to have gained some confidence in the conversation continuing. It's as evident as the smirk on his round face. "Yeah, what a weirdo," he laughs. Jack puts his discomfort into his elbows and moves the armrests of his chair further outward despite the protest of pain in his back.

"Weirdo!" Smoker repeats and laughs loudly.

The Shadow must think it's at Trillers expense because his body visibly relaxes.

"Oh, totally, would." The Tard cheers, and the woman he says it toward rolls her eyes and shakes her head.

"Yep," Luggy continues, "but she wouldn't," laughing at The Tard.

The Shadow turns around toward the strand, leers at the women walking away. Jack pleads silently, begs him not to say anything, but The Shadow yells, "Hey baby!" to the woman, breaking the rule of the game.

Jack's chair folds along the crease in its back panel as Jack leans strongly against it and pushes the armrests out to the side, his ribs howl back at him.

The Shadow continues droning, utterly unaware of how ridiculous he sounds and how uncomfortable he's making Jack feel. "Anyway, he is down at the pier with big signs hung up all over the place. He's been in the newspapers a couple of times," no one pays attention to him. "What a weirdo, huh?" He says 'weirdo' again as if it worked the first time.

No one speaks for a full minute, Jack continues to grip the chair, and The Shadow's lurking grows along Jack's forearms in humps of corded muscle as Jack tries to crush it in his hand. A group of older friends rides past. They all exchange shakas, nods, and let them know to what street they're headed. The Shadow waves as they pass even though he doesn't know them.

"Mind if I grab a beer and chill?" The Shadow leans against the wall. It should seem like a casual way to stand, but with him, that's impossible. Unfortunately, nothing is ever going to change that within the eyes of the boys on the patio. Jack feels sorry for him first and is relieved that he isn't himself on the other side of the wall second. It's only a slight difference in position, but always too close not to worry.

"Actually, my mom only lets me have five friends over at a time."

"Well, there's five of us right here." The Shadow replies, hopefully. He misses the point. He doesn't understand this is all at his expense.

"Actually, I like to keep that last spot open just in case one of my friends comes by. You understand, right?" Mutt cuts him off.

The confusion falls away from his face quickly, pushed aside by deflated ambition. He isn't adept at hiding pain yet. "I guess." The Shadow creeps away.

Jack's chair unbends, and everything returns to form, even as he feels sorry for the boy.

"Lurker," Luggy says with a low, drawn-out voice.

"Mother fucker musta thought it was white boy day." Mutt has a movie quote ready. All of the boys laugh. The Shadow is only a couple of houses away. Jack suspects he hears them but hopes he doesn't.

"I'm just glad he didn't shoot us while we were in school."

"Yeah… Talk about dodging a bullet." It's Jack's best line of the day, and he tries not to smile.

Jack's the only one who watches as The Shadow marches away until he turns up a hill. Jack sees it for what it is, though, a descent. Reputation imposes a trajectory that doesn't exist. The need to theoretically calculate such a thing best defines adolescence but is too often carried long past that age. No one ever mentions it, but it seems to be more important than anyone is willing to let on.

"What about spilling a drink on yourself? Think that would work?" The Tard asks, and everyone seems to know what he's referring to, bringing back the old thread; it's the hours upon hours that the boys have spent together that allows them to speak without explanation. An outsider like The Shadow could never overcome it.

"You kidding me?" Smoker questions.

"Timmy The Tard." Mutt ridicules in a mocking clichéd voice of someone with lower intelligence.

"No, No, bro," Luggy responds. "The fall is bigger. Gets more attention. And really, it's always questionable if it's on purpose. That's what makes it funny. Spilling a drink, people will just think you're a slob. And what are you going to do with your wet shirt all night?"

"Crackie should do it. Never seen a guy lose his shirt more. At least he'd have an excuse." Mutt teases.

"He only buys itchy brand," Smoker jokes.

The Tard detours the subject. "Fuck dude, you still have your shirt on now. Throw it off and get some mit to stop and dialogue."

Jack squeezes the chair again. He wonders if it was worth coming here. "We got Mutt. He gets the most ass out of us all anyway." Jack jokes.

"Crackie! Crackie! Crackie!" They chant. Jack knew before that it would come to this, in one way or another, to have to unveil himself as living a life completely different than theirs, one without the most critical element, control. Only one thing he can do, smile through it and make them believe.

"Fine, mousties for everyone" Jack found the perfect time to say the new word everyone else has been repeating and checks off a box in his head. He takes off his shirt and stands.

But before he can leap the wall, Smoker blurts, "What the fuck happened!?"

"Dude, you're all jacked up, bro," The Tard sounds concerned.

Mutt teases, "Dude put your shirt back on," and laughs.

Jack laughs loudly, "You should see the other guy... his hands are really swollen from punching me so much", and then he continues. "I fell off my skate last night. Bombed a hill, got speed wobbles. Bounced on the concrete a couple of times." Then Jack says the line from a movie he had practiced delivering when he figured he'd have to explain the bruises to his friends. "It's merely a flesh wound."

Unfortunately, The Tard asks casually, "thought you were at a date party last night?" Jack freezes.

Thankfully Luggy follows up quickly with another quote from the same movie "Is that an African or European swallow?" He makes everyone laugh, and Jack sits back down.

"Hey, guys, did you hear Welldubs is having a rager tonight?" Smoker holds up his phone, filled with responses. Now it's the kind of party to which Taurus might show up.

"She really came through, didn't she?" Luggy smiles.

Jack sees A.I. running back toward them.

She turns up three blocks before Mutt's. Jack assumes she cuts behind to the alley to avoid running past this house again. To prevent people from discussing something inherent in them through no fault of their own. Something that makes other people uncomfortable, and so it is best hidden. Jack looks over at his shirt on the ground and understands.

Mutt says enthusiastically, "I have some boomers, a stem, and a cap for each of us. Might even trip an hour or so."

"Perfect" Jack lies and the bruises on his body remind him just how vulnerable he will be.

Some younger girls pass, 15 or 16. They have the developing curves of a woman but hadn't thickened into adults.

Jack had seen them at parties before and knew their names, and there's no question that they knew all of the boy's names in turn.

Jack stretches his arms, sucks in his stomach, and unnecessarily turns, elongating his torso, despite the bruises that run along his spine and ribs screaming in pain. He sees the girls notice. While he has his father's broad frame, he also has his mother's thin skin, and every knot and groove on his stomach carve lines down all to way to his low hanging board shorts, which sit just above his pubic hair.

They smile and giggle as they pass. One hides her face in her friend's hair. Jack shouldn't worry.

CHAPTER 15

September 5, '07

The boys ate the mushrooms and stayed on the patio until after sundown. Jack had no choice but to stop worrying about crossing paths with Taurus, Road Dog, or Ringo. In that state, there wouldn't be anything Jack could do. He had reluctantly but voluntarily laid himself at the alter for potential sacrifice. It took some time to let go of the anxiety, to stop seeing swastika's tattooed on every shirtless 20 or so. It was just after the incessant giggling started when his vision began to change and the light poured into his open pupils that the short patio wall grew, and all there was in the world was Jack and his friends. Calls of "Roberto" carried themselves into the fading light painted on the sky.

Unfortunately, they left for Weldubs, and the good feelings stayed at the beach.

Jack found a place in the back of the party away from the front door so that if any skinhead showed, Jack would be out a window quickly. His friends moved around the party freely, and Jack came up with several excuses not to ever join them.

No one came. At least no one from Taurus' gang. Smashley showed. She tried staying with Jack, but when it was apparent Jack didn't care if she was there or not, she found Smoker and attached herself to him.

She was the one who kept dragging Smoker to the back room. Laughing at his jokes and touching him, with periodic glances toward Jack. The flirting didn't bother him, but the whispers were whole other matter. Every time she pulled away from Smoker's ear, Jack's breath stopped. Jack couldn't help but stare at them and wait to see if Smoker looked at Jack with regret and sadness. Finally, the boomers wore off, and Jack freed himself from the back room.

He checked the pantry for food he no longer needs to take and grabbed a couple of cans of soup. Then he thought it would be fun to find the change bowl again, for old time's sake. A mission to occupy his time at a party he didn't want to be at, drinking beer for which he is no longer thirsty. And so Jack crept away from the party but gave up on the money he no longer needed and now sits in the downstairs hallway of Weldubs house. He can still hear the music, the laughter, and the pointless yelling.

He has heard it for years. You are only important when you reside on the tips of other people's tongues. So everyone speaks as loud as they can, and the volume forces other people to be interested in what they're saying, and in that way, become interesting people. The only problem is no one can hear anyone else talk over their own voice, which makes them all only interested in themselves.

The beer he holds is warm; he hasn't sipped since he sat down, and all of the condensation has dried off. He compares it to the soup in his pockets that so easily passes for beer.

It took some time before he figured out that no one would notice or ask. His first couple of times sneaking them out of a house, he waited until the very end of the party, stuffed his hands in his pockets, and kept his back to anyone he passed as he made a quick and silent exit. It really should be obvious. The open beer he's drinking is clearly not the same as the soups in his pockets. The beer is longer and thicker than those cans.

It wasn't until one time Jack accidentally passed Luggy on his way out that he realized no one would ever assume he carried cans of soup stolen from the pantry. Jack froze in fear and hung his head in shame. Luggy looked down at the bulge in his pocket, commented about road sodas, left Jack, and headed toward the kitchen to presumably grab a drink for his own way home. After that, Jack began to go as if he hadn't anything thing to hide.

It must be the beer that's blinding. Jack practically waves them in everyone's face all night. There isn't a point at a party where he isn't drinking one, holding one, raising one to a friend. And most importantly, no one at these parties would ever think anyone would ever take soup home with them, or more so would ever need to take soup home with them in order to eat. It's the assumption they can't see past, more so than the beer.

Then something completely unexpected happens. While Jacks sits, measuring what people will notice, Bree steps off the stairs.

CHAPTER 16

October '03

The small apartment's carpet is beige, the walls and the popcorn ceiling have been freshly painted white, and the noxious chemical smell lingers even with the windows open. Jack closes the door. His friends had just left. There is school tomorrow, and they needed to get to their homes for dinner. He picks up the empty beer bottles and roach clips. He was happy to hear them celebrate the fact they had a place to go hang out. Luggy said that this would be their 'clubhouse,' a place where they were free to do whatever they wanted. It's only his second day there, and his friends had already come over. Jack was worried it would be too far for them, but The Tard promised Jack that they would come, and he never let Jack down before.

Bree was there too, the day before. To see his place and to help set up the essentials. He didn't make any progress after she left. She said she wanted to come over again to finish unpacking, but he won't let himself invite her back over for at least a week. Even though she said she would be alone today anyway because her parents were going to "Some kind of marriage thing," Jack made other plans. It's all part of his self-imposed limit on letting her see his crumbling life.

Boxes remain stacked on top of one another, on the small table that will be the dining room table, but was previously the breakfast nook table.

They are in the shower, on the stove, and on countertops. They are stacked in front of the unconnected TV and piled against the barren white walls of the apartment. It is too many boxes for such a small space. Jack's telescope didn't make the cut. Neither did a large number of his favorite books.

The deep L-shaped couch extends beyond the wall opposite the TV and blocks a decent portion of the hallway that leads to the bedroom and bathroom. The other half of the sofa pushes right to the TV, making it unlikely for anyone to sit there. Jack sits down on the couch that doesn't quite fit in the room, puts his feet on a box as a footrest, and waits to hear the phone ring. His mom promised to call when she landed, which should have been that morning.

She hadn't spoken of work in two years. Not since she took time off for Jack's father's sickness and then for bereavement. Then seemingly out of nowhere, she mentions a work assignment that takes her far away to another country on a different continent.

She said that it would only be two months. "It won't be long I promise." Her voice thick and groggy. "Plus you have been taking care of yourself now anyway, I don't see what's the big deal."

Money must have gotten tight because they sold the house. Probably too much to ask her to support everything on her own. Jack thought he remembered his father in the hospital mentioning the home being paid for so that Jack wouldn't worry. That Jack would always be taken care of, his father called the house Jack's birthright. That was after the chemo didn't have the effect the doctors were hoping it would. "Don't worry, Jack." His father said, "It will all work out. I promise. Even if I'm not around much longer. In that case, you'll be the man of the house, and I'll need you to look after your mother. And take care of yourself, and take care of your house. It's your birthright, and if there is any comfort in me not being able to look after you, it will be because the home is ours. We don't owe anything on it. No one can take it away from you."

The circumstances must have changed. Jack's mom said that they needed money, which is why she took the job.

Jack hoped that things would change when he heard her say that she was taking a job. He hoped that moving out of the home where she could never forget would help her, even if that meant him giving up on living close to the beach. Close to his friends. Close to Bree. Also, if that meant giving up the only home he has ever known. The house that helps him never to forget.

But Jack is a lot of things, and stupid isn't one of them. He knows that they signed a year-long lease. A year in this tiny apartment that is too small for all things in his life. Jack would happily sleep on the couch. Gladly give up his bedroom and put his clothes in the linen closet in the hallway or store them under the sink in the bathroom. He hopes he is wrong. He closes his eyes and wishes that he is wrong. A year in a single bedroom apartment when his mother is supposed to be home in two months. He knows that she isn't coming back. He knows where the money for the house will go. He knows that there isn't a job. He knows that she has been gone for two years and not two days. And the saddest part is that in all that change, nothing is going to change for the better.

He takes in the clean and empty white walls and measures the space against the boxes piled up. Somehow he needs to pour his old, more significant life into this new empty small one. And the fumes from the paint make him lightheaded.

CHAPTER 17

September 5, '07

Bree walks off the last step of the staircase and takes a stride toward Jack. She stops the moment she sees him and turns the other way. It's clear Bree didn't think it through because she walks toward the other end of the hallway, a dead end, so she has no choice but to turn back toward Jack and the stairs to escape. She keeps her head down the entire time. Jack can only see her hair obscuring her face. Her hand hits the staircase rail, and her body turns toward the exit, all without ever looking up. When her foot hits the first stair, Jack yells, "I'm sorry!" loud enough to cut through the music and the party's indiscernible chatter. She stops then and looks at him for several heartbeats and shallow panicked breaths as Jack squeezes hard the perfect beer can he holds, which dents in his hand. She straddles the staircase and the floor but doesn't say anything.

He doesn't even realize, but his mouth opens, his breath harness resolve and words pour out without edit. "Do you ever feel like you're drowning? You can't breathe. And as hard as you try, you can't quite reach the surface. But you can see it." He hears the cracking of the aluminum can in his grip as he squeezes the half-drunk beer he holds again and again. "You're not too far below. You can see the waterline and the sky, and the air you need is so close, but all you do is sink further and further away." Bree looks to the top of the stairs, toward escape, but doesn't move.

Jack further dents the beer with his thumb following the curve near the top of the can. "No one can see you, and no one can hear you, and so they keep going along with their lives as if everything were okay."

Bree doesn't respond. She lets her back foot rise to the first step. She looks down again and then back at Jack. He hasn't seen her all summer. He can't move. Can't walk to her. He can see she isn't angry but sad. Then without a word, she makes her way up the stairs.

Jack lowers his head as regret unhinges his neck. The beer can he holds, once perfectly formed, shaped like all of the others, is destroyed. Ridges and creases run over its once smooth surface, and it can never return to what it once had been.

Jack finishes his beer. He empties its contents for the sole purpose of completely crushing the can, which he does in his hand. The top and bottom don't wholly align but meet each other as the rest of the can has been smashed inward. There is no way to fix the damage done.

CHAPTER 18

September 6, '07

The morning is warm, and Jack has already turned on the fan to cool. The blades hum. The air they push hits Jack but doesn't cool him. Sweat gathers in the back of his knees, his neck, and in the bend in his arms. It also covers his back, gluing him to the white leather of the couch. It is going to be a sweltering day.

He is on his back with his feet resting above the thickly padded headrest pressed up against the wall. Jack just got home from a night extended by MDMA cut with speed at Welldubs party. He is lying down to go to sleep. His eyes are closed. He doesn't see the door open or hear it.

"Nice couch," Someone says in a soft and honest tone.

Jack opens his eyes. A stranger stands in the doorway. Jack sits up quickly, ready to stand and confront the Intruder. Jack has several inches on him in height, and although both are thin, Jack is much broader with thick muscles in his shoulders, back, and arms. At 18, he's most likely four or five years younger than The Intruder but stronger.

But the long night and the lack of sleep slows Jack. Also, the way the Intruder compliments the couch gives Jack pause. It's out of sync with the picture in front of him. The Intruder wears jeans, white shoes, and an unbuttoned short-sleeved collared shirt, which shows numerous tattoos on his neck, chest, and stomach.

Then the anger falls into the Intruder's voice. "Do you know who the fuck I am?" He demands.

"Huh," Jack replies.

"I know ya hearing me, motherfucker. Do you know who the fuck I am? Do you know what this is?" He points toward his waistline. Jack quickly recognizes the three letters tattooed in block mat black ink just above the Intruder's low-hanging jeans. Jack has seen them in a similar block style spray-painted on the back of stores, common walls, and dumpsters in the area.

Jack must have forgotten the rules and left the front door unlocked. He tries to remember when he closed the door, whether he reached up for the deadbolt. Still, at that moment, he can't, and trying has left him little concentration for the words that are thrown heavily at him.

"I didn't ride the fucking Skittle Bus over," The Intruder barks wide-eyed. His eyes are black as bullets with only pupils showing, keeping their focus hidden. The Intruder, who stands, while Jack sits, does not lower his head to realign the height difference. To Jack, The Intruder stares over his head, seemingly at the wall behind him. It, and the other walls that make up the small living room, are plain white and littered with dirty handprints and dark knicks, from the frayed beige carpet to the white popcorn ceilings. There are no pictures or paintings. Only a television that sits directly on the floor and the fake plastic plants that knight it blocks the wall next to the door. The big white couch that Jack sits on helps cover-up three years of greasy smudges from his and his friends' hands.

It never occurred to Jack to clean the walls. The handprints have gathered so slowly over a long period that he has been blind to them. Even if he did notice, there is no understanding of how to remove them. Which kind of cleaner to use and no one he could ask.

"You think we haven't been watching you? Huh? Bro." The Intruder says "bro" in a mocking manner, drawn-out like an unrealistic stereotypical surfer. Otherwise, his face, mannerism, and movement are prefight sharp. And then he pats the handle of a gun tucked into his waistline. Behind the Intruder, the television continues, unaware, silent but not muted, and the light off of it bounces back and forth. It's on some show that doesn't matter much more than the voices it carries into the room with it.

It is so apparent. Jack can't believe he didn't notice it right away. He stares at the gun, and the lagging recognition pushes the back of his head deep into the plush white leather couch. Only after The Intruder pats the handle does Jack realize how visible the gun has been. The dimpled black grip of the weapon has a glossy finish, which sets it apart from the black mat ink that looks dried and faded on his stomach. Yet somehow, the block lettering of his cheap tattoo first hid it.

Jack continues to stare at the gun. The Intruder takes notice. "Oh, you like it, eh, carnal? It's pretty, huh." His skin had acne not long ago and had scarred where it had raised and fell. He pulls out the handgun and points it at Jack.

The barrel grows. Jack's head pushes further back into the sofa. The fan clicks when it finishes rotating and begins to swing back. Jack hadn't noticed the click all morning. Now he can hear the blades cut the air, and he feels the air on his skin. Jack sees the fake plant to his left waver out of the corner of his eye, its sinewy leaves fluttering.

Again he feels the air rush against his body until it passes down the other side of the couch, the fan clicking once more. The Intruder says something that Jack can't hear. Jack's nipples are hard, skin about to jump off his chest, and covered in goosebumps even though he is sweating. The other fake plant begins to waver. The fan clicks again. Plastic snaps against plastic, and Jack can feel the air pass again, this time from right to left. The Intruder opens his mouth again and says something. The light from the T.V. rapidly changes its brightness. The blades of the fan whisper loudly.

"I said, 'Do you understand?' This shit. Your shit. It's over, Cerrado. Consider it a warning carnal. No one will find you. It's a big ocean out there, and it's deep." He lowers the gun toward the ground or, more accurately, points toward the floor and the apartment below. "Nothing personal, It's like my grand Papi always said, 'menos burros mas elotes.' Listen, I would hate to have to come back, but if I do, I'm taking the couch with me. It's not like you'll be missing it." The Intruder laughs as he slowly walks back through the front door, closing it gently behind him with hardly any noise, betraying the impact of the collision he had just caused.

Jack remains stuck in place, glued in place.

The fan continues to push air, and he still can't ignore the sound, "click"…
"click"… "click"… There is no stopping it.

CHAPTER 19

September 6, '07

Without sleep, Jack left the apartment after giving the Intruder 15 minutes to clear out and made his way to the beach.

Now he rises and falls. The rolling swell rocks him back and forth, expanding and dropping like breath.

He sits beyond the surf line, suspended on his board, while his eyes sink to the bottom. The water is dark and cloudy, and he can't see past his feet, white and glowing under the greenwash. Somewhere below is a floor, and he wonders if that is where the ocean starts or stops.

He lets the gun barrel fall past his feet into the murk below. Threatening whispers, swastika tattoos, and unknown trips all disappear as well.

It is all the things that gather on the floor that causes a wave to break. Depending on what it is, rock, reef, or sand, and how it lays, the wave will form to it. A wave is just a mass of water moving until it collides with something else, and that hidden element gives the wave its shape, defines it.

It would all be so much easier if he just fell off his board and let himself sink as well, toward the corbina fish, flounder, and sand sharks below. Jack stares past his feet toward the pressures that lay on the hidden sandy bottom, and he asks himself again, Is that where the ocean stops or starts? Too murky to tell, he is left uncertain of what he is looking for, an end or a beginning.

Large waves scrape the bottom of the pier, and surfers sit beyond it, waiting for waves that usually break much closer to shore with less shape and size. The air is fat with water. The sun is hidden by the in-between. It is neither hot nor cold, nor sunny or dark, an ambiguous sky that can turn in all directions but has nowhere to go. The sky fades into the water, and the water reflects the sky.

Jack gazes backward, staring at the shore as it turns from water to sand to concrete, washing up a continuing slope. The hills roll like cheekbones, and the gradual incline gives everyone a view. Cascading windows stare out onto the beach, one house in front of another. The climbing houses look like an audience, every window an eye, every alley or street mouth agape to Jack.

Home stands on top of home, a mass of wood, glass, steel, and brick peering down on the water. So drawn to the beach is the town that it looks like everything is sliding down the hill back into the water. The beach is the thing, the very thing that allowed the town to be unique. The sand is a resource of demand, and the water an affluent accelerant.

Addresses start on the strand and increase easterly. To people going west, house numbers read like a countdown in a race of marching homes heading to the water, pushed from behind by everything that wanted to take its place. On a collision course to where Jack surfs.

The funny thing is that the beach used to stretch for miles from the water. Back to his apartment. Rolling dunes with sparse patches of grass and large swatches of ice plant from the old Spanish salt road that he now lives next to, to the same sand underwater that Jack now floats above. It's the same sand used to make Waikiki beach. It's in the concrete of the coliseum and the freeways that criss-cross Los Angeles. They used it to build LAX, and it has been poured over the old Spanish salt road to make the busy roadway Jack hears from his apartment.

There are marshes to the north. And just to the south is the dominant watershed of Los Angeles. But here it is, a desert. Desert with concrete and water poured over the top.

Jack blows on his hands to warm them. Air warmed by his own body flows through his fingers and palms giving him temporary relief from the chill in his hands.

He adjusts the watch he wore out on the water. It is a mistake, an accident, and an oversight. He never took it off from the night before. He looks at it. A heavy and silver diving watch with an abalone face. The shellfish used to abundant around there. His grandfather spoke of abalone diving with his son, Jack's father, when his father was a boy. But there isn't any left in that water.

A tangle of seaweed floats past. It isn't grown there but from some distant kelp forest and carried along by this swell. Jack picks it and lets it fall back into the water. Unmoored, it is free to roam the vast ocean on any passing current.

So much of surfing is waiting, and it is at that time that Jack unravels the tendrils of his brain and sets them adrift. He crawls inside himself, letting his mind flutter between plans for the future, ideas for the imagination, and the memories that saturate his soul like the salt in the sea.

Recently Jack has begun to see a story in everything. People and places expand beyond the breadth of description. Their history holds dimensions larger than anything presently presented, carved in large swathes behind his eyes.

Out on the water, Jack can see his father pushing him into broken wave after broken wave so that Jack could catch the whitewash and stand up without having to paddle into a wave himself, back when he was too small to catch a one on his own. Bree is out there too, with her father, sharing a boogie board, laying on their stomachs, and riding the white water as well. Their mothers are on the sand cheering after every wave, even the ones Jack doesn't manage to get to his feet. Then it's he and Bree in the shallows wearing snorkels and masks, looking for rocks and shells on the bottom and comparing what they found to see whose treasure was best.

Jack saved her once. Some beginner on a long board without a leash fell and the board hit Bree as she popped her head out of the water with five dollar bill. She was out cold. Thankfully they were in shallows and Jack pulled her to shore before any adult or lifeguard hit the water. She jokingly called him "Hasselhoff", referring to the actor from the show about LA lifeguards.

Jack can also see himself and his friends in storm surge with waves that are walls of crashing water in which no one has any business being out. They just like getting thrown around, at being at the whim of something larger than themselves, the freedom from control. Or it's the pier. Even with the changes, Jack can see himself jump off naked and swim to shore before he or any of his friends get caught.

Yes, Jack can't help but see it all everywhere he goes, even if he doesn't want to. Even if it would be easier to let himself forget that those days ever existed because they were never coming back.

It is the sound of others who draw his attention. They holler and splash, scratching to get into position for an outside wave. They are the surfers he saw earlier on the brim of the beach. He can tell by the way they held their surfboards that they aren't any good. Probably not born to the beach.

A wave begins to form, and they furiously paddle out. Jack takes a less direct angle. He is sitting north of everyone to go in the direction the water pushes and not against it when he has to paddle. To surf is to know the air, water, and ocean floor.

The water rises, pushed up by an unseen sandbar. The ocean that lays before it begins to suck over the wave, bowling like a cupped hand. The wave changes directions slightly, turning toward Jack. He mirrors it and places himself at the center of the wave's highest point.

His back arches, shoulders, and chest raise slightly off the board freeing his arms for long strokes. He paddles to the left as the rolling water crests, and he matches its speed.

The wave seems to stop for a second, and then the bottom drops. Jack pushes down on the board, and in an instant, he stands on his feet.

The lip of the wave falls over, but before it crashes down upon him, Jack slides down its face, just out of the reach of the chasing broken water.

He bends his knees and leans back into the wave. One rail of his surfboard digs into it, and water spews out from underneath the other side.

The board gains momentum, and Jack crouches lower. He turns his shoulders, and the board climbs the face of the wave, throwing himself against the lip a second before it comes down. For a brief moment, he is weightless. From behind, the other surfers see him cutting through the lip as water sprays in a fanning arc around him.

He maneuvers around the wave, dancing with the water, in and out of danger. Always a shift in weight in front of a thick descending lip of sea. He can hear the hoots and hollers of people on the water as he passes them on the wave of the day, leaving his mark on the wave as it pulls water from in front of it and throws it down at Jack.

Again his board drives down the face, and at the bottom, he turns back into the wave scaring the water. Underneath the water, the wave hits an unexpected sandbar that pitches it higher and longer. It pulls with it the things he tried to let fall to the bottom, the ones he has tried to let sink. The Intruder, Montana, Taurus, and Smashley pick up from the ocean floor. Jack can see their faces stretch as they are pulled up and over the lip of the wave. Their jaws stay at the bottom of the wave while their foreheads rise with the wave. Their mouths and eyes open wider as their heads grow thinner and longer. It looks as if they are trying to swallow Jack whole. They are in a wall of water about to come crashing down on him, and a large froth of all that he has past chases after him.

He has a chance to escape. To drive his board faster and find a pocket for himself inside all of that turmoil, a place whereby some miracle of nature, waves form a haven inside of themselves. A spot where the wave will carry him as it breaks over like a protective shell, and all that harm that would fall upon his head becomes a crown. He has to be decisive and immediately trust his instincts and forge ahead. But he can't. He already gave up.

The wave comes crashing down. Jack bounces along the bottom, which tears at his shoulders, back, and arms like sandpaper. He collides, again and again, head over feet and ass first, elbows raised to protect his neck, like a ragdoll until he pushes up against the beach at the waterline.

Water drains from his nose and ears. The sand is harsh on his feet. Blood begins to return to his fingers and toes with tiny pricks. As if Jack's hands and feet are pincushions slowly gathering needles as he crosses the beach and heads to the showers outside the restrooms.

The concrete under the simple metal showerhead has worn a darker gray from the water, in distinct contrast against the lighter sections that remain predominantly dry.

He reaches down and cups a small amount of wet sand. He smears it into the metal knob underneath the showerhead and pushes it in for the water to come on. It is a trick his father had taught him. All children who grew up there know it.

The water only stays on as long as the knob remains pressed. Inside of it is a spring that acts as a timer. The sand fills the space inside the metal knob, and the friction prevents the spring from pushing out, freeing Jack's arm from holding it in.

He rinses off while he holds his surfboard under his arm. Standing with his back under the showerhead, he runs his hands through his hair. Jack again blows his warm air onto his clenched fist.

Then he finally notices, and if anyone were looking, they could have easily read the pain on his face. He is no longer wearing the watch.

The sand relinquishes, the metal knob pops, and the water stops. Jack stands there for a while without turning the water back on, and his body continues to collect needles.

CHAPTER 20

December, '04.

The old mahogany cupboard with a dark walnut finish creaks when it opens. Tiny yellow carnations in the middle of blue Fleur de Lis' stagger along the white lining paper. The front corner of the cupboard paper has come off the base, which Jack unconsciously flickers with his thumb.

Baking soda lays on its side. Jack stands it up and slaps it out of the way, and shoves a can of pitted olives to the side next to a box of instant mashed potatoes.

Jack lowers and tilts his head to see a large oblong dark circle in the very back from an old soy sauce package that had recently leaked. Some particles have gathered in the corners. He grabs the instant mashed potatoes and stares at them, measures them before he tosses the box back in frustration. He doesn't know why he bothered to take them. He had grabbed a can of chili that night too. Thought that they might go together. It would have been much easier to put a second can in his pocket than leave with the box. This was at a house party, and the cans look like beers in his pocket. He promises himself no more boxes.

Change is the best. Found in couches, on hallway tables, and kitchen countertops. Jack won't take all the coins in a change bowl, but he will grab a couple of dollars worth of quarters. No one notices him take it or that it has gone missing. Two house parties a weekend make three to four meals he can buy at a cheap fast food joint. Plus, whatever he can grab from the walk-in pantry. It's Friday morning, so that means he is low on both coin and goods. He doesn't bother to close the cupboard as he turns away.

Jack opens the refrigerator door again, knowing full well what he will find. There is a ketchup bottle, mustard, ranch dressing, half a tub of imitation butter, and an old onion. The light inside comes on, and the fan's motor buzzes. There are brown smudges in the veggie crisper, and a white ring, maybe from spilled milk, on the second level plastic self, and an endless number of stains everywhere.

So empty as they are, the refrigerator and shelves, that these blemishes have no place to hide, and it becomes pretty evident that they are all that remains. So to stand there looking, one can't help but see, not only see the emptiness but also the marks of what once was.

He lingers in front, hoping he missed something previously. The buzzing serves as an auditory reminder that he is wrong when he closes the door. The condiments rattle in place after the soft thud of the vacuum seal.

The services like phone, television and the internet continue. Still, the deposits for things like food and clothes are few and far between. Jack assumes that the bills are auto-drafted and therefore don't need thought from his mom. The other funds, which rarely come, show Jack just how often she thinks of him.

The first couple of deposits Jack went through in a matter of days. Pizza for him and his friends when they'd come over to pre-party. New shoes that he didn't need. A video game. Movies and concessions. He quickly learned to budget and prioritize.

Back then, the deposits came every two weeks as if they were portions from a paycheck. Jack doesn't know if that truly isn't the case. In her messages, his mom has occasionally mentioned work but without any detail. Such as the name of the company she works for, her title, her boss, or any colleges. She has written, "sorry I haven't reached out more I've just been busy at work." Or recently, "sorry, I can't make the trip this time, I have work." She only made it back once in the last year. She passed out on the couch, spilling her wine all over herself. Jack changed her and put her in his bed. As he tucked her in, she apologized. "I'm sorry, honey, I'm cursed. It's best for you to stay away from me. I'm destined to destroy everything I love." "Who cares about the couch, mom?" She passed out before he even finished speaking. Then he cleaned the sofa and slept on the floor.

It was the best weekend of the year.

He'd welcome her return even if that meant a role reversal; he the caregiver, her the recipient. But he has lost all hope that she will ever come back.

He finally has concluded that he has lost both parents, and for all intent and purpose, Jack is an orphan, left to fend for himself, living meal to meal, and trying to keep that secret the best he can. He is lonely and embarrassed to admit that to Bree and all his other friends. They must know, though, because The Tard always seems to have an extra sandwich in his lunch, which with how he eats could be a rounding error. But Mutt, Smoker, and Luggy routinely grab too much from the cafeteria, like an extra slice of pizza or two salads instead of one, and that makes Jack believe that they know.

His friends called him 'Trashcan' for a bit, and Jack ate their leftovers with gratitude and shame. That's the thing about his friends that some people don't realize. As cutting as they could be, they always looked out for each other. Maybe because they were so alike, so similar, and with each meal they give Jack, he becomes less like them. That's why when he eats The Tards extra sandwich and tastes the oil and vinegar The Tards mom sprinkles on his lettuce, the sour flavor of the vinegar overpowers the rest.

Jack checks the time on his watch. Only 20 minutes until school starts. Mutt picks him up in the morning for the surf team. Even though Mutt lives on the beach and Jack far from it, but it isn't that season. Mutt offered to drive Jack regardless, but Jack refused. So now Jack skates to and from school. It's not the fastest transportation, so Jack needs to leave now.

He lingers on the watch. Its iridescent face picks up the fluorescent lights that run underneath plastic sheeting that make up the small kitchen's ceiling. He can sell the watch at a pawn shop, but he won't. There is one he has walked to several times, always turning away before the storefront. The timepiece is all he has left of his father. His mother threw everything else away.

Jack begrudgingly texts Bree, hoping she can bring him a breakfast burrito.

They talked on the phone the night before, and she offered, but Jack had initially declined.

Jack was surprised when she first told him that her parents were divorcing months earlier. And yesterday, it had become official. Even though Bree had a boyfriend, she told Jack first. "What did Repo say?" Jack asked about her boyfriend after Jack consoled her. "I haven't told him yet." She answered, sniffling in the last of her tears. That surprised Jack because she and Repo had been dating for several months and spent so much time together. Jack offered her a hug through the phone. "Maybe you can come over this weekend? It'd be nice to have you." She answered. "Maybe," he responded. Jack thought about the days he saved from being with her, the self-imposed threshold of asking too much. And he could justify spending an entire day and night with her without worry about overstepping his boundaries when she probably would rather see Repo instead. That's why Jack turned down the breakfast burrito when she offered later in the conversation. He can only ask so much from her, especially now when dealing with more pain in her life.

But he's already broken that promise, and all before school even starts. He grabs his skateboard and opens the door to see an eviction notice, and quickly reads that he is a month behind on rent. He knows his mother paid a year in advance, so those 12 rental cycles have come and gone. It might as well read that his mother has completely forgotten about him. The only difference being that it is a message Jack received a long time ago, and being late on rent is something he didn't already know.

He heads out for class trailed by the mocking buzz of the refrigerators fan and all the images of smudges left by all that has gone missing. Unless Bree gets his message in time, he'll hear it all day.

CHAPTER 21

September 6, '07

After surfing, Jack found two hours of sleep on his couch. The pins and needles from the cold water never went away, slowly crawling up his extremities, like a static signal to his brain. He made his way to the bathroom to take a proper shower. The pinging of disconnected hands, arms, feet, and legs usually fades when warm for most people.

But Jack can't thaw. He has felt similarly before, and he knows what's needed.

Jack stands naked in front of his mirror. He sees that the bruises on his body have already begun to clear. The cold water certainly helped in this matter, soothing and releasing the trapped blood.

The rest of the picture is wrong though. The mirror is flawed somehow, but it is indistinguishable in what way. It is probably just too big and too cheap, and everything in it looks flawed as well.

He looks vaguely at it, at the peripheral, at the bare walls, the dimpled plastic shower door, the yellow on the ceiling. The silver faucet head pops up out of the white-tiled sink, straight and attentive, alert like prey on the bottom of the mirror.

His revolver is on the counter next to a lighter. For some reason, his gun doesn't look dangerous anymore. It could be the flaw in the mirror that makes it seem like a toy. Or it could be the Intruders gun. It was different. It didn't have a cylinder of a revolver that feeds ammo as it spins. The weapon that the Intruder pointed at him looked so new to Jack's by comparison that Jack's gun seems antiquated now and somehow less dangerous. Somehow it seems easier to pick up, easier to cock, and easier to pull the trigger.

Jack picks up a lighter instead. He flushes flint to throw a spark and opens the gas with his numb hands. Jack can't feel any of it, so the process is like watching a stranger perform the task but using Jack's arms and hands. He lets the flame burn for a bit before he moves his scrotum and plunges the white-hot metal into the fleshy part of his uppermost thigh. It leaves a red smiley face on his skin, and the pins and needles begin to recede in that leg. He does the same for his other leg, complete to a red smiley face and smells burnt hair and skin. The flame comes back on again to land inside his right armpit and then inside his left.

If it were the winter, he'd have so many other options, but Jack doubles down on the places already visited, and then he takes out the alcohol wipes, and everything burns yet again. The pain has broken through, and the feeling returns to his body.

Jack wonders if it would be better just to let it take over, to remove himself entirely from all the pressures he's felt, ones that leave no room for anything else. What if there was someone he could ask for help? Someone in his life to keep him afloat?

There isn't, and Jack has no words to change that. Cracking open his sternum would have been easiest, nowhere left to hide, freedom via exposure, like an old salt creek dried in the sun.

And all that has been unspoken is allowed to escape. And everyone would know how Jack has felt all these years. Escape, he lingers at the thought and looks at the gun. Would it feel like watching a stranger pick it up and cock it? What would his friends say? Would they make fun of him? Would those remarks chase Jack through the grave? Then he thinks of the Intruder, and a naturally crooked smile crawls across his face. Yes, he is ready to be removed. He already feels free.

CHAPTER 22

September 6, '07

The boys approach the liquor store slowly to make sure that no one is inside. The clerk always makes them wait until the store is empty to buy alcohol because they are so obviously underage. They stand in the asphalt parking lot that is so small it only has two spots for cars and a bike rack, a cost of being so close to the beach. Jack's newfound freedom placed him where he would have been otherwise, on a beer run with Smoker for a barbeque at Luggy's house.

Across the street, a surfer towel changes, and a woman walking, passes him with a disapproving glance and shakes her head. It's probably the way he squats that looks weird. He is stretching the fabric of his boardshorts to wick it into the towel he wears to help dry them. She has no idea, but every surfer does it. As far as Jack is concerned, she doesn't deserve to know that trick or any other trick taught to those who grow up on the beach.

Jack looks inside the store through the windows covered in posters. Not much about the store had changed since he was a kid who lived around the corner. They still have posters for Volleyball Opens as old as thirty years hanging in the windows. Mixed in are half-naked women holding some kind of beer or alcohol, still stuck in unnatural poses they have held for decades.

The posters have faded, the colors run dry and thin, and the images appear worn out. It looks as if the pictures have been taken with a filter. One reserved for moments that have passed long ago.

That through time alone has become lighter and more inviting, a softer and simpler version of reality where context has been bleached away. This store had always looked like that even when Jack was a kid and would come here with Bree, and her brother, Adam, to buy candy when he lived within walking distance to the water. They searched for change in sofas and drawers, car consoles, and desks. After Adam passed, they went together, even though his mom would not have allowed him to go without someone older to watch. So he snuck out because he knew that Bree needed it. It was a better time, as golden as the posters themselves.

When a customer comes out, the boys head in.

"What up, John?" The bell rings as the boys walk into the store, alerting the clerk that new customers have arrived. The homeless John Doe is inside too, but it doesn't matter to the clerk or the boys to buy liquor.

"Hey, kids," John says. He is dirty and looks to be in his late seventies, but there is no way to know how much of that is hard living. No one knows for sure how old John is, just as no one knows his actual name. He dresses in clothes that were once popular decades earlier. And, a beat-up Dodger hat with a white ring of salt sits on his head, like a crown.

The boys walk by the counter where John has placed an assortment of junk food, canned goods, and one bottle of high-quality bourbon. They go directly to the refrigerated beer and start grabbing 12 packs.

"Are you going to sell liquor to these kids?" John directs the question to the clerk behind the counter.

Jack, placing a case of beer on the white linoleum floor, catches a glimpse of John's feet. He stares at them in disgusted fascination. John doesn't have any shoes. His feet are worn leather with thick yellow nails capping gnarled toes, red with abuse, covered by a layer of dry white skin that has died a long time ago but has failed to leave his body. They look like flesh boots.

"Don't listen to the burnout. God John, no wonder you look horrible look how you eat." Smoker says as he picks up the first case and brings it to the counter.

"Don't worry about him," The clerk assures the boys.

"They're underage," John says to the clerk.

"Well, see, my buddy and I were black marines...." Smoker continues.

Jack stops listening. He knows the movie his friend begins to reference and the quote that will soon follow.

Instead, Jack sticks his head back in the refrigerated glass and pulls out two more 12 packs of beer. John responds again, but Jack doesn't hear him over the noise of the cooling system. When he pulls out the last 12-pack, he hears the clerk mid-sentence. "You're right. These kids aren't 21. They're 22." The pause in his cadence sounds like he's telling a joke, and because he lets the boys buy beer, Jack laughs.

"I am so sorry," John says in a grand sarcastic fashion. "You kids ever have a black eight ball?"

"What's that?" Smoker asks

"Grab an Old English forty and a Guinness."

Smoker, "No offense, but I'm not comfortable putting my mouth where yours has been."

"Don't worry, I don't want any of it, and I'll buy it," John offers.

Smoker hands the clerk the money he has for their drink and the underage convenience fee and carries out two 12-packs and a 40 of malt liquor. Jack carries the other two 12-packs and puts the can of Guinness in his pocket.

"Did you kids see what's happened to the pier?" John asks as they walk out of the liquor store, the bell ringing before the door closed behind them.

There are rumors about John. Every kid has heard them. He has been a fixture on the strand since they were kids, going back and forth, collecting cans out of the trash. He was supposed to have once been wealthy, but no one knows what happened. Alcohol seems like an apparent reason.

"Yeah, they're working on the coffee shop right now," Jack answers, and the trio turns up the alley.

"That's exactly what this town needs another coffee shop, huh?" John jokes.

Smoker adds, "That would be the fifth one in three blocks."

They position themselves behind a large green dumpster blocking their view from the small street adjacent to the liquor store. The alley is small, maybe 15 feet wide. Cars that come down this way usually have to turn around because of the dumpster.

Litter, mostly empty beer cans and cardboard boxes, lay on the ground. A large metal crate covers a drain in the middle of the alley. The boys stand near it, and John has his back to the yellow wall of the liquor store they had just exited.

"I used to fish on that pier every day. No more, they won't allow it, which is why I bought this crap." John raises his left arm, the one holding the plastic bag of food, to emphasize his point. "It's those damn new lights, the string lights that drape. Can't cast."

Smoker says, "Well, they probably didn't think it through." Then he holds up the 40 and asks. "So what do we do?"

"Yeah, didn't think it through. You two grew up here, right? I've seen you around. You guys graduate this year? You look that age." The boys don't respond. John continues, "I went to Costa too, you know, a long time ago." John speaks slowly and without urgency. He doesn't seem to be in a rush to go anywhere. He places the grocery bags on the ground, and the gentle thud of the cans settling seems slow as well.

Jack answers after Smoker doesn't, "Yeah, we just graduated."

John smiles, and crow's feet cut through his skin in tiny white lines from his eyes down to his jaw in sharp contrast to his dark complexion. His face wears the marks of a lifetime spent in the sun; liver spots cover his cheeks, and freckles blend into a beard that never wholly materializes. He is not as tan as much as he is blemished.

John directs, "Open that bottle of malt liquor." Smoker cracks the lid and snaps it off. John continues, "Just drink a little more than the neck of that forty," He looks from one end of the alley to the other. "You know I've lived here my whole life. Seen a lot of changes."

Smoker takes a drink and hands the bottle to Jack. The malt liquor pours over his tongue, and the alcohol tastes bitter and stale. The carbon burns the back of his throat. Jack hands the bottle back to Smoker, who drinks until he meets the mark given.

"Now open that Guinness," John says to Jack, who still has the can in his back pocket. "Pour it into the forty." The hiss of the can fills the alleyway, and then the sudden snap of aluminum puts it away.

"Can you hear that?" John asks, but before anyone can answer, "That's a band saw working on a house on Fourth Street. There's a drill for a place off Morningside. And I bet those hammers are on Third. Man, this place grows to die."

Smoker looks lost, and Jack does as told. The amber liquid turns a more pleasing, fuller brown.

"Funny, it kind of looks like coffee, huh? Maybe you can get it at the new coffee shop. Take a sip." John smiles.

Jack obliges with a small, polite swallow, his mouth still sour from the last drink. His surprise manifests as another much longer pull off the bottle. The flavor has turned as much as the color.

"It's way better." Jack holds the bottle out to Smoker. The disbelief on Smokers' face falls away once he pulls the bottle from his mouth. Smoker speaks excitedly, Crap that's a shit ton better! John Doe."

"Anything for a Marine." John smiles at the small victory, playing along with the quote Smoker gave earlier. "Black Marines," John laughs to himself. Jack wonders if he ever saw the movie.

John asks, "Have you seen all the roses beds that have been replacing the ice pant with?"

Smoker answers, "Yeah, what about them?"

"You can't sit on the wall with the rose bush like you can with ice plant."

Jack speaks up. "Guess that's up to homeowners. They get to make that choice."

"I once had a strand house. "

"Yeah, what block?" Smoker asks.

"Thirty Sixth. Got it for whisper and sold it for a song. That was after I lost my wife. We didn't have any kids so, I figured I didn't need it anymore." John speaks without resentment or the anger that it festers. Jack takes notice. "I preferred being on the sand anyway, sleeping under the stars, back when there were stars, grunion runs, and bonfires. Do you know why they are redoing the pier?" John asks.

"I don't know. I guess they needed to," Smoker's tone is dismissive. He seems ready to move on.

"You know that the original pier was twice as long and paved in cobblestone? It matched the stone used on the sidewalks of downtown. Storm blew half of it away. Anyway, they did some retrofitting not long ago, so why do they need to change it again?"

"Honestly, I don't care." Smoker holds his hands out to the side, palms up. "And I don't really care about the roses. Doesn't matter to me in the least."

"Tell me, black marine, have you ever been to Nigger Park?" John shockingly changes the topic.

Jack shuffles his feet. He steps on the metal drain, and he feels it shift under his foot. The clang of metal ricocheted off the walls below and rang back into the alley in protest.

"What the fuck are you talking about?" Smoker hands the bottle back to Jack. Nigger is a dirty word that kids were taught to never say. And for the most part, they don't, especially around a stranger. They only say it among themselves reciting lyrics. Even when they're telling inappropriate jokes, they use the term 'black.'

"It's the park on 26th street. Behind the Lifeguard headquarters and the metered parking area." John continues.

"Why do you call it Nigger Park?" Jack asks. He takes another drink.

"I didn't name it. It's been called that because back in the day, it was a black community. Then, there was a fire, and the houses burnt down. The town decided it needed a new park and they put it there. Eminent domain, the land was annexed, and the black families had no choice but to leave." Underfoot the metal crate rattles in the hollow space underneath as Jack again shifted his weight from one leg to another.

"No fucking way," Smoker goes in to poke holes in the story. His hands rise above his waist and his shoulders up toward John's face. "That doesn't make sense. You move a whole community to put in a park that no one can really use. It's all on a hill except for the basketball court, which takes up the only level ground. In that park, you can't do anything but sit down. It's too steep." Smoker's assessment seems perfect, except he left out the part where if the ball rolls out of bounds, it ends up rolling all the way to the beach.

John continues, "Back then, it was part of a neighborhood called El Porto.

All of the black families worked in the nearby sanitation plant, and there was nothing else around. But this town was growing, and it was only a matter of time until it moved north. So they burned down their homes."

The metal drain clangs again, the sound unbroken by an empty space, but no one else seemed to hear it.

"Bullshit. You are so full of shit." Smoker calmly dismisses him.

"Molotov cocktails while most families were at church. That way, no one was hurt."

"Why didn't anyone stop them?" Jack speaks so fast that the question comes out unprocessed before he hears how naive it sounds. The drain rattles again, and this time everyone hears it.

"Even if that were true, do you know how many black pro athletes live there now, anyway?" Smoker sputters. Jack silently teeters on the grate leaning one way and the other.

"It's the same reason that they're changing ice plant to roses. Same reason why they changed the pier. Why my diet has gone to crap, as you said. Too many Mexican families and bums, like myself, spend their nights fishing there. So they put up lights that make it hard to cast, and because no one can safely cast, they say no one can fish there anymore."

"You're saying that to reverse engineer no Mexicans and homeless people, they put in new lights to outlaw fishing?" Smoker remains skeptical and his hands remain in John's face.

Jack asks earnestly, "Why would they do that?"

"They think it makes this a better place to live if we're not around. We no longer fit the description of the town. Poor people who have to fish to eat. And they'll give you a reason why it makes sense without saying what they really want. It's like that black eightball your drinking. They dress up their motives in color and call it progress to make palatable." Jack looks down at the bottle he holds. Its full, creamy liquid is nearly halfway drunk.

"You know, when I was a kid, this place used to be just a beach town. Back then, no one cared too much to make it anything else. It was a beach by LA. Now it's LA by the beach." There it is, missing before, late, but they're all the same. Jack hears the bitterness in John's voice, heavy with resentment and anger. It falls away immediately under its own weight, probably rolling into the drain Jack stood over. The drain rattles again, bringing up the sound from beneath until it echoes from within, where Jack stands.

"Fuckin loon." Smoker elbows Jack for a laugh, but Jack is too busy looking at the yellow wall of the store. It is very high compared to how narrow the alley is. The colors look old and faded, just as he remembers they did when Jack was a boy. Back when he didn't have to know these things when life seemed so much simpler.

CHAPTER 23

September 6, '07

Jack has to piss. After the black eight ball, he crushed two more beers when he got back to Luggy's house. The boys play a drinking game where you throw the lids of beer bottles into plastic cups weighed down by the water. He leaves his friends and the game after a loss to go to the guest bathroom. Curiously, the door is locked, so he heads upstairs to the ensuite bathroom in Luggy's room.

After walking up the circular staircase, he pauses for a second to admire the view. Perhaps the best view in town. Even as bad as he has to go to the bathroom, the vista is something he can't let pass without giving it his full attention.

After a heartbeat, he turns down the hall toward Luggy's room. When he passes the slightly open door of the master suite, he hears an indecipherable protest. It's a low guttural shriek that would not have alerted anyone outside of the hallway. Concerned, he pokes his head through the crack of the door and steps into the door jamb. Luggy's stepmom stands startled next to the bed.

There is a large glass of white wine sitting on the end table next to the closet on the other side of the room, and the bottle from which it came sits empty on the end table next to which she stands. Jack saw her open it earlier when he and Smoker came back from the liquor store not too long ago.

She's frozen in position. Arms crossed over her chest, and she covers herself with a shirt that she is not yet wearing. Jack can see the hanger lying on the other side of the bed, opposite the door, next to the closet. The wine bottle, glass, and hanger are literally the only items not perfectly placed in the room.

"Oh, Jack, it's you." She relaxes her posture instantly, almost mindfully. And her sugary southern accent pours through.

"I am so sorry, Mrs. Claudino," he apologizes profusely, lowering his eyes to the ground and shifts his weight back and forth on his feet. "Is everything okay?"

"It's okay, sweety. You just startled me, that's all. I saw someone pass by with the door open, and here I am not quite completely dressed yet."

The room remains in a particular order as if no one lives there. Only the curtains sway in the breeze in front of the bay doors that overlook the patio below. Everything else seems stiff, locked in its proper order.

"Sorry, I didn't mean to… I really didn't even see you in here before you called out." Jack turns himself halfway back through the door.

"It's fine. We just had an impromptu Graduate like moment," she laughs, and Jack isn't sure if she is embarrassed too or not.

"Oh, ok." Still, Jack turns ever so slightly further into the hallway with his head down, ready to escape the second politeness allows.

"Jack," She says louder with astonishment. He has no choice but to look back into the room to stay where he is.

"Don't tell me that you have never seen the movie The Graduate." She smiles with her arms still crossed in front of her, pinning her shirt against herself.

"No, I thought you meant something about graduating this year." He answers honestly.

"Oh no, it's a movie about a woman who is not happy in her marriage, the guy is probably cheating on her, and a young man who she seduces. Y'all should see it sometime. It's a classic."

"Ok, I'll look for it. Sorry again, I was just on my way to Paul's bathroom. I really didn't see anything."

"No, that's okay. Come in here and use mine." He doesn't move. "Go ahead, hun. It's not like I am naked."

She moves aside the shirt she held in front of her. "Look, this bra covers more than most of the bathing suits you see on the beach." The bra is black and big, and unlike many bras, he has seen, there is no lace, nothing see-through at all. The cut of the bra is not sharp or low and covers most of her skin, but the cups do hold her up well, creating a high and long fissure between her breasts.

Other than that, she has dressed appropriately. She wears a long skirt that runs down past her knee, and the waistline hangs just below her belly button. "Hey, what do you think? Pilates." She says proudly, and she turns her torso to the side and slightly arches her back while she points her legs slightly in the other direction, elongating the lines of the stomach. Jack knows because he has posed similarly but always under the guise of stretching. At least she isn't pretending to do otherwise. He tries not to be embarrassed for both of them for such overt acts.

Jack stays where he is, standing in the doorway, as he notes the details of the picture in front of him, trying to figure out an appropriate response to a seemingly inappropriate situation. He can't move forward into the room and is too polite to turn around. His lack of an answer has nowhere to hide in such a tidy room.

"You look nice." It's the best he can do. And in truth, she is an attractive woman. From what Jack has gathered over the years, Luggy's father, who the kids call "Pops," left his wife for her when Luggy was in elementary school. She had been the other woman, ten years younger than Luggy's mom, until Pop's left his wife to be with her. Jack can see the beauty that she retains to drive a man to act outside of his previous commitments. Still, Jack can also see small lines forming around her lips and eyes and the elasticity of her jawline drooping ever so slightly.

"Thanks, Jack. I work out every day. Have a trainer at the club. He's an asshole," she laughs, "but think he gets good results." She holds up her arms, flexes her biceps, and laughs some more. "Come on… give 'em a squeeze." Jack complies. Her muscle is hard while her skin is soft and supple. "As firm as a bad mattress, right?"

"Bigger than mine." He manages to reply gallantly, hiding behind what little charm he can conjure at the moment.

"Jack, hun… speaking of the club. I heard a little rumor about you." She pauses, reading his face. "My friend Cindy told me you like older women."

Now it's Jack's turn to lock into position, frozen in the doorway, hands pressed against the inlay and mill worked white molding, heart loudly beating as if it were knocking on the door to get out. Such a fitting name, given that its homonym is "jam." Jack's breath stops for a second, and he tries his best to keep the shock out of his face.

It is a tenuous place to hold. A door jamb is the smallest section of a home, and it disappears completely when in use. While standing in it, one can't lean forward or step backward without removing themselves from it. So to stay in it is to maintain an impossible position designed to eat itself.

He immediately tries to process the conversation about him that may have happened. What did Cindy say exactly? How would they even start talking about it? He still needs to answer her, but what can he say without knowing what she has learned. "Is that true?" he asks.

"I don't know. Is it?" Jack can read her confusion and trepidation. Her reticence in saying more. Perhaps if he spoke more frankly, she would return that directness to him. It's the first time in their short interaction that she didn't seem so confident. The first time she sounded authentic since he came to the room.

The yelp and covering up were overly dramatic, and the way she instantly relaxed betrayed the belief that she ever was startled. The posing with the shirt and dress had too much showmanship to be spontaneous. Jack knows because he recognizes this kind of insincerity, moment molding, from his own experience doing it. She is good at it, even if a little obvious. The question she asks is brilliantly innocuous. A conversation that passes entirely as small talk. She probably thought through all of it first, this question, or a similar one, but still, she can't hide the interest in his coming answer. Interest that exceeds light conversational curiosity.

He wishes he didn't have to provide an answer, but there is nowhere to go and nowhere to hide. "I like older women." He contrives a smile to cover the panic bubbling just below his skin and then lies, "but I have a girlfriend now."

"That's good to hear." Jack can see on her face that she didn't practice or think about this possibility. "I hope things are well with you." She pauses and smiles as if a thought came to her. "Please let me know if things start to go awry. I'd be happy to give you anything you need at that moment. No matter what the cost."

He tries to thank her with his practiced smile, but it hardly holds. He lowers his head and slinks toward the master bath, passing the large mirror next to the closet. Next to her wine glass and hanger from which her shirt came. He can see her standing next to the mirror, looking at her older but well-maintained body, drinking her wine, maybe thinking through a conversation that she hoped to someday broch. One that is a non-starter because of a promise he made himself, about a line he would no longer cross, regardless of his desperation.

As Jack stands over the toilet trying to relax, he thinks about all the people accounted for in the house. His friends that he left in the living room. Her husband, who Jack, saw in the kitchen by the locked guest bathroom. There is no one else in the home to use the downstairs bathroom. He can see her put down her drink and run from her spot in front of the mirror to look through the door and make sure it was Jack who walked by. The door only so slightly cracked that no one would have bothered to check in if she held her tongue. And no one would see her standing there in her bra.

But how did she know when Jack would walk by the door? Then he remembered the pause he took to look at the view. The loud sigh he let escape when he realized that he would soon be saying goodbye to that steel-blue water laid out below. And the words he muttered when he thought he was alone, "Forgive me." Yes, that must have been it—the alert she needed to check the door and stand next to it with her shirt off. Yes, everything was perfectly placed in that room and locked in its proper position.

CHAPTER 24

February '06

He tries to get her to go inside. She pushes him out further on the balcony. "What's the matter? It's such a nice night," she says.

"It's nice inside, too," Jack counters. He moves toward her right side and turns sideways to squeeze through the space between her and the glass sliding door that leads back into her home. She slides back over, cutting him off. She grabs his face and then playfully slaps his cheek.

"Uh, uh, ah." She coos at him, letting her finger run over his lips. Her hands slide down the front of his shirt and then into his pants. "Ahh, see, I knew you liked it out here." Her hand is around his growing erection.

Jack prefers it to go away. But she has been rubbing her chest against him and rubbing her pelvis against his. Jack thinks he can hear voices from the neighbor's patios and rooftops. Each home sits on a small lot. The price of land close to the beach is high, and the plots have divided repeatedly over the years. Now houses are built out on stamps of land not much larger than the home's perimeter. The houses, in turn, grow several stories and close to the neighbors. They all have decks to maximize living space and take advantage of the views and ocean air. The deck that Jack and his date are on is only yards from the nearest neighbor and in full view of five houses across the small avenue. He swears he can hear them on their balconies, rooftops, and in the alleys below. And he is confident that they can listen to him and his date. At least they left the light off and stand in darkness.

"Cindy said you're 18. You're 18, right? Right?"

"Yeah," Jack lies.

She looks unconvinced. "Fuck it. You're hot as hell."

Jack pushes her against the glass door pinning her arms. She whispers her pleasure in his ear. Then he uncouples and moves toward the open door back toward the inside of her house.

She grabs his arm. "Where are you going?" She teases, grabbing his hardon over the denim fabric of his jeans, pulling him back toward her.

"Come on..." he chuckles, "let's go back inside."

"Not yet. Pull down your pants." She starts unzipping his fly for him, and her fingers begin to unfasten the button.

His hand flashes to hers before she can completely undo his pants. He grabs them and moves them away from his waist.

"Hey!" It's a break in character for her. "I said we're staying outside!" She commands.

Then sweetly, amorously, she tells him to take off his pants. Jack feels her warm mouth on his cock. Wet tongue under the tip and her lips tightly moving back and forth. He can hear the flesh meet in the open air and swears that murmurs are coming from across the street. He feels pleasure in her mouth and guilt in the hushes emanating off the neighbor's balconies, their buzzing shock, and dismay.

She pauses and looks up at him, her hand stroking him. "Do what you did before. Pin my arms and kiss me. Then lift my skirt and fuck from behind. Do it hard! "

Jack does as he told. Their skin slaps as it meets, his bony pelvis against her meaty, perfectly rounded ass. "Tell me you like my ass."

"I like your ass."

"I work so hard for you to have it. To want it. Tell me you have to have me."

"I have to have you."

She ratchets up the distress. "You can't have me. I'm married." Then more directly, "Tell me you'll take me because you can. And there's nothing I can do to stop you."

"I'll take you."

"Please don't!" she pleads. After a second or two passes, "What are you waiting for? Take me, dammit!" Jack thrusts harder. "Like you mean it!" She commands.

He lets go of her breasts, and grabs her hair, and pulls hard against it. Her head bends backward. He kicks her legs out wider and brings one of her arms behind her back. Then when he thinks he might have moved her arm too far back, he lets go and grabs her neck, and gently squeezes. She bucks backward. Her moans too loud to be discreet on a quiet night.

He chokes her harder to quiet her and cuts the volume with his squeezing hand. He isn't sure that he's gripping too hard and worries that she won't let him know before he hurts her. She breathes hoarsely and quickly until her body quivers and stops. Out of breath, she removes him from inside her, turns, and addresses him. "You can finish in the bathroom if you want."

"That's okay." He pulls up his pants and tucks his erection into the waistband to hide it.

"I'll let you know when he is out of town again. I really liked the thing you did with my hair. Let's do more of that."

"Okay."

"Money's on the entryway table next to the gong. Thanks, babe." And she kisses him nicely on the cheek.

Jack heads downstairs, grabs the money, and exits, leaving a little bit of himself behind that he'll never get back. Walking down the street, he can still hear them. Can hear them on rooftops, on the balconies, and in the alleys. He can hear them all. They groan at what he has let himself become—the dismay of all the people who he has let down.

CHAPTER 25

September 6, '07

"No, no, no!" Pops incredulously shakes his head. "The grill isn't hot enough for the steaks yet. Now get out of there."

Mutt moves away from the large built-in stainless steel grill, handing the barbeque tongs to Pops. Pops seems to have a way of doing things without flexibility. Jack can see why a man like him would assume that he should never be questioned. Everything around him seems to prove him right. The town is full of them now.

"So, you boys ready to go off to college?" Pops asks. He has the habit of speaking with a low, jutted jaw that doesn't move nearly as much as the words he speaks require. Jack wonders why he does so because Pops always had a reason for everything. Still, every utterance that comes out of his mouth is correctly pronounced and enunciated.

"Are you kidding me? The amount of new ass available to us is worth the price of admission alone." The Tard says quickly. Pops seemed to like him best out of Luggy's friends.

"That's why I'll be coming out to check on you, son." Pops says disapprovingly but winks, "Without Moms, of course." He cracks a wry smile. All of the boys laugh, even Jack, though a cadence late.

They all stand on the front patio of Luggy's house, each holding a beer that Jack and Smoker went to buy. Except for Jack, who sits on a lounger next to them. Raised well above the street, showcasing the best view in town, with the Pacific laid out in front, Palos Verdes to Malibu. Pops lives at the top of the hill.

"Seriously," Pops continues, "As individuals, you are only worth what you can give. Those who can give the most are worth the most." By the looks of his house and following his statement, Pops must have given a lot. He continues, "A college graduate is going to make on average four times more than a high school graduate."

Pops' jaw barely moves, remaining slightly open and low but not slack, and his lips stay pursed and still, despite pronouncing several different syllables. His mouth doesn't seem to work at all for the words that it produces. Each one comes out like all the others, without inflection, so that his tone remains smooth, set in an unwavering rich timbre. When he talks, all of the boys stay quiet and attentive. The only other sound allowed is the flame burning under the hood of the grill. The way his friends hang on to every word is unusual for them. They are quick to dismiss and joke. But not with Pops. It is as if Pops' words were precious. Jack can imagine them painting the sky as they leave his lips, one word following the other, a spoken golden road.

"Don't you have to be a high school graduate first to become a college grad?" Mutt sarcastically asks. His internal editor never works.

"Thanks, Mutt. You have a keen sense of the order of operations." Pops' mouth spits its sarcastic retort without moving by some act of magic or sleight of hand. Jack is pretty sure that Mutt annoys Pops sometimes. Still, he is always welcomed over and engaged in conversation like the other boys. Jack, on the other hand, is sure Pops doesn't care too much for him. Pops only talks to Jack when he happens to be standing next to someone else.

"You go to school to get a degree and then a good job. It's that simple." Pops clicks the tongs together like castanets.

The steaks lay in a pyrex dish on the grill. They are thick and well-marbled. "You are all going to become important pieces of our community, and that is only as strong as the members who make it up." Again the tongs click. "Remember, life is a competition, and competition brings out the best in people. It is Darwinian. Only the strong can survive, and that leaves the individuals with capacity in control." He takes a rag and wipes down the grill. "There are a lot of people who make excuses. Why they didn't make it in this world. Excuses are like assholes."

Smoker jumps to answer, "Everyone's got one."

Pops waves his tongs to indicate that Smoker got it wrong. He corrects him, "They all stink. Let me tell you, the cream always rises, and dust settles. Never let anyone tell you you had it easy. They have every opportunity that you boys have."

Jack again looks around the massive home and can't imagine anyone with so much question themselves. Or anyone, even those with half as much, begin to question him either. "Be strong. Take what you can. Otherwise, someone else will. At the end of the day, only you and all the other deserving will be stewards. Forget Democracy. We live in a Meritocracy and reward those with the capacity for success. It is freedom at its best." Pops smiles, opens the hood, and begins to spray some kind of oil on the grill. "Or in Jack's case, marry rich." It is the first time Pops addressed him since he showed up a couple of hours earlier. Jack laughs, happy to right. Pops didn't like him.

"Pops, you played college ball, right?"

The Tard asks, "How much ass did you get?" There is not a better question to ask Pops to answer.

Pops sarcastically looks over both shoulders as if his wife might be listening. "Let's just say I got my share. I mean, I wasn't any scholarship athlete, but I played plenty, and that made a difference. But more importantly, with basketball and my father having been alumni, I was able to attend a school that my grades would never let me." Luggy's father is tall and slender except for a slight protruding potbelly that stands off his body. Jack can tell he had once been an athlete. "That's where I met most of my business partners. I was able to make connections to people that have been instrumental in my work and company. Access to capital, investors, and industry influencers. I'm telling you there isn't a magic formula other than skill and hard work. And the courage to be great. The ability to allow yourself to crush those that stand in your way. You'd be surprised at how many people don't believe that they deserve success."

Jack finally places what he is reminded of by how Pops holds his mouth in a permanent circle. Pops enjoys sitting on his large patio, drinking neat whiskey, and having a cigar. When the wind is low, he blows big, full smoke rings. He holds his mouth precisely the same way then as he does when he speaks. Jack can now picture the words he says as hollow wisps of smoke. That can only exist in the gentlest of conditions, instantly crumbling against the push of even the slightest breeze.

"Look at what you guys were able to accomplish this year. State Champs. Probably the best high school team in the country. "

"Not many other places raise their kids to play beach volleyball." Mutt chimes in and undercuts the praise.

Pops continues ignoring Mutt, "Look at Tard. Played both Baseball and Volleyball at an All-American level. That's the definition of a winner. That's the person who's strong enough to lead." Pops addresses Tard, "It's a damn shame you aren't going to play both in college, son. Not sure what UCLA is thinking."

The Tard frowns and, to his feet, says, "Yeah. I'm pretty bummed too. They think there is too much overlap in the season."

"There was a ton last year too. But you managed it perfectly. See, that's what I mean about excuses. If you ask me, that's the problem with institutional control. It keeps people from being able to accomplish all that they are capable of. It places limits on us that wouldn't exist otherwise." The Tard lifts his head and smiles.

"Yeah, he's screwed with his scholly and all the fans," Mutt holds his hands to mimic breasts.

"Mutt, it's a shame you were just too short to be on the team. What did you play? Surfing? You and Crackie getting high before school is what they should have called it." Jack's not going to say that it didn't happen. It did. But only on days with no surf and only after he figured out that there was no longer any point to school. "Jack, it's a shame you were too short too. You showed a lot of potential back in the day." Pops throws on the steaks, and there is an immediate hiss of the raw meat as it starts to sear.

Smoker questions, "Too short?"

Mutt adds, "Yeah, you start 'playing surfing' too." Mutt holds his hands up in quotation to help deliver the joke.

Jack prefers that they didn't say anything. There is nothing to be gained from this conversation.

"Jack, what are you? Six foot?" Pops address Jack as he sits.

"Six three" Jack is a hair short of six foot four but doesn't like the idea of rounding up. He's always felt smaller than that anyway.

"No, you're not." Pops' round mouth broke into a smile. Jack wonders if it is supposed to ease his statement. Jack is still sitting down. So, in his prone position, it isn't apparent just how tall he is. At the moment, with everyone else standing, he comes up far short, and he feels the difference as he looks up. "Son, stand next to Crackie," Pops commands.

Luggy moves over to Jack, but before Jack can stand up before he shows Jack to be the taller of the two, he blurts. "We're the same height, so yeah, he's at least six four." Apparently, Luggy didn't mind rounding up.

Jack would prefer to get a measuring tape than to go on with this exercise. That way, it would be visible, not just a suspicion, that he is continuously measured. The conversation is exactly that, a calculation on the heights he has reached and how, no matter the reason why, people like Pops still see Jack as someone who doesn't measure up.

Jack hears the grill burning lines into the meat.

"Plus, he can jump out of the gym," The Tard adds.

Mutt counters, "Too bad, he is so tall." Jack can't wait to hear Mutt's different contrarian position, "He'd be an amazing surfer if he were only, like, three inches shorter."

Smoker counters, "There are guys who are have been six two and dominated."

Mutt, unlike Smoker, actually surfs and doesn't just wear the clothes. This is an argument he can and should win. "Crackie's six three. Most guys are six foot and shorter. Powerful and balanced, like gymnasts. Face it. It's not a tall man's sport."

Pops cracks, "Well, Mutt, you should have been really good then."

Mutt lets his "can't give a shit" expression answer. Pops continues. "Well,

Crackie, maybe you are tallish. Jack can smell the charring of meat, and his mouth watered a little. He knows he must look, like some drooling fool, stupefied and lacking in response. Pops then looks at the other boys and continues, "But he must have been short in other ways." A loud crackle came from the grill, fat drippings exploding in the flame as the meat renders.

Jack takes in that feeling, the one of being weighed and measured and subsequently found lacking. Then he listens to the juice of meat catch the flame of the grill and noisily burst. Disappointed by the fact that Jack cares about this conversation at all, even after he decided to let go of everything, in particular disappointment itself. As the hiss of the grill continues, he reminds himself that soon enough, there will be no more room for disappointment. No more for judgmental conversations. No more room for anything. And the flames under the hood temper just a little.

Then something peculiar happens. The conversation returns to the long paternal conversation that Pops is prone to give.

Smoker leads him back with a question. "So, you're saying that strength is our greatest virtue?"

"What I am saying is…." He ponders bending one arm, lifting the tongs above his shoulder while folding his other arm across his chest, placing its hand in the crook of his bent arm. "What I am saying is forget virtue. Forget morality. It's vapor. Think of merit in terms of a scoreboard. Do you know what birds do when resources are limited? They destroy other nests. That's nature. That's Darwin. To think that you or anyone else is going to change the world is short-sided. As if there is some perfect version out there we can obtain. There are no guiding principles that we need other than to live your best life. When you do, you'll get to decide morality. You get to determine the direction we go as people. Progress isn't some linear direction, it's a moveable target, and you'll be the ones who place the bullseye. It's simple. You'll win. And because of that, you get to decide the rules. Winning is the only virtue, and everything else is fiction. The only lives you can try to perfect are your own. Trust me, the rewards are great." Jack sees Smoker flick the gap in his teeth but remain quiet.

Jack almost speaks up. He is shocked to hear Pops say it. He thought of all the people he knew; maybe Pops would be the last to speak those words. It's the prayer of the desperate. Words that remove context when the context is insurmountable. Everything around Pops, his view, his house, his cars, should have eliminated those words. Only people without these things are supposed to say them. People who are trapped in situations with no recourse but to do whatever is necessary to survive. It's a conclusion that Jack came to, one he had no choice but to come to.

When there is no way to win, you change the rules and let the outcome become the only guiding principle. To hear Pops say it feels like a death row pardons, forgiveness, and justification for all that Jack has had to do. If that is the one true guiding principle, then Jack can stand up taller when another man tries to take a measure of his life. He does his best not to speak out and say, "thank you."

Pops begins to tell a story about a time in college, one that requires him to continually check to see if his wife is about to come in earshot. Jack stands and walks toward the balcony's edge looking only at the tops of the homes below. How many other magnificent homes, with golden views, are occupied by desperate men? Where would they be without it? Jack wonders if there is a point to winning if that desperation never turns. Never becomes something else, something worthwhile? Then he thinks about Pops and the words that either form as vaporous smoke or stamps of gold.

And he again takes into account everything around Pop's life that points to him being right when others may be wrong. He imagines the impression this view gave its owner. To have everything else beneath him, and something so big and powerful as the Pacific Ocean seemingly bent at the knee rolling up to his feet like a beggar. Jack hopes then that Pops is right. After all, he has it better than most.

Jack's phone buzzes. He picks it out of his pocket to send it to voicemail. His thumb goes to the button instantly. Instead, he stares in disbelief. It isn't a number he has saved as a contact, and nine times out of ten, that means it is a customer or a girl he no longer wants to see, but this is a number he recognizes right away. One he has memorized. Then he freezes. What can he say? He is completely unprepared. Then he answers anyway. "Hello? Bree?"

CHAPTER 26

April '06

It's Saturday on a crisp early spring morning. Jack is on campus in the room in which he took sophomore Spanish the year before. Honeycomb balls and miniature pinatas hang from the ceiling. Multi-colored donkeys with student's names and other personal information occupy most of the space on the wall, as well as maps highlighting countries where Spanish is the given language.

He sees Bree at a desk just underneath a map of Columbia, but she won't look at him. Her head has been down since he walked through the door. She pretends to fill out some pre-test information when no one is supposed to fill out anything until the after test begins in ten minutes. It's the first time that they have been in the same room in two full seasons.

There is an empty desk next to her. Maybe Jack should take the open seat? They won't be allowed to speak because of the test, and that might be advantageous. She can't protest. Ask him to move. Or tell him how much she hates him at this moment.

This could be the first step taken toward an apology. Maybe she'll just get up and take a different seat. But space is filling up. There won't be any empty chairs. Jack hopes that she'll see the action as he intends, the first move in reconciliation. His closeness approximates expressed remorse for what he said and reassurance that he needs to be close to her in all aspects. This salvo is both literally and figuratively him coming to her.

Jack hurries to sign in before that seat is taken. He hands the proctor his registration. The proctor is older with her hair up and readers hanging around her neck. He hopes she moves quicker than she looks.

"Okay, hun, do you have the payment?" She asks.

"Payment?"

"Sorry, but you have to pay to take the SATs, honey."

He can feel his eyebrows rise, and blood pours into his face. "My mom was supposed to make a payment online." Jack's mom promised the last time that they spoke that she would pay for the test. How many months ago was that? Jack can't remember. "How much is it?" When the proctor answers, Jack thinks of the cost for the test in terms of meals missed. Then he asks, "Why do you need to pay for something required for college applications?"

"Well, you need to pay the proctors, like me, the test creators, the people who grade them. And it's not like applying to a college is free. They charge per application."

"They do?"

"Are you signed up to retake the test already? The spots fill up quickly?"

"No, I'm not." Panic tightens his chest.

"Where are you applying?"

Jack thinks of the schools his friends have mentioned and says mostly the same list back to the proctor.

"The UC's? Don't worry, you'll have plenty of time until then. Just make sure you take it before November to get the results back in time."

Jack feels the relief pour through his face. He has time to come up with something by then. No matter what challenge has presented itself, he has always managed to figure it out. But still, it doesn't feel right to him. "I'm in every advanced placement class. Carrying one of the highest GPAs in school, I bet. I just don't see why I need to pay for something that I worked so hard to do well on?"

"Well, I'm sorry, but no one is entitled to anything." She laughs softly, and he assumes at his expense. "Plus, to get credit for the AP courses, you're going to have to take the exam for those. Each one of those is going to cost more money than the SAT."

How'd he forget? There's too much in life to keep track of every little detail. Jack's taking five AP courses, and tests begin in about two months. He sees the numbers immediately. Money for rent. Money for food.

Bills that had been shut off over the last year and the sacrifices made to get them back on. Considerations for which no one else in the room has ever done the calculations. Regardless of what level of math that they might have reached.

Will that be a question on the test they get to take? How can a number be more than the sum of other numbers while simultaneously carrying the smallest value? How many of them have to answer that question on a monthly, weekly, or even daily occurrence? How many clients can Jack get in that given time?

For every client, he gets there is a 50% chance that they know someone to whom they will recommend his services. And for every client, he has only half of those have a transaction in a given month. Even if the money is excellent per transaction, what dollar amount can he expect to receive in thirty days? How quickly can his business grow to account for the delta between what is forecast and what is budgeted?

That should be on the test. That should be at the forefront of the mind of every child sitting in those chairs. The ones that handed over their checks with no more thought than it takes for them to reach into their pockets, grab the paper between their fingers, and drop it into the hands of the proctor. No idea where the money in the account came from, what was done to obtain it. How much its disappearance will affect how they eat, where they live, and how they live. No understanding of what not having that check means. What schools they can attend. What jobs they can get.

How would they explain this to all those in their class, why they didn't take the AP exams? Why didn't they take the SAT? Because there is no explanation. No written portion of any test would allow such creativity in writing that will ever make the answer to this sound plausible. So anyone who would have to provide such a solution is doomed to fail. Doomed to never pass on account that all the answers they can give all point to wrong ones even when they are accurate.

The piñatas and honeycomb balls sway on their strings, and the donkeys kick their back leg as they mockingly bray. Jack wishes he could take a bat to the room, to the pinatas to the paper tissue honeycomb balls. Smash them to pieces and send them bouncing off the walls. Explode their papier-mâché guts into the air.

Take a bat to the desks in which he sat while wasting so much time. To the advanced placement courses, he won't get credit for taking. To his peers, oblivion. To all the parent's protection doted on their children, stripping away the kid's sense of reality. How things really are.

"See" The proctor smiles at Jack. "It's not as bad as you think. The SAT is actually cheap compared to all the other things you're going to need to pay for. Now just make sure your parents know next time that you will need to bring a check with you to pay for the exam."

Jack is living in an equation with no correct answers. As he leaves the door, he looks back over to see if Bree has looked up. Her head stays down. The door closes behind him in a thud, and his plans for the morning, for his life, are no longer visible.

Jack then decides that if he can't be right, he needs to ask himself, just how wrong does he need to be?

CHAPTER 27

September 7 '07

The morning after Luggy's barbeque, Jack stays in his apartment and thinks about all the things he should say to Bree when she picks him up at 11. He isn't even sure what he expects to get out of this outing they have planned together. How could he, though? She had only called him the day before, asking to get together before she goes away to college. What does she want? What does he want? A chance to say goodbye and tie up loose ends? What else could there be? Not much.

She said that she was leaving in two weeks, and there is no way he'd be around for her to come back on the break.

Still, he thought it best to stay quiet, listen to what she wanted to hear, and hopefully be fun, be someone who she would like to see again before she leaves. He is fully aware of how weird he acted with her at the party. How strange he must have come off. He so desperately wants to fix it.

He is surprised when he gets in her car, and she suggests they go to the tide pools. The ride there is full of stalled conversation and small talk. He turns up the radio to fill the silence.

They park on a black asphalt road on top of the cliffs of Palos Verdes. Light brown dirt has swept over the curb on the beachside of the street by the days' gentle ocean breeze. Otherwise, the street is all black, the kind of dark found only on a newly paved road.

Jack looks down at his wrist, and as his jaws clinch, he feels the pressure of the enamel pushing down. In response, Bree's eyes narrow, and her mouth parts slightly as if it were loading words. He realizes how easily he has been read and allows his cheeks to soften.

It's too late. "What's wrong?" She asks cautiously.

"It's no big deal," Jack says without a hint of disappointment. He smiles, "It's just that I lost my watch the other day. I went in the water with it, which I usually don't do, and it must have fallen off or something."

"Well, that sucks. Was it nice?" They stand outside of Bree's red convertible, a description that makes the car sound much more impressive than it is.

Jack answers. "Yeah, it was, but that's not it, it's a diving watch." He shuts the car door, and the thud resonated louder than expected.

Of course, she knows the watch of which he is speaking. How many times did she put it on? A dozen or more?

"Oh," Bree's short and restrained response is an opportunity to move on. To let that be the extent of that discussion. Knowing her, she's probably trying not to pry. He doesn't take advantage.

Jack continues, "I'm just bummed that I took it out surfing." Instead of looking at her, he looks at his bare wrist. And he speaks to that, to the light hair that disappears against his darker skin. He really could use the watch. Wear it as a token of fortune on this crucial day.

He continues, "I just forgot to take it off, such an idiot." Jack speaks lightly with a smile. His tone is insincere, but at least he is not droning on. Jack hates himself for bringing it up and regrets it instantly. He only has a small window with Bree. There are so many other things he'd rather talk about.

"Where were you surfing?" Bree asks, pulling back on the dark green leash attached to her chocolate lab "Sierra."

"Northside of the pier, why?"

"That's a heavy watch."

"Yeah, it is."

"How long ago."

"A couple of days. During that north swell."

"You were northside?"

"Yep."

"What did all the spongers say when you were out there?" She refers to the body borders who typically stay on the north side of the pier, which runs a black ball flag -no surfing allowed- most days. The surfside is the southside, where they create a surfing-only zone, and no one is allowed to swim or bodyboard there.

"Well... who cares?" He jokes, and she laughs. He is happy to be off to a good start. "Actually, they were way in on the inside. The lineup was well past the pier."

"Do you know when it fell off?"

"Pretty sure it was on my last ride, thing just closed out on me, and I got put through the spin cycle."

She thinks for a bit. "How far out?"

"Pretty close to shore. Past a group of spongers posted on the shoulder, just hoping I would fall so they could drop in and take it themselves."

"Hmm. The current hasn't been too strong the last couple of days, and the pier is a great barrier. A lot of things gather around it. Your watch might still be around there. I can go for a dive there. I don't want you getting your hopes up, but maybe I can find it?"

Jack wonders if this means she's forgiven him. It might mean more to him than the watch itself, which was once the most cherished possession. He tries not to get visibly excited and gathers himself in a short inhale and silent exhale. "That would be awesome, thanks." He sounds perfectly measured and politely appreciative.

She responds, "I know how much your dad wanted you to have it." It sounds to Jack that the offer is more for his father than for himself.

Once they get to the trail, she lets Sierra off of her leash. The dog bounces into the brush and disappears. How wonderful it would be to get that watch back to get just a little bit of his life back. To have a piece of joy to carry with him during his last days.

"Where is the best place for diving, Hawaii?" Jack asks, stepping onto the trail. It feels like a good question. She is going to college there, so it makes sense to ask it.

"I love it there, the vibrant color of the fish and reef, but I prefer kelp forest."

They navigate a short narrow, and winding descent. The conversation gives way to concentration, so there is a delay before he follows up with "Why?" The sound of rock underfoot fills the gaps in the conversation, relieving Jack from any pressure to keep it out of silent, dead lulls.

"Hawaii is amazing." Bree smiles and crocks her head to the side, indicating that she's searching for how to explain. "But when I am in the kelp, I feel removed. I feel like I am the only person who has ever been there. The light filters through the water and kelp, and it's like I've faded out of existence, and I can watch the world from a secret place that no one else knows about." Jack is amazed that she spoke to him like that, completely unfiltered; after all, it had been some time since they were close. He wanted to say something, but nothing would have made him sound the way he wanted to. His practiced smile didn't say anything in return.

Jack leads Bree along the dirt path next to a mealy green shrub high above the ocean. "Watch your step," he warns, the rocks slide a lot." The two-foot-wide trail steepened sharply, and Jack made sure his first step wouldn't loosen dirt or the stones embedded in the path, sunken during rains, and left a prisoner in the hard mud. When his left foot touches down next to his right, both legs slide several inches, but Jack bends his knees to compensate and regain his balance.

"Wow, you look like a pro," she teases, "I'll try to be as agile as you." She has a handle on sarcasm so that it doesn't cut, and her smile during its delivery dulled the words even further.

"Alright, I'm no ballerina."

"That's not what I heard." She giggles and leaps down next to Jack, slightly bumping into him with her hips. Jack steadies himself by holding onto her hips as she leans forward. His hands linger longer than his balance requires, and he allows them only as much time that would remain short of conspicuous.

The breeze off the water picks up. It wraps around Jack's body under his shirt. There and gone instantly. With the breeze and the sun's warmth, unencumbered and glowing, the hair on the back of his neck rises.

"Damn, you should have played football. You could have been the best linebacker ever to come out of high school." The allotted time for their embrace ends with the sentence, and he lets go of her.

"Do you think I could have dated a cheerleader?" She steps back away from him with the question, and he hopes he has let go in time. They move on, concentrating again on the trail, watching his feet fall, hoping for another slip.

The first part of the trail is the steepest. Afterward, a dull decline lays out to the cove below. To the left is a rock beach one hundred yards long with a still water line of mint green. Straight ahead is a gleaming ocean with pulsating reflections bouncing up from the sun. Through a bending path, down to the right comes a large rock jutting into the sea, half-covered with water. That is where the tide pools thrive.

"I used to come up here all of the time with my Dad, but I don't ever really come up here at all. It's not far." Jack speaks as they stop on the middle plateau; the smell of the ocean carries in on every cool breeze. There is no one else around.

"No one leaves the bubble. People think that Torrance is another country." Bree replies. Sierra bounds by them. She navigates the terrain much faster than they can, and the dog again leaves them behind.

They reach the bending dirt path next to the stone beach. Each rock had been worn smooth from the tide and bleached by the sun. Some green seaweed floats lazily at the waterline, while a couple of pieces of driftwood have already beached themselves. Next to the stone beach, a large brown flatbed of rock sprawls into the ocean, holding pools of water and life. The tide has moved out, and most of the rock is dry. Both Bree and Jack step onto the rock removing their sandals, and walk to the biggest pool barefoot. He feels the chalky stone as his toes grip the earth. The balls of his feet land naturally to support his stride with no sole to get in the way. Without shoes or sandals, he feels connected and free as he was when he was a boy running wild over the same rock without a care in the world.

"I loved coming here when I was a kid," Jack treads the border of nostalgia carefully. He has a goal to be fun enough that she'll want to be around him more. "I used to pick up crabs and skip stones. I think I wanted to be a ship captain."

"It's amazing how many things change, but some things don't." Bree smiles at Jack and dips her toes into one of the pools.

Jack looks into the tide pool and sees his reflection broken in the ripples of her foot. "I used to think of things that seem so ridiculous to me now," his voice was full of the reminiscent tone that he had just tried to avoid. It makes him sound sentimental, and he usually works for dry and detached.

"Like what?" Bree removes her foot too quickly, and a sea urchin near her toes closed in reflex.

Jack stands on the opposite side of the tide pool. "Nothing," he responds quickly. His reflection has become clear again. He catches himself staring. Looking back at him is an indifferent, smug face with no time for stupid stories.

"Yeah?" Bree seems to want to hear more. He stays silent, though. Bree begins after a little wait. "We all think of weird things that we don't share with anyone, but I think we would all be more interesting if we did. I have this strange thing I think about all of the time. Actually, I don't really think about it. I just feel it."

"What's the difference?" His shallow question did not seem interested in its answer. Jack shuffles his feet left to right with his head down, focusing on a crab walking sideways across a rock.

"Let's just say that is not a fantasy or a thought of mine, more like a premonition. I always feel like I am, I guess like I am already dead."

"You kind of look dead, but just in the face, so it's not a big deal." Jack makes a joke. Sierra runs past the pair chasing seagulls off of the rock.

"Shut up," she thankfully laughs, "I mean, in the future, I am dead."

"Yeah, Einstein, we all die, but not all of us truly live," Jack says this last part in his best Scottish accent. He had a movie quote handy.

"No, it's the past right now, and I am reliving my life the instant before death. You know how they say your life flashes before your eyes when you die, well that's how I feel sometimes. I get to see it all over again." She rubs her arms lightly, alternating from one hand and then the next. "Do you ever have deja vu?"

"No, they have shots for that," Jack roars over the bark of the dog that resonates soundly from its chest. Jack speaks like a jabbing boxer.

"I have it all the time, not necessarily with big things like the first kiss or your drivers' license test, you know things that would stand out in your life." She seems to have ignored his comments and moves past them as if Jack didn't speak them.

"I was your first kiss. Glad to know you don't think about it." He had meant to sound sarcastic, but he hears dismay and hopes she doesn't catch it. Jack watches the crab scurry for a dark crevasse to hide.

"When I get the feeling, it usually happens when everything is quiet." Bree continues through Jack's interruptions. "Just doing something that allows my mind to slip like hanging out with my family or friends, walking down the street looking at shadows on the ground. Sometimes just at a cash register following the clerk's hand, move the groceries over the scanner like I was at a tennis match."

The breeze comes in stronger, whipping Jack's hair about his face, flicking it against his forehead in an uncomfortable manner. Jack turns away from Bree and the wind.

"I get this feeling that's cool, and my skin tingles like it's trying to get off of my body." Bree grabs both of her elbows with a light squeeze and gently rubs her biceps. "I don't know, it's really weird, and I don't tell too many people about it. But it's so strong that I can't ignore it. I just let it pass and enjoy it because I feel so alive when it happens. I actually try to hold that feeling as long as I can. Usually, it ends with a shiver. I don't know exactly what it means if anything at all, but I feel it so strongly that there must be something to it."

The wind tapers off, and Jack turns back toward Bree. "That's really weird." He says flatly, sounding like some asshole as if Bree isn't cool enough to talk to him. He silently curses himself. Why is Jack doing this? He doesn't mean to, but he can't turn it off.

"Do you know why I wanted to see you today?" Bree asks in a different, more somber tone. Jack hears the warnings going off in his head. She seems disappointed or upset, and he isn't surprised.

"What are you talking about?" He responds as if he doesn't know how he behaves.

The seagull that had been chased away lands on a rock that sits in the water. From Jack's viewpoint, it looks as if the bird perched on Bree's shoulder. Sierra barks again.

"At Jenny's, what you asked me,"Bree initiates eye contact. He looks down in response. "It was… different. I want to know why you asked that."

"Don't worry about it. I was just drunk." His words rang back at him, unguarded.

"Please."

Jack shakes his head, wearing a cocked smile, and he shrugs his shoulders. He picks up a crab squeezing its shell to see how much pressure it can handle.

"Here, look at this," Bree says after some silence. She walks around the pool to Jack and hands him an old piece of paper folded in half with an Angel drawn with the particular chaotic strokes of a young boy. "You gave that to me when my brother passed away. Do you remember?" A wave thrusts hard against the rock as if it is trying to knock Jack into the water.

"You have this in your pocket every day?" His joke is not at all funny. He knows it. Sierra barks again. Jack opens the letter and reads a line he put in quotes at the top, before the script of the message. "Yea, though I walk through the valley of the shadow of death, I shall fear no evil, for you are with me; Your rod and Your staff, they comfort me."

Another wave crashes into the rock, spray mists Jack's face. He stops reading as he knows the rest. "This is so lame," he protests and drops the hand he held the letter in down by his thigh. His throat swells and dries in protest.

"No, it's not!" She seems even more disappointed, and Jack begins to think of ways he can change that. "It reminds me of my brother and how much I loved him. I can't tell you how many times I read it after he died. I kept it on the nightstand with my favorite picture of him. I still read it sometimes." She trails off and looks out at the water. After a second or two, where only the sound of waves hitting rock speaks. Bree looks back at Jack and continues, "What's lame is you totally disregarding it. Why do you always pretend to be such an asshole?"

Jack stands, stunned.

"Give it to me. I'll read it." Bree reaches out to him.

"No," he says petulantly. Sierra bounces around the rock, barking at the commotion. The bird cries back in response.

"What? It's my letter."

"Yeah, so what? I wrote it." He leans back and holds the letter away from her. It crinkles in his grasp.

The bird squawks again and again, with Sierra answering each caw with a resounding yelp.

"Jack!" she commands, "don't ruin it!"

He is resolute. Defeated, he doesn't also need to be embarrassed.

She reaches around his back and pulls the letter from his hand, and the paper pops but doesn't break.

"This letter is why I wanted to see you before I went away. I love this letter. It reminds me of my older brother." Bree starts to cry softly, Jack can't quite hear it in her voice, but her big green eyes began to shine and turn red around the edges. "I have held onto this letter because when I read it, I think of him. It helps me remember what he was like. How he always took care of me, made me laugh, and for some reason, it can be hard to remember, but this letter you wrote does that. Then I feel good, I feel alive. I'm happy and hate to think some asshole wrote this."

"Bree," she starts to read where Jack had left off. "I'm sorry God took your brother. He must have needed him in heaven more than we needed him to fix our bikes or take us to get candy. My mom says that God has a plan for all of us, that things happen to us for a reason. I wouldn't be too upset if I were you because if my mom is right that we have a plan, then I know that your plan will be the best of all because you are so good, and God has to know this. I'm sorry that we will not see your brother for a long time, but when I heard he died, I grabbed my stuffed animals, the ones he always used to put on shows for us, and I tried to do his voices. Don't tell anyone, but I saw him. He stood behind me watching until I turned around, then he disappeared." Bree smiles as she reads. Two tears run down the left side of her face. One sat on the cusp of her cheek, and the other ran into the valley of her lip. "I'm not scared to die, and I don't think your brother was either because he was so brave. Remember the ice plant fights would have, with him versus every other kid on the block? You shouldn't be scared to die either because God wouldn't take you. After all, I need you so much. Love Jack"

Bree folds the letter back up and puts it back in her pocket. She wipes the remaining tear from her face, and they both stand in silence.

Jack's barefoot kicks the ground, and it bounces back against the hard stone. He has blown yet another chance.

Bree continues, "Why do you always pretend to be such a prick? It's like you're playing a role, some lame cliché, 'the beautiful and misunderstood loner'."

Jack pauses before he speaks, and in the cadence, he can't help but think that it's precisely what he has turned into, a lame cliche. "You think I like being some kind of loser orphan who pushes coke?" Jack shoots back defensively. But he knows in some way he did. In some way, Jack embraced it, he may have been pushed to it, but at some point, Jack saw himself as a man with no one to answer to, someone who didn't need anyone. He closes his mouth, biting down on any further words that would just make things worse.

"The other night, I didn't want to even see you. To be disappointed by you again. But you spoke openly, honestly. Weird, yeah. But honest.

And it gave me a glimmer of hope that the person I used to know that I used to be so close with was still there. I have really missed him over the last couple of years, and I thought he was long gone. Killed off by some cigarette ad personality living in a music video."

"Sorry," He apologizes.

She continues without acknowledging him, "And finally, you finally apologized to me! What took so long? Like you didn't care all those years how badly you hurt me! Like you didn't really care about me at all. You were my best friend!" Jack hangs his head. "Is this how you really want to live? You have either really turned into a cliche, or you are pretending to be one. I'm not sure which is worse." A large wave slams into the rock bed with a thud that resonates in the space in-between the surrounding stones, in all of the deep crevasses that remained hidden to everyone who ever walked there.

"I'm sorry," he says again. It's a hard thing to speak, but with each word, the next one comes easier. "I'm sorry I don't know why I would say anything like that to you. I don't know why I would act like that, act like the person I have become. I wish I could stop." That is the truth, chiseled to the marrow. It made it sound like an easy task to accomplish when spoken so simply, making the statement misleading.

"Why can't you?" She stands close to him, only half an arm away. He fights the urge to grab her.

"I don't know. Sometimes I think I'm just broken." Jack hears the words spring out of his mouth but never before entertained the thought or come to that conclusion. Yet, it had been spoken so clearly there is no denying them, leaving Jack only left to wonder about their origin. There is a sense of freedom in saying it, but the consequence of truth is equally miserable. He can be himself, sure, but that is a sad young man with little hope. What good is that?

The water makes a sucking sound as it retreats from the hidden empty spaces and escapes to see the light of day again.

"What do you mean?" The red in her eyes have darkened, the green behind it flashes in the sunlight.

Jack pauses. He doesn't even know what he means entirely. "Remember that video game we used to play where you have to jump from cliff to cliff with a fire chasing you?"

"Yeah, I remember it... If you move too slow, you die in the fire, and if you miss time your jump, you fall and die?"

"That's right. That's how I feel all of the time, as if something is trying to run me down. So I just kind of just turned off. And I don't know if I can turn back on." Jack puts on a smile, hoping that would lighten his words. He looks out on the horizon. "If I can just swim out as far as I can and get away from everything for even a little bit and drown all of the bullshit. Let it all sink below and never have to feel this way again." He swallows hard several times to remove the dry, dull lumps from his throat.

"Don't say that." Her sniffle is abrupt, as are her words.

"It's not that I want to die. It's that I wish I felt alive, and somehow I am neither." Jack turns and looks at the dog pawing at a shallow pool, water splashing everywhere. He, too, has made a mess.

Bree hugs Jack. He closes his eyes and smells her hair. When he opens them, he sees the seagull flying away; wings stretched wide, holding the wind under them with a reserved strength that carried it high overhead. To a height where Jack and his problems must have looked tiny and insignificant. The same reserved strength, a gentle persistence, he feels in Bree's arms wrapped around his lower back, she too, has a breeze in her touch.

"Why is it so hard sometimes?" His heart thumps in his chest.

"If it weren't, would we even care? Or would we just get bored like we do with everything else?"

"Yeah, but some people have perfect lives."

"Things are only as perfect as they pretend them to be." She lets go of Jack and pulls her arms back from between his.

"I'd settle for a life decent enough to pass as okay."

"It's the struggle or the willingness to struggle, the belief that it's going to be worthwhile that makes it all so beautiful. How do you appreciate anything if you never lose it?" She sits down and puts her foot in the water.

Jack moves next to her, sitting closer than expected, joining her by putting his feet in the water too. Sierra lays down on the rock bed, no longer interested in anything other than drying off in the sun.

The waves continue to hit the rock, but the thud becomes billowy and hypnotic, and Jack sits silently without a care as to the words that do not pass between them. The sun litters their backs and legs. This is the start of Jack's favorite time of year, early autumn. The air held the crispness of fall and the warmth of the summer, and it is the ripening of the world, the sweetest time of year.

Jack speaks first, keeping his voice light. "You know everyone thinks they have a lot to offer. Every weirdo, loser has thought they were something special regardless of how idiotic they were. And there was probably one person who did, who was just as stupid as them. Who pushed that stupidity on the rest of us, telling that idiot just how talented he was, how much potential he had, how he was brilliant. Behind every asshole is someone who believed. That's the scary part."

"I don't know about every weirdo or loser or anyone else. But ever since we were little kids, I thought you were smart, compassionate, and kind. Maybe I'm one of those idiots who believe, but I still believe in that kid. The one who was my best friend." Her body moves, her torso turning toward him, her legs spread wider, so the closest one to him almost touches Jack's leg. "You were always there for me. When my brother died, you were there. When my parents divorced, when they were fighting, I looked forward to escaping to your place and making tacos together. I needed that. I needed you."

"You needed me?" Jack's astonishment manifests as a question he asks himself out loud.

She answers for him, "Of course I did. You know, for someone so smart, you can be absolutely stupid." Being called stupid has never made Jack so happy. She continues, "Why do you think it hurt so much for you to just throw our friendship away? It's not because I didn't care. It's because I cared so much."

Between the sun warming him and the water refreshing his feet, Jack can't imagine a better place to be than at this moment. The ocean continues to serenade them, and Jack leans to his side, leans closer to Bree. It takes all of his strength to prevent himself from falling into her lap.

"You know what's amazing about this tide pool?" She speaks after enough time passes for a handful of waves to crash.

"What?"

"All these little creatures live in two completely different environments. The water is in, and it is out. Dry. Wet. They have adapted to live in both. Exposed to the air or buried underwater. Even something so tiny and insignificant as a hermit crab can be one of the most resilient things alive. I think that is amazing. Most people would think of them as small and insignificant. I think it's more likely that people underestimate things around them, including themselves, than overestimate them."

The breeze off the ocean carries moisture with it, and as Jack thinks of a reply because outside of a couple of words she has done most of the talking, his parched mouth relents, and he feels so comfortable he does not want to ruin the feeling with some words that he is about to make up. Terms that offer nothing more than allowing him to speak when he might feel obligated to do so.

He lays back on the rock. The sun warms his face and neck again, and he feels a thawing. He almost falls asleep when a thought jumps into his head and instantly out of his mouth. "Why, after all of this time, did you want to talk to me about that letter?" It may have been the best question he ever asked.

She doesn't respond quickly. If it were anyone else, Jack would assume the response is being crafted and polished to minimize content and maximize the effect. "I needed to talk with you. I mean really talk, before… I don't know. Nothing feels like it's going to be the same anymore."

Jack's silence speaks in agreement, and then he changes the subject. "You still want to know what I used to think about that's totally weird?" As he sits up, his feet push further into the water.

"Yes, I do." Bree smiles softly. The black spikes of sea urchins swaying under her reflection stole his attention, and a red starfish hovered above Bree's head like a halo.

"Ok, but don't laugh. I have this weird fantasy that I am really sick. I don't talk about it to anyone, but they can see it, so they know. It's obvious that I am struggling through something, and people offer to help, but I turn them down. Then when it's the end, and I'm in a hospital bed, and people are saying their goodbyes, they break down and cry, but I don't."

She smiles. Jack picks up a crab and holds it to her face, and she blows it a kiss. Jack let it go back into the water.

Next, he picks up a shell, and with some growing confidence, jokes, "Think I can hear the ocean?" With water so close and audible.

She smiles and laughs, "Maybe," she says sarcastically, and then continues, "but the blood we hear in our ears is really almost the same."

Jack knows she means the sound that we actually hear with a shell to our ear is the blood flowing through our capillaries, but he doesn't really follow. "What do you mean?"

"Our blood is mostly water, with primary electrolytes of sodium and chloride, the components of salt, playing a large role. It has the same density too."

"I love that you know that."

"It makes sense, right. Life came from the ocean. The saltwater in us is a memory of what we once were." She smiles, and Jack follows slavishly. "And you were once the captain of a ship," she laughs.

"I think maybe people need to start calling me Captain," he states flatly.

"Aye, Aye, Captain." She laughs again. So does he.

Water runs over the edge of the rock, and some of it makes it back into the pool that they sit around. The tide has come back in, sending those on the rock on their way.

CHAPTER 28

July '05

Jack is sitting on his couch. "You're a slut." Jack flatly states without anger but with hurt and surprise. The news is shocking, and so are the words that come out of his mouth in response. There is no thought behind them, no measurement. They speak only to his utter and absolute crushing heartache. He stops when he realizes what he said, that Jack blamed her when he shouldn't. He shouldn't have been surprised at all by the news she shared. Bree has been with her boyfriend for more than a year, since Freshman year. She is nearly 17, and most of the other girls in their class lost their virginities sometime much earlier. But Jack has been chaste and turned down sex several times. He is just waiting, waiting for them to get together eventually. He is confident it would happen sometime. Hopefully, sometime soon. But he has ruined it all with three simple words that he didn't mean to say. Three little words that aren't truthful at all. Words that don't convey his sadness and regret but somehow blame her for his feelings.

"What did you say?" She sounds just as shocked.

Jack stammers for a second, and he knows he should immediately apologize, but his loss won't let him. So he just repeats what was said, as she asked him to do like he is reading back a note that someone else had left, one with words he doesn't own.

"Fuck you," he hears her cry on the other end of the phone. They don't talk on the phone every night, but they speak more than twice a week. And that doesn't include Taco Tuesday, which they do every week.

Jack is hesitant. Her sobs hurt to hear. Much more so than when she told him that she lost her virginity to her long-time boyfriend. And she didn't blurt out the words to throw it in his face. She shared the news in a way any good friend would tell another that something wonderful and massive had happened to them. She called Jack, her best friend before she even mentioned it to him. "You're my best friend, and I want you to be the first to know."

"Go on," he was excited to hear what she would tell him and sits up. Happy for the glee in her voice and that she seemed to be suppressing her excitement at the news. How wonderful it must be if she is holding back her joy and energy. What fantastic new information does she have to share if it gave her such happiness to even think about it? Then she told Jack.

"What?" He mustered through his shock.

She told him again with the same blissfulness as before. "I know it's a little shocking, but I can't believe I'm no longer a virgin. I had to tell you first."

Then the venom came out. The rejection that Jack foisted on her in three little words.

Now it's just sobbing on the line. He wants to tell her that he doesn't mean it, that he spoke incorrectly. That she is, and always will be, his girl. But he doesn't. He stays silent. He holds his words back, afraid of how else he could make things worse, scared of the things he has to say.

Instead, he wears a muzzle made out of fear and regret, preventing any further harm even at the cost of any future atonement.

Jack hears her hang up. He holds his phone to his ear long after.

CHAPTER 29

September 7, '07

With the top down, the air bends over the car's blocking windshield as it plows through the oncoming atmosphere.

Wisps of it trickle through Jack's hair and ears, but mostly he remains shielded and comfortable in the air pocket, the bubble, that the car offers to them both as they drive home. Bree took a long way home, avoiding any major roads. Portuguese Bend offered little traffic and an open-ended, panoramic view of the ocean. It felt like the car rode on top of the water, and Jack floated along too. When they came over a hill, just before they began their side street maze home, all of Los Angeles could be seen in the distance. The blue San Gabriel Mountains jutted up like fortress walls, and all the peat moss foothills, full of Southern California chaparral, rolled in high clarity, giving way to the flat city streets in between. Only sandcastle clouds dotted the sky, and Jack saw the Hollywood sign, some thirty miles in the distance. Visible only three or four times a year, usually only after heavy rain. He couldn't read it. Still, it was unmistakable in its bold white lettering.

Once they made their way to the flatlands and passed King Harbor, they turned onto Valley Drive, the street Jack grew up next to, which cuts diagonally through the South Bay's beach towns.

Valley Drive runs next to what was once the old railroad tracks, with Ardmore Road constituting the other bookend street on the other side of the tracks. The train once ran beachgoers to the old Redondo swimming hole from deeper parts of the city.

These were the people who ended up staying there and growing these communities from distant LA outposts to beach neighborhoods. It wasn't in fashion, and they carried with them no-cache, just an appreciation for life near the water. Most people might assume that was an eternity ago. Jack knew it wasn't that distant. His father told him stories of growing up on blocks of open lots full of trees, dilapidated homes, and living near a biker gang.

At some point, well past the usefulness of the train had run its course, the tracks were removed, and the city laid down wood chips calling the newly refurbished land the greenbelt. Bree and Jack spoke about the last train they saw to run on the old tracks, the pennies they used to lay down, and the ice plant fights they had when they were kids. They also talked about the cars that don't realize that both Ardmore and Valley have sections that turn into one-way streets and the high number of them that end up driving the wrong way. Bree brought up the fact that it was Jack's Mom who gallantly chased down cars going in the wrong direction before any damage could be done. It was a nice memory. He made a note to think of her like that more.

"Growing up here was fun," Bree says, "but I liked it more when we were little."

"How's that?"

"Everyone here grows up quick. Everyone wants to be an adult so early. And some of the girls were always so bitchy to anyone who didn't see things the way they did. I never understood it. Why were we so quick to stop playing?"

As content as he is behind the protection of the windshield and safely tucked in his bubble, Jack falls comfortably silent. So after they talk about the ice plant fights, and the pennies flattened by train, and growing up in the area, Jack silently slips into himself. And lets himself feel a future as pleasant as he, on that sunny day, with trickles of air caressing his head. A future where he a Bree ride together.

When she turns down his street, Jack jumps at seeing the Intruder out front throwing a ball with a couple young boys from the neighborhood. "Just drop me off here," Jacks says, lowering his head. He hopes to God no harm comes to her. How would he ever forgive himself?

"Are you sure?" She sounds confused.

"Yeah, this is where everyone drives me off. Otherwise, you end up going a block further before you could even turn around, and it's kind of sketchy around here."

"This isn't that bad of a neighborhood. My mom grew up here. My grandparents' house was like four blocks over when they were a young family." She continues to drive forward despite Jack's protests. A couple of guys of similar age and appearance lean against a car parked just outside of Jack's apartment.

"Drop me off here," Jack protests again. This time it's not as polite but stern and sudden. His hand goes for the wheel.

"Jack, what are you doing?"

"Just please stop. Please." By now, everyone on the block can see them.

And when she stops, Jack quickly opens the door to get out.

Bree looks around. She can see all the people in the street. Whether she thinks that's troubling is unknown. But she asks, "Is everything okay?"

"Yeah, yeah, it is. Do me a favor, please use this driveway to turn around."

"What's wrong?"

"Nothing. Can I call you later?" And he hopes that he can.

"Yes, please do."

She turns the car around as Jack asked.

Jack walks the block, and when he passes the Intruder holding the ball in a throwing stance, he hears him say to no one in particular, "You know what I like about this block? No random dudes come over at all hours waking these ninos. God, I hope that shit doesn't change. Cause I'll know the second, it does."

Jack tries his best not to run into his apartment.

CHAPTER 30

September 8, '07

Jack didn't think he would call her so soon. They had just hung out the day before. Jack stayed in last night watching some television, eating the soup he had taken from Welldubs house. He didn't even ask any of his friends if they wanted to hang. He needed time alone. Time to sort out the breakthrough with Bree, and equally time lamenting that it came so late and that the next week or two would be his last with her, last with everyone.

She said to come over in the afternoon she had many errands to run, and Jack thought to ask to join her, but he didn't want to overwhelm her, so he surfed with Mutt instead. They met up with the rest of the boys for burritos from their favorite Mexican spot, a cheap place, in the parking lot of a motel, with great food. His friends were going to smoke, to get "crispy" as they were now saying, and see a movie, but Jack had plans. They pried, of course. "What're you going to do?" They asked. And when Jack told them he was going to see Bree, "Hang with Bree again." He couldn't help but smile. It hardly fell off his face the rest of the day.

He heads down her walk street, and Jack stops in front of his old home. There are some changes to the façade; the windows and doors are different, and the paint. Like most of the houses, it is now a muted grey, almost white, when it used to be peach orange. The bronze hood over the chimney has fully oxidized green, and the color cascades onto the newer paint. The patina grew from exposure to wind, rain, and the salt carried in the morning fog—the elements to which it was exposed. A change so gradual and subtle, one needs a longer view to understanding the difference between then and now.

Overall the changes to the home are only superficial, as thin as the chimney's patina, and don't betray his memory. They only serve as a reminder that he doesn't live there anymore. That someone else sleeps in his room. A sign that a thin coat covers his life, grown by exposure to the elements.

"Change in the bathroom, and I'll be right out," Bree says as she heads toward her bedroom. Prints and paintings hang on the yellow walls, and the only furniture in the front room, a dark oak bench, and a small table against the wall opposite the front door. Fresh sunflowers sit in a vase on top of the table and highlight the earthy yellow in the entryway. Jack knows it is just like her mother to have fresh flowers throughout the small house. Her home is one of the only houses left on the block with both a front and back yard, probably the origin of the sunflowers.

Jack changes quickly and waits on the bench in the front room. After some time, longer than expected, Bree returns in her bathing suit carrying two towels.

"Sorry, I had to send an email real quick."

"That's okay. It's just nice being back here. You've kept the place the same. No major changes. Feels like I'm 12 again."

"Yeah. We might be the only ones who haven't gone through a full remodel. I mean, none of the old families live on the block anymore. It seems once the kids reach a certain age, they move on. New families come in, and everything is a teardown, regardless of how nice the house is, regardless that they spent a fortune on it, they tear it down anyway."

Jack as serious as can be, says, "Don't tell me they got rid of the sour grass in Mrs. Ellington's back yard?"

Bree smiles. "Why did we eat it? It tasted so bad. And that's where her dog would pee." He shrugs and chuckles. She continues, "come on; let's go." They head out, and the western sky is a blood orange bent into blue right above it.

"Shoot, I think the sun already set."

"Yeah. Looks like it just happened. Come on, let's get to the water. Maybe we can catch it," Jack is ready to do anything with this girl. He wants the day to last forever, even if that means chasing the sun.

They rush down the block and cross the last street. The sun is down by the time they pour onto the strand.

"Darn it. We missed it. I really like catching sunsets. It makes me feel like I've completed my day. I dunno, sorta like closure." She speaks toward the water.

Jack glances over at her as she stares out to the distance. He agrees, "There's something about it that I can't put into words. Feels like everything else stops, and you have a moment to catch up. And you're exactly where you're supposed to be."

"Yeah, that's it, the feeling of being present." She nods her head.

Jack continues, "But really, it's just an illusion. We're adding our own feelings and meaning to something that actually isn't happening."

"What do you mean?" She asks curiously.

Jack explains, "I mean that the sun isn't actually setting. Relative to us, it isn't moving. Right? We're all hurtling through space. Being cast out from some single point of origin. But in our solar system the sun is stationary. And we're just rotating to make it appear as if the sun were moving."

She seems to measure his explanation, then says, "I guess you're right. Maybe it is just a trick, but it's so pretty, magical even, and we only have it for such a short time."

"That's not true, either." Jack stops to make sure he isn't going to sound like "a know it all asshole" but continues trusting her not to take him the wrong way. "Yeah, you and I only have it for a little bit of time. But it never really goes away."

She looks confused. And Jack knows just how smart she is, so he takes responsibility for not explaining himself thoroughly and sets to fix it.

"Picture this. Total darkness. Nothing but space." He sees her close her eyes and smiles at the faith she has given him to invest entirely in his little moment. Smiling, he continues, "Then add earth, Blue and green and white at the poles. Now add the sun, bright and massive. Now the world turns on its axis, so see it begin to rotate. Think about the light the sun throws off of it and how it hits us. Zoom in on North America but picture it at night. The earth turns toward the east, so light first crosses the eastern shore pushing out the darkness in front of it. That's sunrise. It continues all the way across the land and now covers the whole country. Call it midday."

"What about Hawai?" She jokes.

"Forget Hawaii," He teases back.

"Boo!" She laughs but keeps her eyes closed.

Through a broad smile, he starts again, "See the darkness of night on the Atlantic as it comes over the land, pushing the light in front of it. In between is a thin gold band. That's sunset. Watch it fall into the Pacific. Now keep picturing it as the gold band crosses Hawaii."

"Yeah, Rainbows!"

"Crosses Australia and New Zealand and then Japan and the rest of Asia. See it cross the Mediterranean and Europe. All the way back to the Atlantic, over the US, and back into the Pacific Ocean. Did it ever leave us? Did sunrise ever leave us? No. Now zoom out a little. See earth as a sphere. See sunrise on one side and sunset on the other. At all times, there is a thin gold band surrounding us. We don't always get to see it. We only get glimpses of it. But it is always near. Surrounding us all."

She opens her eyes. "Thanks for mansplaining the sunset to me."

Jack starts to defend himself and apologize. But she interrupts, "I'm just kidding. I never really thought about it like that before. One of those things that should be obvious but falls outside of our personal perspective, so we don't see it like that. It's nice. To think it never truly leaves us makes me happy."

"What is it that makes us feel this way, you think?" He asks. "No one ever says high noon is my favorite time of day. And that's when the sun is the strongest."

"Because of the combination of day and night. They give each other definition and balance. The shadows accentuate the light, and the sun provides the night depth. Each one is more potent because of the other. I'd probably feel the same about sunrises if I were ever awake for them." She giggles.

"I am. Will be in the surf by then if it's good enough. It's nice, real nice. But there's something about the sea. Maybe if we lived on the East Coast, it would feel the same. But the thing about the sun setting into the ocean is that it paints the water."

Jack pauses to look around. Enough light remains to cast shadows on the beach, in all the indentations and footfalls. The sky lies still as no wind blows, and the clouds anchor themselves full and picturesque. From Malibu to Palos Verdes, both seem far away and quiet. In between lays the ocean, still and purple like plum rice paper. With something ready to be written.

"Hey, look, it's red tide." Bree points to a small wave breaking, and inside the billowy whitewash, green lightning flashes at impact. "Let's go in." She announces, and he follows.

Purple sheen surrounds the couple as they wade into the water that has retained the warmth of the day. Jack keeps much of his body submerged, wearing the water up to his neck. Bree swims over to Jack, hugging him from behind. Her arms across in front of his chest, her hands hold his opposing wrists. After a long silent period, long enough, in fact, that the small space of water between has become noticeably warmer than the rest, Jack turns around and kisses her cheek. Then she playfully dunks his head under the water.

"How about a pier jump?" Bree asks.

"All right," he agrees.

They run along the hard-packed sand wet with the outgoing tide, firm because of the water deep within. Leaving a footprint with every stride as they cut through the night. With every kick of leg, the red tide-soaked sand flashes brilliant green—freedom in every stride, every step of the way taken with unencumbered bare feet.

They climb the concrete stairs quickly, and the new lights layout before them like the lights of a runway to their upcoming leap. They don't waste time and run straight to the end of the pier, past the new apricot benches and the gray guard rails to the unfinished new coffee house that only needs finishing touches to be complete. It looks like one of the forgotten beach houses without the company signs, with its wooden shutters and small stature. The simplicity of the design feels comfortable and old.

Jack and Bree stand on top of the rail. Jumping off of the pier carries with it a hefty fine. Both of them leap without hesitation. Jack lays his body horizontal, one arm extended towards the black western horizon, and the other reaches out to the town. Before impact, Jack pulls his arms in, breaking the surface with his hands, and his body follows into the water. The ocean catches Jack, and its buoyancy pushes him back up to the sky with a deep inhale of night's sweet air. Jack looks over to Bree, who has already begun to swim toward the beach. They quickly swim to the shore and run back to her house, leaving glowing wet footprints along the way.

Underneath the outside shower on the side of her house, warm water pours over their bodies. They have to stay close so that both can fit under the shower at the same time. Water splashes off of Jack's body, bouncing onto Bree's, and vice versa. Jack's skin relaxes as the water washes away the salt that has already dried, pulling his skin tight. Their bodies brush against one another, not intentionally, but neither make any attempt to avoid the contact. Bree turns her back to the showerhead rinsing her hair. Jack stands behind the showerhead, water pouring out beside his ear, and watches her with all his attention. She holds him captive, with no thought or memory, no other plan, or worry entering his mind. He watches the water stick to her skin, rolling down her entire body. It flows from the nape of her neck, down her back and ass, before dipping into the inner thigh, releasing below her ankle.

Bree turns towards Jack, and he closer to her, the water now hitting him between his broad shoulders. Bree presses against him, starting with her thighs, then stomach, and she stops just as her breasts playfully brush against his abdomen. Water bends around Jack, from his shoulder down his back and onto Bree's arm, now wrapped around him. The warmth trickles between them, pooling in places where their skin touch. The kiss happens slowly at first. Their heads come together as if pushed by the water, and when their lips touch, they press softly. Tongues speed the passion, and they both hold each other as tightly as possible. Although every limb tangles and their bodies press firmly against each other, they can't get close enough, feel enough of each other.

Then she pulls back. Still holding each other. She looks up at that night sky and says, "Starlight star bright first star I see tonight I wish I may I wish I might have this wish I make tonight." The star that she speaks to is the brightest in the sky. Jack knows it, meaning he knows its name or, more appropriately names, because it is actually two stars that combine to shed that light. Sirius is a binary star, with the predominant of the two producing more light than our own sun. The other, dimmer one, the remnants of a sun that has run its course and exhausted itself, burned through itself, and collapsed. They revolve around each other closely, as relatively near as Jack stands next to Bree. And it is evident between the two which one is which.

Jack knows this because of its position in the sky. Part of the "Dog" constellation, sometimes referred to as the "dog star." It is the origin of the phrase the dog days of summer, as it rose in ancient times during the middle of that season. Now it rises much later in the year. So through the passage of time alone, the label is no longer applicable.

She puts her head back on his shoulder, and Jack silently makes a wish too.

CHAPTER 31

September 9, '07

Jack hears pounding on the front door. Unlike Plexiglas, there is no weight behind the strikes, just an impatient pace in their frequency.

Jack is sitting on the corner of his bed. He slept in for the first time in a long time. He even had a dream. Carried on a wave without having to push his board or pump his legs for speed. The shore is close but not getting closer. The wave's crest falls over, the sun rests just out of the opening, Jack smiles. He is nestled inside the hollow portion of the wave, propelled by the broken water falling just behind him. The same water that has fallen over his head like a canopy, keeping him hidden and safe. The wave doesn't end.

He rubs his eyes and thinks of his kiss last night, her promise to see him before she leaves, smiling at her as she drove him to his apartment, after a quick stop for milkshakes and french fries. That wasn't that long after the kiss. They held each other in the water, for who knows, to Jack, it felt like an eternity, but it probably wasn't more than a couple of minutes. Then they got dressed, hopped in the car, stopped for a snack, and he got out and floated to his bed, carried by night's feat. Falling asleep quickly and staying asleep through a good portion of the morning.

Jack moves slowly to the door. Whoever it is has slowed their pace. They keep a persistent rhythm, with a cadence of a relaxed heartbeat, like the pace of Jack's heart as he meanders to the door.

"What the fuck? Smashley says exhaustedly as if she wore herself out, hammering on the door.

"Sorry, I was just in bed, and it took me a while to get to the door."

"I'm not talking about having to bang on your door. You haven't been answering my texts."

"What texts?"

"Don't be stupid. I've been texting you since yesterday afternoon. Where... is... my... key?" She throws her hands toward him palms up and motions them up and down with what can only be read as impatience.

"I didn't realize you were texting me. I guess I didn't look at my phone yesterday."

"What did you lose it?" She's condescending.

"No, I was just with..." he slows down, "I was with someone."

She must have been focusing on what she would say because she misses that last detail. "Well, I've been trying to get a hold of you. We have a date party today. You'll love it. Catalina cruiser. Day drinking. Food. Then back to the house for a dance party. Also, I needed to get my handbag yesterday. I left here the other night, and I needed it yesterday! Gosh!" She is very animated, clearly frustrated. "You wouldn't answer the phone. And it looks like you lost my key?" She pauses. "Who were you hanging out with?"

"What do you mean, you lost your key?" Jack realizes that he has missed an important detail too. He is confused.

"Do you not know what the word lost means? Who the hell were you with yesterday?"

"Bree, that's who I was with. What key are you talking about?"

"What the fuck? That's what you're into? Weirdo tomboys? Consider us even for the whole Smoker scenario." She is louder than she needs to be.

"She's not a weirdo. You don't have a key."

"Well, now I know why you didn't answer any of my messages... You dick!"

"What key are you talking about?" He repeats himself, still confused

"My key. The one I leave under the welcome mat! Well, now I know what you were doing when I was standing out here, pounding on your door like an idiot. For God knows how long. Yelling for you. I had to tell your neighbors to fuck off when they told me to be quiet. In this ghetto, you can get shot for less. I just needed my handbag…"

Jack doesn't follow her. He stopped listening when she said she had a key under the placemat. Instead, Jack pictures the Intruder standing over him, the gun barrel growing, and Jack stuck in place, unable to gets out of the way to escape the oncoming and crushing danger. How he had tried to remember locking the door, the panic, of trying to hear the words the Intruder spoke while simultaneously sorting out how the Intruder got in, in the first place. She left a key. He had been so ardent with the rules, and she left a key for anyone to grab. To unlock and open the door, and Jack, to unknown dangers, and the venom of other men. "You left a fucking key here!" He yells back. He loses the other words he has lined up to yell in his fit, unable to string together his thoughts coherently, shaking with rage, fists balled.

"Yes, I left a fucking key here. That's what people do. They have keys to each other's homes so that they can come get the shit they need when they need it. And don't fuckin yell at me. I wasn't on… A what? A date?" She laughs. "Maybe I'm just not nerdy enough for you. Anyway, you're going on a date with me today. I'll pick out your clothes. No beach bum shit, either." She heads toward his bedroom.

When she passes him, he says, "Get out." Then his voice raises, "get your bag and get the fuck out!"

"Excuse me? Don't fucking talk to me like that." She stops in her tracks and faces him.

"Get the fuck out!" He repeats himself.

She slaps him. And after a pause, she smiles. Then she teases him, "Guess you don't care about Smoker going with on your loser trip?"

"I guess not."

"I'm going to tell him. Don't think I won't. I'm going to tell him how mad you got when you found out. How you called him a bitch. You know what else. He's a better lay than you."

"You would know that, not me."

"I can't believe how pissy you're getting just cause I left a fucking key here."

He opens the door for her to leave when she steps out. She quickly realizes, "My purse!"

He closes the door on her soundly. Goes to his bedroom, finds her bag, takes a step toward the living room before pivoting and grabbing the alarm clock. Once outside, he throws the bag and the clock into the street before he slams the door again.

"Real fucking mature, asshole. Fucking loser."

Jack lays on the couch with his feet pushed against the wall. After another half-minute of her yelling, she leaves. He stays prone for some time, thinking of all the exposure one can't guard against, no matter how well they adhere to the rules. Life is going to open your door, and the elements will find you no matter what. There are no safe places.

CHAPTER 32

September 9, '07

Jack pushes the crosswalk button, liberally chasing each press with another, at one of the slowest lights on PCH. Skateboarding to Mutt's, he already passed the first set of hills walking up the incline and riding the descent slowly, turning back and forth easily, maintaining a casual speed. He keeps his skateboard's "trucks" loose. The trucks are the mechanism that regulates how much weight and pressure will cause the skateboard to turn. Stiff and the board hardly responds. Loose and the board reacts to every shift in weight and balance. The gains in mobility come at the cost of speed. There is only so fast a loose board can go without getting "speed wobbles" when the board shimmies violently and throws the rider from it. To counter, Jack takes long, exaggerated turns and power slides when needed to make sure he doesn't lose control.

He still has the larger set of hills that rise off of Pacific Ave to go over, a climbing slope three blocks long, but it's mostly downhill to the beach, from there.

Jack left quickly after Smashley's exit. Who knows what commotion she stirred last night, and who is going to hear about it. At least now, he is free from her, and if he's honest, Smashley is free from him too. He isn't so naïve to believe that he hasn't been horrible to Smashley, too, flirting with girls in front of her so that she had to fight for him. And she has no idea of the potential damage she might have caused. It's not like Jack ever shared any of that with her. As happy as he is that it's over, that he's set himself free, he is as glad that she is also free from him and all the damage he has caused her.

Jack considers jaywalking against the long light and keeps an eye for an opening. However, there are too many cars on the road to safely make his way across, so he waits vigilantly, repeatedly pressing the button. Then one car pulls up to the light next to him. Stopped and waiting to cross the busy intersection too. Jack hardly pays any attention to it except for the loud bass he can hear emanating from its speakers. He's still pushing the button when he looks closer at the driver and the passengers in the front and back seats. His thumb stops when he recognizes the Intruder in the rear. Even with sunglasses covering his black eyes, his face is unmistakable.

Its shape and features burned into Jack's memory. His broad nose, acne scars, and closely shaven head. The Intruder looks up, and a second later, taps the driver's shoulders and points Jack's way. The person in the passenger seat opens the glove compartment and grabs something that Jack can't see.

Jack's frozen hand remains glued to the button, even as the rest of his body turns toward the car. His broad shoulders are parallel to the danger, presenting himself as the biggest target possible. He closes his eyes. The freedom from his life he seeks is only feet away. Two cars pass him in the closest lane in a whoosh of sound. Then he hears the car door open, the bass pours out freely, louder than before, like the pacing drum of an old war machine.

For some reason unknown, because there is no thought in his mind, he turns blindly and steps onto the busy street.

Perhaps it is the promise of another outing with Bree. If anything, he just needs another week at the most. His subconscious may be calculating this without him knowing because, at the moment, he is wholly focused on the car bearing down on him at fifty miles an hour. It is only ten yards away and closing quickly when he finally crosses the next lane, which had just vacated. The sound of wind-breaking is a vacuum into which Jack lurches. The car's horn behind it blares and quickly slows down as Jack scrambles over another lane toward the center divider, barely making it there in front of another vehicle. Now Jack is in the middle of it all with the breaking air serenading him in surround sound and the racing traffic vibrating his perch. Still, the bass is not far away.

Somewhere in the recesses of his mind, the part that is asking for one more week is another calculation. The rising hills two blocks away and the long red light where his chasers wait. They must have been calculating, too, because their wheels screech as they make a right turn.

Jack knows the first left they can make is only three blocks away. They'll have to wait for a break in traffic to make the turn. Jack can only hope that one doesn't come for them because it won't take long for them to catch up. Jack needs to leave the center divide as soon as he can to have any chance to win that race. Still, the southbound cars bear down on him, and he feels the air they drag with them push against him as if it were trying to knock him off his place. Finally, luck finds him. Just as the Intruder's car turns and its music softens, the light changes. Jack throws down his board and gathering it with his feet all in one fluid motion. He pushes with his right leg as quickly as he can, gaining his top speed within a couple of strides.

The stop in traffic also means that when the car gets to that turn, it will soon have the break they need to catch up quickly. Jack is already going as fast as he can as the hills he'll need to climb loom in front, offering no quarter. In a minute, he is two streets from PCH, and his chest burns. As the incline begins and his speed wanes, Jack picks up his board even earlier than he hoped.

Two blocks of a sharp ascent lay in front of him, and he now runs. His legs pump as fast as they can and without any protest, but his lungs are having a harder time keeping pace. Before he can see the car, he hears the bass again. Still faint but growing. The chasing car has made its way back. It is three blocks behind when it rolls a stop sign and turns right onto the same street Jack now climbs.

Jack passes the first inclined street. One more before gravity works in his favor. The bass is getting louder, but he can barely tell over the strenuous huffing coming out of his mouth. Now his legs burn too. He is near the peak. The car is only a block away. The bass thumps faster as if it were pounding to its pursuit, like a ramming ship gaining speed. His lungs are on fire. He can't move any quicker, and his pace slows down despite the oncoming doom. He would stop and throw up if he could. Sweat pours off his forehead, and his clothes stick to his skin. Only a half-block away. The bass is loud and echoes in his sternum, and he even hears the engine's roar. Finally, Jack is at the top.

He doesn't drop his skateboard to the ground as he would normally. That would require gathering it and straightening it with his feet. Seconds lost when he doesn't have them. Instead, he jumps in the air and places the board underneath him, stepping down on it with the same force as if he were dropping into a wave. He uses bodyweight to generate as much momentum as he can, as fast as he can to get to a full speed quickly, going down this steep hill.

The car is only feet behind them when Jack suddenly turns onto John St. The car, unable to turn that fast, goes straight. This isn't an escape. They will be able to turn back only one block ahead. But this does give the car an extra stop sign that will hopefully slow them down at least a little. The wheels on the skateboards hum as the greased bearings inside them turn over and over at the top speed Jack has hit.

He has a plan, a route in mind. This is close to where he grew up, and he knows every alley and street by heart.

Going at such a high speed, Jack feels the board begin to quiver. He has no choice but to power slide to get back just a little control. Jack turns his hips, pushing all of his weight into his feet, and the board slides perpendicular to the street, perpendicular to the natural turn of the wheels themselves. He brings his board, legs, and weight back underneath him. It works, it is only a short and slight decrease in speed, but the wobbles disappear for now.

Jack turns right at the next corner, putting him on the same road as the chasing car. He has a hunch, and it pays off immediately. Even going down the hill as fast as he can, even quicker than his board will allow, still isn't fast enough. The car's speed is unbeatable. Jack is going to have to outthink them. Once Jack turns, he is face to face with his chasers. But they are both going too quickly to change course, so Jack passes them on the sidewalk before they can do anything to stop him.

They turn their car slightly toward him but eases past the front bumper with room to spare. They will turn back onto the same road only a block away and get there very quickly. Jack can't let his board slow.

Jack has a choice. He can go down Sixth St., which cuts across Valley and Ardmore and the Greenbelt and allows Jack to stay on his skateboard and keep his speed.

Or Jack can turn right again and cross the greenbelt on foot, giving up all his momentum in an instant. He turns right. The chasing car is back in pursuit and heading straight toward Jack as he turns. The speed wobbles come back, and Jack feels the imbalance in his toes and heels.

He should power slide again, but the car is only half a block away. He might lose his board, his balance, his speed, everything. He risks it and lets the wheels turn as fast as they can. The board wobbles dramatically, violently. With only yards to go until Ardmore, he feels it slipping out from under him. He can't hold on any longer. He has already lost control and totally at the mercy of when it will throw him.

Jack stares at the house on the corner. With every roll of the wheel, he gets a better view of the upcoming street and the oncoming traffic. He won't be able to see much until he passes the house, and at that time, it would be too late to stop or change directions. Totally at the mercy of the timing of everything around him. He looks behind him. The pursuit is only a house away. The bass is loud again, yelling at him and bearing down.

Finally, the street pours out onto Ardmore. A car flashes into his field of vision, feet away and charging. Its bumper is knee-high, and as Jack stares at it, at the grill, black like open jaws, and the lights like the dead eyes of a shark, it seems bigger than the car itself. He can no longer feel board shake underneath, can't hear the bass thumping from behind, frozen and staring at the wide-eyed. Fortunately for Jack, who cannot move his body, the board and all its speed carry him past. The driver is only able to hit his brakes after Jack slips past the front bumper.

The board violently shakes underfoot, even another second, and he would crash. Jack ollies the curb holding onto the board in his hand, throwing his body onto the ice plant growing on the margin of the wood chips lining the greenbelt. All his momentum topples him, and he bounces through the plants and painfully onto the wood chips, rolling several yards still clutching his skateboard. All momentum is lost. Jack is entirely prone and still on his back, but he pops up quickly, jumping through the ice plant like he did when he was a kid. He is back on his skateboard off of the green belt on the same sidewalks he used to explore when he was very young.

There is a chance that the car has given up. They can't follow him or turn around as this is a section of Valley and Ardmore that turns into one-way streets. They won't be able to cross the greenbelt until driving another four blocks before they can circle back on Valley. Still, Jack doesn't know, so he moves quickly. He has another short to descent in another two blocks. This is the last descent before he can make it to the beach and disappear on the strand where no car can follow or keep pace.

He moves fast through the walk streets before coming to a road that runs parallel to the beach. He allows himself to slow down just a little. He is so close to the beach and his escape. But he hears the bass again. It makes the hair on his sweaty neck stand on end. Jack sees the car turn one block over. They still pursue him. Jack lets his board roll freely on the last set of hills. The car is close behind. Engine, bass, and lyrics all roar so close.

Jack makes one more turn. He goes down the alley behind the liquor store where Jack drank his black eightball only days earlier. It would make sense to avoid going somewhere hidden to bystanders and witnesses, but this is his town. He knows every inch of street, ally, and curb. The car is close, and its bass crawls on his wet scalp. Good, he thinks to himself. He needs them close. They are right on his back heel, about to hit him when they slam on their breaks. The squeal echos in the narrow alley with the high walls. The alleyway with a dumpster that blocks cars from being able to pass through. Jack has one last obstacle. The drain grate on which he recently stood. Its openings will eat his small wheels throwing him dangerously from his board. He ollies again, leaping over the potential hazard, as he did with the Greenbelt curb on Ardmore, but this time he keeps his board underfoot and lands squarely on the wheels keeping all his momentum. Coming out the other side of the alley, only one block from the beach. One block from the strand. One block from freedom. He doesn't bother looking back. Either the car slowly reversed out of the alley, or the passengers got out on foot.

Either way, they aren't catching up. Jack has found freedom. His heart pounds as he turns onto the smooth flat concrete of the strand. Sweat drenches his shirt, and he feels it run down his legs. It's the desperation that he thought had left him a long time ago, the will to live. Jack lets it pump his legs and fill his lungs as he moves ever quickly to Mutt's house.

CHAPTER 33

June, '06

Jack lies on the white couch in his apartment. His feet up against the wall. Television on. A book from the library open on his chest. He's holding his phone to his ear and hears the rejection clearly.

"Sorry, bro, but I don't need you," Montana states unapologetically. It was Smoker's idea that Jack ask.

Smoker knew Montana better than Jack did. Jack always tried staying on the other side of the party or bar if Montana was there, and for good reason too. Smoker was even the one who connected them when they didn't have each other's phone numbers. Jack called him after he sent a text asking if it was a good time to talk.

Jack retorts, "You know how many times I've been at a party that people tried to get ahold of you but can't? I'll just be another delivery system. You can't be in two places at once, right?"

"Yeah, but what about what about the money I'm gonna lose by cutting you in?"

"You won't lose money unless you're strapped for surplus. If there's not enough to go around between us, then I wouldn't do it either." Jack had already given thought to potential objections, and this is one for which he already had a rebuttal. "But if there are sales that you're unable to get to under the current circumstances, I can be the one sweeping in lost opportunities."

"Yeah, but we know a lot of the same people. If you sell to someone, I no longer get that transaction. And to cut you in that rate is way less than I would make if I just sold to that person. Are there enough new clients where I am not just cannibalizing my own business? I'm not even sure I am missing on any new business. Eventually, I get to everyone."

"But that's it. That's what I am saying. You don't." Jack pauses and silently wonders if he is pushing back too hard. Then he continues, "There are nights when people want to party but can't cause they can't get to you. So you're right. You didn't necessarily lose a customer, but you lost a sale. Yeah, you get the next sale, but you might have missed one or even two before you get around to them. So instead of clients, think of them as a number of potential transactions. Are you maximizing transactions?" He makes sure to emphasize the rise in his voice that demarcates it as a question. He wants to make sure that he isn't telling Montana but only suggests that it's something worth asking. And deferring to Montana's answer, instead of the answer Jack can provide and overstep his place.

"And we might run in the same circles, but you know those are big circles. I could be in some part of the town at some party, and you can be in another part of the town and some other party or bar, and we can coordinate so that we don't overlap. And I'll totally defer to you."

Montana is quiet for a while. Jack stays silent, too, appreciating the thought Montana gives to the conversation. It's a good indication that Montana may decide to include Jack. And not only that, but also a good sign that Jack would end up partnering with a person who takes this very seriously and thoroughly views his business as such. Montana sighs, "But I'd be introducing new risk. A big fucking potential life-altering risk. I know who I am. I know the rules of this game. You don't know shit. Even if I teach you, I don't know if you're gonna follow em."

"Please, I need this. I really do. You'd be saving me. I mean it. I won't let you down either. I won't slip up. I won't go against your wishes. I'll be a soldier, and do exactly as I am told." These are the reassurances that he planned to give.

"If I did this and you fuck me over, I would have to kill your ass. You know this, right? No 'sorry,' no 'we're friends,' no nothing because that's what you would be agreeing to right now."

"I'm begging you. I need this." Jack didn't practice this, didn't anticipate those words passing his lips. But he can feel the overwhelming desperation, and really, only a sliver of it has fallen into his words. "I won't slip. Think of it as franchising, like a fast-food restaurant. I pay you for the right to sell your shit. And I need this more than you, so I'll be just as fucking adherent to what has worked for you as you are."

He has said all he can. So he just closes his eyes and takes a deep breath in, and hopes this will be the freedom he imagines it to be, the one he so desperately needs. And he holds the phone close to his ear so that he doesn't miss the response.

CHAPTER 34

September 9, '07

After the chase, once he landed safely on the strand, Jack didn't waste any time getting to Mutt's. So he was still wet with sweat and raw when he showed up—greeting everyone with a high five before making his escape to the bathroom to clean up and calm down.

"Nothings on," complains Smoker, scrolling through the TV at a pace with which no one else can keep up.

Jack grabs one of the mossy green balls lined up on the metal desk. Red hair hides inside an entanglement of light green yarn. Jack presses the weed into the glass bowl at the base of the water pipe. When he pulls his hand away, the ball sticks to the tip of his finger, dragging it out of the bottom of the bowl. Jack again presses the ball down. "Sticky shit," he says to no one in particular. It is the only thing Jack has said since he got there.

He did his best to hide the evidence of his escape, to move so quickly that no one would notice the wet spots under his arms and in the inseam of his shorts, marks of fear and panic. He knows that's what's expected. That there is some silent agreement they share between them. An understanding that theirs are lives of leisure and excess, and the only threads of danger are the ones in which they create. Which they all did, and then they compared them. Whatever they wove as intrigue, they held up for everyone to see. The lone caveat being one could never complain or show that any of it was more than they could handle. And that is where Jack always lost.

Then Jack puts the flame into the glass bowl of the bong. The green contents crack and burn, and the fire bends into the bowl drawn in by his breath. Red embers turn black and gray while the chamber of the bong fills with smoke.

Jack's finger presses in once again, and with the last remaining power of his lungs, he sucks the ash through the small hole, pulling the glass bowl out of the bong and clearing the smoke from the tube. Holding in his breath, Jack clenches his teeth, not yet ready to let go. His head grows lighter, and he releases the smoke from his lungs into a long cloud, while another, unseen mist crawls up the arteries in his neck and passes into his head.

Jack begins his fall immediately, tumbling into himself, into some deep recess, until he is far removed. Jack has found the remnants of who he once was somewhere deep below and can see out those old eyes and know their past thoughts. The rest of the world appears to him as a projection that lays over his eyes without ever touching as if he looked through a camera's lens.

Jack passes the bong back to Mutt, clears his throat, and leans back on the bed against the wall. He uses the term "crispy" and crosses it off like a to-do list. His friends take turns smoking and speak as they do, but Jack doesn't hear what they say. They are in the periphery like a picture when only images at a certain distance are clear, and everything else remains just out of focus.

The soft glow of the TV has caught Jack's eyes, and the rest of the room falls away. Pupils dilate to let in as much of the light emanating from the screen as possible, and his eyelids slump transfixed as he stares from the back of his skull.

The TV continues to jump, and the images juggle like a thousand balls in the air. Every voice Jack has ever heard comes through the screen. Every person he has met, every thought he ever had, heard in between the flipping channels.

He knows them well. He has long watched them with intent like a sociological study. They are the ones who never speak about themselves because everyone else wants to. They are the ones who laugh because they are with the right people. They keep their sentences short and never repeat themselves but make others do so. They never apologize, and they never say "no" because it is already implied.

It is not always the same, more like variations on a theme, but the characters on TV are close enough for Jack to know that he and his friends keep showing up on the screen. It helps reinforce Jack's quiet assumption that the world borrows from him and those like him.

Jack looks around the room to see if anyone else sees what he has. The others are visible but far away in the frame, looking at the computer that invaded the room without vetting. There are new sites where you can build a profile of yourself, a digital copy. Anyone could be on it, and that is what made it worthless. His friends have no idea. No inclination that it's a culture coming to replace theirs. One that they can't control simply by being born in the right part of the world.

The TV stops jumping, stuck on what appears to be a movie. Jack has never seen it, but he already knows the plot. The characters are just too familiar. He smiles at them, and they smile back, and for a second, Jack sees himself on the screen, cool and quiet, a leading man.

Again Jack holds the lighter and the water pipe, and with one more breath, he blows out the rest of the world. Someone turns off the TV. Jack follows all the other boys out of the room and down into the garage. There is an extra bike for Jack, the one painted black, and everyone else grabs the one they rode over to the house. The clouds in the sky haven't dispersed but are thinning into a haze that chokes the sunlight. It is overcast, but the air is warm, and the beach is crowded for an ugly day.

Jack accidentally leaves his sunglasses upstairs on Mutt's bed, and the sun filters through the high thin clouds in bright but muddled light. He does not speak up. Jack doesn't ask the group to hold up until he retrieves his shades. He's sure that they'd wait, but it isn't worth being left behind. The splintered light echoes through the low-hung heavens so that the source remains hidden but reflected. The light burns a thousand separate holes in Jack's eyes. He goes along with them quietly, uncomfortable as the light bounces off the high clouds at him in indirect angles. It is an escapable spotlight, and it is a day lit in reflection.

They ride in a staggered two by two formation as a moving roadblock. Their bikes crawl along the strand at such a slow pace that if they move any slower, they won't be able to maintain balance. Jack's legs fall on the pedals, pulling them down with weight, not pushing with muscle. The rotation of the crank is only a byproduct of him being there on the bike. Blocks of rose bushes line the concrete strand they brazenly take command of, a personal path to a kingdom long ago conquered. The private gardens have overtaken the prevalent ice plant in the same manifest destiny the boys used to commandeer their town.

Earlier that summer, Jack had been sent into those bushes. Mutt crashed into him, and their bikes would not come apart. When Mutt pulled hard to his right to free himself, Jack followed and flew over the handlebars. He pulled thorns out of his skin all night and still had scars over his wrists and hands.

He joked in a deadpan delivery that the scars were a failed suicide attempt. The girls always laughed after he smiled and told them the ridiculous reasons why, always some mundane indiscretion, like stubbing his toe, as if that were reason enough. Then, as they laughed, he would tell them that he did not have much or anyone, which made them laugh even harder.

Over to the right people walking, keep pace with the cavalcade. Some serious cyclists complain as they pass, and the boys answer back with sarcasm. Jack, though rides mute, as he watches everything roll through at the distance of a lens. He looks out over the strand, past the several high canopy tents set up on the beach, and out to the light blue boxy lifeguard tower that sits some fifty feet from the water. It looks like all the other lifeguard towers that dot the sand, except this one is on the street that Jack used to spend his days with his family when he was young.

His father taught him how to surf while his mother taught him how to play volleyball. Each one took their turn teaching Jack while the other became the cheerleader rooting them on from the sidelines. None of his friend's parents were so free with affection and enthusiasm as his own. Whether they were surrounded by strangers or alone they never hid their love and appreciation for their son.

The summer months were his favorite, and he always fretted when it ended because he and Bree went to different schools. She attended a public school while Jack went to a private Catholic school. At least there he had The Tard.

But summer months were spent on the sand and on the walk street, chasing each other on big wheel bikes, playing tag, and staying outside well past dark as each home turned on lights so that the children could play deep into the night.

Jack sees a group of middle schoolers only a couple of blocks down and closer to the water. Unlike high school kids, who end up congregating on specific blocks according to their grade, the middle schoolers stay close to home and pool together in pockets. Jack didn't get to the beach as much as a middle schooler. With his father's passing, he seldom made it out in the water. The Tard would drag him out of the house to hang out with other friends, even if that meant that the Tard didn't go to the beach near his own home. Bree did something similar too. Besides being at his house with him, she made him go in the water, usually for a sunset swim, if she noticed that he hadn't gotten out yet.

Now Jack thinks it's so strange how he avoided the very water that is now his only refuge. How many days did he waste when this was his backyard? Why do we deny ourselves relief at the exact time when it is most needed? The pain is the reason. The pain of loss. When he lost his father, the pain was there to remind him. It was all he had left, and when that was gone, there would be nothing. That's why he held on. Even all these years later, he still holds on.

The bike pack continues north to a swarm of outgoing freshman girls lying next to the strand. Year after year, the freshman congregated there. Just as they sat in the same spot at school lunch, too, next to the main office just off of the quad. It is designated to be that way, simply because the class before them did so as well.

All of the girls say "hi" as the boys ride past. Luggy says something funny that Jack doesn't hear. He is looking down at the line of concrete cut through the sand, but he hears the girls laugh in response. When he looks back at them, his hand clutches his stomach, and then it jumps back to the handle of the bike. Jack sees the foam grip rotate around the metal frame. He then realizes that he has torqued the handle as if it were a motorcycle's accelerator. He didn't feel the shame that bent his wrist and balled in his forearm, hidden deep within himself as he is, but he knows it is there, and he wonders if it will go away on its own.

By summer after freshman year, Jack more than made up for time lost on the beach the year before. He lived on the beach. His apartment was too far to come and go. He left early, and only after plans with his friends had run their course would he give up and return home. He didn't have a curfew. There was no one there to enforce one. All he had to guide him was a desire to spend as little time at home as he could. That meant sleepovers, dinners, and parties. Whatever reason to stay out was reason enough. Smoker, Luggy, and Mutt all behaved similarly, and Jack grew closer to them by the sheer amount of time spent together. Not that the Tard wasn't around. He was, but his parents kept him on a shorter leash. Bree was around the beach but not the parties, which was fine for Jack because he preferred their time alone together.

It was so simple, the gratuitous use of a day when nothing mattered, not even the angle the sun held in the sky. And that time on the beach accounted for endless hours of dialogue. They spoke about a lot of things as they lay in the sand or drying off sitting on the strand wall, and it was often concluded that they were what and where others wanted to be. They were aristocratic land barrens that owned nothing more than a lifestyle. The beach installed confidence warranted or not. Back then, Jack believed it, maybe more than anyone else. He loved the idea, and given what else was around him, he needed something and clung to it like an unstrapped life jacket.

Several blocks pass and Jack is lost in thought. Water sprays onto his back, in between his shoulder blades, and pulls at him from his deep recess. As the water drips off his body, he falls back into himself, like being lowered back down on a rope. Giggling sophomore girls pump their water guns at him.

The spray only travels three feet from the sand across the southern route of the strand, the girls look at Jack, and he can tell that they hope he will say something. Their eyes are large and optimistic, and their small smiles seem eager and ready to respond to whatever Jack has to say, but he keeps quiet and continues his getaway at a snail's pace.

After a turn of the pedal, their faces blur as they fall behind and out of focus. Jack looks at his front tire and watches the tread circle. By the summer after sophomore year, life had developed a pattern too. One that was framed by events that circled every year. Fourth of July to start the summer. And it is unlike anywhere else in the world, more like Mardi Gras but with bigger crowds and massive amounts of underage drinking. It's also the day of the Iron Man. Where participants run a mile, paddle a mile, and drink six beers without throwing up. That starts the summer, and the Sixman volleyball tournament is the other bookend. Where the fourth of July spread across several cities like a parade on the strand, the Sixman condenses in several tight blocks next to the pier.

That's when Jack lost his virginity. Just two weeks after his argument with Bree, It was that night that Jack first went to a bar. And it was the first night Jack went home with an older woman.

He was on Ecstasy, still in his Sixman costume, a pair of Stubbie shorts, and a cape. His fake mustache had fallen off, no shoes or shirt, an outfit similar to what most people wore that weekend. She approached him. She invited him home. He never heard her name.

It was the thing that seemed to win over the older guys' admiration, and it was the same thing that always won over all of his friends. Regardless that night, and because the party started before seven am, that day, remained Jack's coronation. His welcoming.

He still had a hometown fair to look forward to, Rally in the Alley. School functions like the winter formal and prom, unlike most underclassmen boys, Jack had already attended, going with a senior who asked him. There were other volleyball tournaments. There was the Beatdown, which pitted the rival high schools in drinking games to see who was the better school. And there was the Barry, which was more drinking games, different ones, but no high school affiliation. The Sandpiper Club -a benevolent social club made of local mothers- modeling show. He was the first person ever to go shirtless. The following year all the boys demanded it. There were big and little events, some required invitation, but that was the first summer where the invitation was expected. And it remained the case throughout the rest of the year—the rest of the years. Jack was minted.

Most of the bike ride up until the point had been mute, but when the group reaches the pier, the sound of the work being done finally pushes through and crawls into Jack's ears. Men yell at one another, saws screech in high frequency, and cranes grunt, and black smoke escapes from somewhere behind as the old lamp posts are lifted out. Jack watches the pole dangle precariously in the air, shifting slightly with the breeze. When the crane lowers, one end of the pole workers help balance the entire 15 feet until its entire body lay on the ground.

Just after the pier, after the bend that inclines slightly, and after a slight unnoticeable decline that follows, a group of outgoing Juniors lay on towels in between the sand mounds sparsely littered with ice plant. In the sand, the bikes kickstands rest on sandals.

Small mounds cover the bottom curve of the tires to keep the bike from lying in the sand and from getting on the chain. A row of them are line just off the bike path, left unlocked. Jack sees the 12 packs of beer covered with towels lying next to the poles of a volleyball court. Most of them watch the game going on while they laugh and talk to one another.

Jack knows just about all of them, just as he knows about everyone on the beach. Everyone is alike in that they have all grown out of the same sand. He knows that parcel of sand too. After his junior year, he laid there drinking those beers, playing in those games, finally earning money. He had the perfect life for it, surrounded as he was by people who liked to party.

That was where Jack turned just enough into more than he needed. Money seemed to put itself in his pocket. By then, Jack was no longer on the volleyball team. He didn't have the funds he needed for travel, so he quit before his junior year. The money came just too late. The nights during that school year were quiet, with no Bree to talk to and no other girlfriend with whom to speak. That did not mean he did not have girls around. Jack constantly did. He just never invited the same one over more than a handful of times. It was not that he did not want someone to get to know; he did not want them to get to know him.

He knew the girls had built up some idea about who he was, and Jack was sure that Jack could never live up to their imaginations, that he would just let them down. And it must be true because everyone he has ever known has left him in some way. That was the one benefit to working with older women. They knew they were paying for a fantasy, and they never stuck around long enough to find out. His prostitution didn't last past that summer, though. Once Jack started selling cocaine.

Some of the juniors see Jack and his friends, some whistle, some hold up beer. Others sarcastically flip them off, but almost all of them turned to look and acknowledge them as they ride past. It's confirmation that Jack had once belonged, had once cemented himself within something bigger than any one person.

Further down the strand, about seven blocks stands the Marine Street lifeguard station. It is a tan building with a brown garage door and a sharp-angled concrete ramp from the sand to the square garage door. The building houses two public restrooms, and beside the protruding square glass hut that sticks out of the western wall, the building is rectangular. Concrete stairs cascade up from the strand to the street that bends, ramps downward where there used to be a basketball hoop, passed the chain blocking access onto the strand and back up. People call it the loop.

There is no one there. So much of the senior class has already left for college. The boys stop anyway. No one speaks. They just stare toward the water. The sand that usually glowed golden lay below them, a bone white. Jack straddles his bike and looks at the shadow he casts on the concrete. It is as honest as anything could be. That is what people see when they look at him, a one-dimensional imprint lacking depth but holding its shape perfectly. But the honesty is not in what they see; it is in the difference between the shadow and the man, the separation between the image and the truth, and recognizing that they are not the same.

The truth is that somewhere along the way, cool turned to cold. That he had spent the last year going after girls to get their parents. Each one he stripped of innocence was an attack on the hope and love given to them by their families. Jack was an instrument of reality set loose on all of those who lied to him along the way. And it had become clear that included everyone he knew.

It was that pretense that colored everyone's vision. That was how Smashely came to be something that she never should have. He was the only guy she never could lure. So she kept pursuing him for no other reason to solve some mystery as to why he never tried. He confused the dogged nature of her interest as acceptance. Something he was short on. She was the first one of the girls who understood that selling coke was the only way he could win and when she said, "Do what do you need to do," he placed his head on her lap like a son would with his mother. She had won her prize. Both came together during senior year for their own wrong interpretations of the actions of each other. They fell victim to perception.

Without volleyball, Jack's senior year days finished at lunch. His friends no longer came over after school or on the weekends. They did not need to. Their houses were as open to the activities they used to hide in Jack's small apartment. And there was no doubt the better place to be.

Jack filled his time on his couch, hoping that Bree would call. She was still with the same guy for most of the year, but Jack had heard that they finally broke up. He hoped she would start going to the same parties, but she did not. Jack looked for her in assemblies and found himself walking yards behind her down hallways Jack had no business being in, but that was as close as he ever got to her. He couldn't bring himself to reach out any further. She was trying to avoid him, of course, but he could have said something, done something, to get her to talk to him, but he did nothing.

Jack imagined perverse situations that might bring her back to him. That Jack, one day, might be sick enough where she would have no choice but to forgive him and come to his aid. Or that her father might pass away, and he could console her. Jack would have gladly offered up his mother and her demise for his depraved and twisted fantasies, which only brought him happiness with a price, but his mother was a loss that he could bear without Bree's affection, so in that regard, a worthless endeavor.

Nothing happened otherwise. There was no big climatic theatrical twist. There was no more an obstacle to overcome than just to keep things as they were, social homeostasis.

As Jack sits on his bike, staring at the ground, he recognizes that his friends look at something entirely different. They are leaving. Their brotherhood is over. And when Jack looks at them, he sees their legacy secured in a volleyball championship banner. Their names on it, embroidered in gold, hanging in the gym for future classes to see. Jack recognizes that gold sewed into their faces, ones that are so eager to look far from where they stood. A view that remains entirely out of focus for Jack.

They would be back in the summer. And more permanently after they graduated, but they would be different for having been away, and Jack would be the same. And that meant Jack would be different than them, different from what he had been told he was supposed to be. Sure, Jack can tag along with The Tard, but it's not the same. Their experiences will be totally different. Jack will be in close proximity to it but not actually a part of it. And that sounds all too familiar to the last four years. Jack bends his wrist again around the foam handlebar as he looks at his friends smiling. They stare out over the water, and he resents them for being able to see horizons he cannot. Oh, how he resents them.

CHAPTER 35

July '07

It must be the drugs, but it's not. There is no way Jack imagines this. They're real and only standing feet away. If it were the drugs, then he would be the only one to see them, and he can tell by the look on his friends' faces how their eyes swell with tears from laughter and incessant giggling that they see them too.

"What the fuck" The Tard laughs.

"Doctor Jones!" Luggy yells.

Mutt adds, "So glad I'm not the only one who's seeing this."

Jack's tongue feels swollen and doesn't quite fit in his mouth, coated thickly in a metallic residue as if he chewed on coins. It is the residue from the LSD he let dissolve on his tongue as he, and his friends, entered the famous theme park, ready for a day of misadventure.

Despite the effects of the drugs, Jack doesn't see things that aren't there. He just sees them through a skewed perspective, from atop a different axis, just off-kilter from reality, but not completely removed. The flowers are a perfect example. They stay in their flower beds as one would expect, but their colors meld, the petals bloom and close when he looks at them. It's as if they're breathing. All living things breathe in their own way, but this looks like the diaphragmatic breaths of a person. They are expanding with inhalation and shrinking with exhalation. Still, Jack remains conscious of the fact the flowers aren't changing. He knows that this is the effect of the drugs of the hallucinogens. He has taken them enough times to understand. So while Jack knows that he is under the influence, and the world is presenting itself differently, he can't rightfully blame the drugs, even if that would make the most sense. It certainly makes more sense than the foreign guests wearing the wax paper toilet seat protectors, the ones found in public restrooms, on their heads like hats.

"Japanese cowboy hats" Smoker can barely speak out the line before he giggles. Everyone laughs.

"Dr. Jones!"

The crown of their heads pokes through the center cutout, and the paper rests on their foreheads and ears. The rest of the wax paper droops like a floppy hat with a wide brim, similar to ones people wear to keep off the sun. It's an odd thing for someone to do, and Jack had to think through the likelihood that he had only imagined them, created them out of thin air. He didn't. They have caught the attention of other people in line. There are glances. People are turning to others in their party and pointing out the hats in hushed tones, and some smiles pop up on the faces of the people who are only now getting their first glance.

"Fucking perfect, dude. Japanese cowboy hats!" The Tard says back to Smoker.

"Dr. Jones!"

But the boys have drawn their own attention. There are comments and glances sent their way as well.

Jack can feel them boring into the back of his head. He can feel their eyes on him, and he can hear their whispers loudly in his ears. They trample him. Feels their weight against his lungs, keeping his breath shallow and quick. He is grateful for his sunglasses that hide nickel-sized pupils, and he wears his usual his silver dollar smile to ward against the penetration of those stares.

"Dr. Jones!"

It doesn't help that Luggy keeps yelling. It doesn't help that they picked the busiest day of the year to visit this magical kingdom. The line that they are in has barely moved. The last sign Jack read put the wait up to three hours from that fence post.

No, they aren't there for the rides anyway. They are there for these moments. Like when the spiked roof of one attraction fell, all of the boys jumped to the ground and laid flat. They were the only ones who did. Everyone else had seen it happen for an hour as the line they all waited in switched back and forth, in front of the spiked falling roof that came from a plot in a movie.

Everyone else expected it when it was their turn to stand underneath it. Only the boys were surprised. They hadn't noticed it yet, caught up in looking at the flower beds, the fine details of the ride, the strangeness of the other guests, and the park. So to them the roof really was falling and they jumped to the ground to save themselves. People laughed then. The boys laughed at themselves. Once they got to the front of the ride, Jack couldn't answer the ride attendee when he asked Jack how many were in his party. He couldn't move his mouth, mute from the metal tingling his tongue. Jack just pointed to his friends and let the attendee count for him.

When they poured off the ride, they stood around the flower bed for a time. There was nowhere else to go. It was so crowded that lines formed in the walkways of the park. Jack heard someone say it was the most crowded day of the year. Then they waited behind people to move. It was a line to get in line. Finally, they boarded the train that circles the park. After several complete passes, the conductor kicked them off. Then they got into a new line. The one they stand in now, the one that they share with the foreign guests wearing the toilet protectors on their heads. The one full of whispers and glances that Jack is stuck absorbing while he stands next to Luggy, who has been yelling "Dr. Jones," gathering more attention than Jack needs or wants at that moment.

"Dr. Jones!"

Mutt, laughing, says, "Hey, hey guys, what do you call a Mexican with a rubber toe?" Mutt waits and continues, "Roberto!' Everyone laughs. Luggy starts yelling, "Roberto." Everyone else starts to shout it as well.

Jack doesn't speak, and he doesn't laugh. He is possessed by a thought that can only generate from a variant axis. In the hours that he been at the park, Jack has jumped from line to line-caught behind throngs of people. Standing and waiting to be processed and moved. Entirely at the dictation of metal gates, posts, and chain link. And at the mercy of the other guests, who he needs to move as well. Watched and judged by all of those who surround him. It must be the drugs, but maybe it's not. Jack has a premonition that he has been in a line his whole life.

Funneled in a specific direction, at the mercy of others when he will move on, and the direction it turns. Choice has been taken from him. Direction and pace have been set forth by circumstances out of his control. Jack has been in a line his whole life, hurdled like cattle and processed at the whim of the place he occupies. It must be the drugs, but it's not. He is sure this is true. And he is just as confident that knowing this doesn't change anything. He'd share it with his friends, but they wouldn't understand. He can't entirely close his mouth as swollen as it is, so the words might slip out. Even if he spoke them, his friends would discard them immediately like loose change, like the coins rolling around in his mouth.

Still, he knows it to be true. He can't see things that aren't there. It's like the flowers in the flower bed. They remain where they should be. So Jack isn't seeing something that isn't there, just that when he looks at them, their colors meld, the petals bloom and close, it's as if they're breathing.

Jack looks at the foreign guests again. They are wearing wax paper toilet seat protectors found in public restrooms. It must be the drugs, but then again, it's not. He is confident that they're real. He has taken LSD and sees things differently but doesn't see things that aren't there. They came to a magical kingdom to do so. Jack heard someone say that this is the busiest day of the year. People are looking at him. He is stuck in line. He has been in a line his whole life. The roof can fall at any moment. It must be the drugs, but it's not.

*****

Once they broke through the stupor and mind-altering coercion of the LSD. When the flowers rested, the boys went back to their car and began drinking in the parking lot about the time the firework show ended. Luggy had taken a fifth of Irish whiskey from his father's liquor stock, and they had one 12-

pack to share amongst them. Mutt apologized for forgetting the weed he planned to bring, and so they only drank. After only an hour, the booze disappeared, and the giggling reticence of the drug was washed away by the sloppy aggressiveness of the alcohol. They left shortly after.

On the way home, They hollered the words of the songs playing and slapped each other's hands. Some pushed against each other or the seat in front of them. Jack stayed silent with the wind from the cracked window filling the space of his still slightly open mouth. The air moved around his head and down his back. It carried him from his seat, lifting him as if he rode outside of the car. And he looked back in through the window at his friends as they drove off together, with Jack outside watching them go away. Jack was far away then. Only the wind seemed real, as if he wasn't there, just retelling the story of when everyone went to the theme park and took acid.

Then the car stops, and Jack is there on the street watching the red brake lights reflecting off of the misty black road as the car rounds the corner and speeds away. He stands in a small circle of a street light that covers most of the intersection and cut across the yard of one of the houses. He turns to go with only the hum of power lines with which to walk.

His friends usually dropped him off there. It saves them from having to cross Aviation, the old Spanish salt road. Jack crosses the southbound lanes first after three staggered cars pass, and their brake lights reflect against the asphalt as Smoker's car had. As he walks the two northbound lanes, it seems to take an unusual amount of time, at least twice as long as the first lanes he had crossed. He is not moving quickly, legs taut, stiffly flexing as bamboo, but he hadn't felt this delay in the first lanes. It seems that they had widened that road without him knowing, an extra four or five lanes for all of that traffic. And when he turns to look back at the street, after he stepped into his new town, his old hometown looks miles away. A distance far enough to confirm he no longer lives there but close enough to continually remind him of the fact.

When he makes his way across, he sees a parked car so new and nice that Jack resents its unknown owner and looks to punish him for whatever luck has come his way. The kicks seem loud to Jack as he raises his right leg and thrusts his hips toward the car's window. With his kicking leg perpendicular to his body and his left under him, bent for balance. His shoes create a slapping sound that echoes in the night. On his fourth try, he hears the window break, and his foot finds no more resistance.

Jack sprints down the street, leaving the broken glass to be found in the morning, sitting in the passenger's seat, and lying on the ground around the tires. Still, they won't see the anger and apathy that kicked it in. Jack has taken them with him to carry them with him wherever he goes.

CHAPTER 36

September 9, '07

After the slow-moving bike ride, the boys stayed down on the beach for the rest of the afternoon. They joined up with some of the older guys playing a drinking volleyball game called ACE. When the sunset and it was too dark to play any longer, they headed for downtown in a pack on bikes.

When they approach one of the main downtown intersections, Jack notices the blinking red hand begins to flash. He knows that this particular light is quick. It goes from walk to red in only a few flashes. From a car's perspective, the yellow is only a wink. It could be that there isn't much through traffic. And most cars are merely circling to park. That there isn't a dominant direction, and the light is designed primarily for foot traffic. Still, Jack knows that the traffic light will change, and the cars will cross in front of him. He doesn't have a downward slope to propel him. This particular section is flat. He starts to pump his legs to gain speed. He is only yards away, and the traffic light turns yellow. He hears one of his friends call his name. The light turns red, and the cars in front lurch and block the intersection.

Jack doesn't hesitate. He knows exactly what he is doing. He feels the tile of the crosswalk underneath his tire. There is a white van crossing in front of him. He already saw it, knew it would be there, calculated it passing directly in his path. It doesn't matter. None of this matters. He is leaving, leaving his friends.

Jack turns right. He is now behind the bumper of the van. Jack fills the space between it and the car that trails behind it. One of his friends calls his name like he is cheering Jack on. Then another calls his name like a question, asking him through only his nickname, "Crackie?", where he is going. Jack knows exactly what he is doing. He knew this pocket would be there. Jack just needed to speed up to catch it, to make his right turn with momentum to help him climb a hill. To gain the elevation he needs, that will put him on a path toward the walk streets. Jack is leaving his friends behind. For the night at least. He knows where he is going and what he's doing. He has never been so confident in his life. Jack is chasing the sun.

He knocks at her window. The light is on, and he can see her shadow on the wall in the room.

She opens the window and smiles. "What are you doing out there?"

"I don't know. I couldn't wait. I know you wanted to see me again, and I wanted to see you, and you just never know what might come between now and then." He desperately exclaims. "I just don't want to risk it. This is where I want to be. Maybe I'm just sick of taking the options as they come? That I would like to decide when and where I want to be. I want to be here. I want to be with you." He speaks as vulnerable and honest as he ever has. Tears well in his eyes, she probably can see them, but he won't let them loose.

"Come on in. Come in." She says and immediately climbs through the window.

He stands fully in front of her, a head and neck taller. She asks, "Jack, are you okay?"

He answers her with a kiss. It doesn't say that he isn't fine. Or that he had been threatened through friendship, one compromised by betrayal, or even more important, that his life is in danger.

That he barely escaped today. No, the kiss doesn't say any of that. This kiss only says that he can be okay. That with Bree, he can be so much more than that.

This kissing leads to touching, body with body, body with hands. Hands pour over every nook and curve, every muscle and form. He kisses her nape, ears, and clavicles. She kisses his chest and neck. He undresses first. She follows.

209

In bed, the sheets collect underneath them. They push the comforter off the side of the bed. Jack kisses Bree's stomach, her navel, then falls back on his knees, heels underneath his buttocks, and studies her body. How each rib lays just below the surface of the skin, becoming more defined with each inhale and disappearing with every exhale. He follows the arc of her rib cage flowing through and giving way to her firm stomach, turning inward at her hips and dipping into her thigh and pelvis, resting above the small patch of black pubic hair. Jack retraces his visual path back up toward her breasts. The contrast in how full and supple they are as they sit on top of those delicate ribs. The soft, sensual desire of man lays tucked in the curve of breast meeting bone.

Rising over her body, Jack lifts himself on hands and knees until they are eye to eye, their skin touches, but their bodies don't rest one another.

Bree lays on her back, her right leg straight before her, and her left leg slightly bent away from her body, elongating her torso. Jack's hands run over her sternum and along the elliptical curve of her rib cage. They move slowly and stick her skin. Jack tries to move his hand with just a light touch, with his fingertips, but he is much too nervous or too excited. He lets his entire palm enclose high on her hip. Jack squeezes and gently pulls her body off the bed towards his and then slowly lets her fall back onto the bed. He rests his hand there, and his thumb lies in the line formed between her hip and leg. She holds one hand flat against Jack's chest and the other covering her left breast. Jack props himself on his left elbow. His broad shoulders are high above Bree, and his back forms a triangle down to his bare hips. Jack traces the line. His hand just ran with light kisses. Bree grabs his head with both her hands, running her fingers through his hair. Jack holds his head on her chest long enough to pick the rhythm of her heartbeat. Bree softly murmurs. He picks up his right foot and slides it from just below her right knee, along her calf and shin, until his calf rests in her right instep. Jack's erection presses into her right hip. He knows she could feel him because he could feel himself swollen with blood and lust. His erection is much warmer than either of their skin.

Jack kisses the thin, soft skin behind her ear and tugs on her earlobe with his two front teeth. She rolls towards him and kisses him on the lips, and her tongue glides along the rim of his bottom lip. Jack follows with his tongue along the top ridge of her mouth. When she retreats, Jack gives chase and penetrates her shallowly, into her mouth, touching her tongue with his, and then they part. He moves his hand from her hip towards pubic hair. Her small strip of pubic hair is shaved close to her body and feels rough on his palm. Jack moves his finger inside of her and retreats much the same way he had kissed her. She grows warm to his touch, and he feels her soft in his hand, and she puts his hand in her. He massages her flesh lightly. He teases her. She has opened her legs, inviting more touch, but he resists.

They kiss again for several seconds. His hands and tongue penetrate further. Jack puts his hand on her clitoris and moves his finger from side to side with a light touch. Their kisses ignite, and tongues and lips hurry with each other. Jack has had enough, and he can no longer contain himself. He lays over her. She is wet and receptive, but he does not allow himself the complete pleasure—his first stroke half of the head of his penis inside of her. The second push moved in his entire head. Bree bits the bottom of her lip and pulls at his waist, trying to get him into her entirely. He smiles and finally fully falls inside of her, and they become as close to one another as possible.

He feels her heels in the small of his back pressing into his kidneys, urging him further. Jack lets his hips move independently of thought at their savage beat. Bree times her thrusts with his. It is unsuccessful sometimes, but on the short spurts where they meet each other perfectly, it is almost more than he can bear. He slows down. He doesn't want this night to end so quickly. He pulls himself out of her body. Catching his breath, he lowers himself on his elbows. Her breasts push against his chest. A small amount of sweat causes them to stick to each other. Jack's penis, still erect, lays in between her thighs.

"I don't want to come yet."

"Not yet," she asks of him.

He rolls off of her body to the side, his stomach still flush against her abdomen. He began stroking her with his hand again as he had done before. She asks him to lift his hand a little higher by placing it in the exact spot she wants. He lets his hand move back and forth while his penis remains aroused and untouched. She comes quickly and quietly. Her pelvis thrusts in shorts spurts, and she let out some moans. He wants to give her a little time, but his patience gives way to desire, and again he is inside of her—the thrusts thunder with the slapping of skin. The lovemaking turns more animalistic. Jack once again places his hand in the spot she had requested earlier. Without his hand, he can no longer prop himself above her. He lays his body entirely against hers. Her head is buried in his neck, and when she orgasms again, he feels her moans on his ears and neck. Jack lets go of himself, and after half a minute, he pulls outside of Bree and finishes on her stomach. He visibly slumps for a couple of seconds. Bree lays still, legs still spread, and her vagina red and swollen. She only stares at Jack and him at her. Finally, he stands up and a towel, and he cleans her stomach. Jack throws the towel on the floor, and the two of them lay dead together. His erect penis begins to fall, stopping with every heartbeat like the second hand of a clock.

CHAPTER 37

May, 07

Prom ended with Jack's date rushing to the charter bus to take them all to the after-party. The bus has more than 50 purple cabin seats with thickly padded head and armrests. There are two on each side of the transport's wide and black rubber walkway. And with the vehicle's interior lights off, the kids ride in the dark, as only the opposing traffic's headlights offer any visibility to their bouncing on their seats, jumping over onto the people in front of them, and yelling at nothing and no one in particular. Each speeding car driving the other way changes the shape of the shadows on the bus roof as it passes. The shadows rise in the rear of the bus and crash in the front, to rise again as a new car approaches. Jack sits silently and has already watched his silhouette rise and fall several times. Bree and her dates, three other senior girls, are on the bus too, in the very back, a good distance from Jack and his date.

Five minutes into the drive and Jack's prom date starts to sob. Jack can't hear her cry, but he can see her hands come to her face and slide tears away with her fingertips. The noise that lends her cover is the excitement saturating the moment, with every seat occupied by some combustible energy, and there's an audible buzz of conversations that have nothing to do with Jack's date's tears. Instead, it's the words that slip through it, through the humming static of chatter that has his date bringing her hands to her face and wetness to her cheeks. But, of course, those were more or less the exact words that made her rush to the bus in the first place. They just weren't said as directly then as they are yelled now in the vehicle's dark hull, like the barking of distant chimps raining down from the treetops.

Jack's date does well to maintain her silence. Jack and the girl on the other side of the aisle, Luggy's date, are probably the only two people on the whole bus who see her. She hasn't let out a sob or a chortle. Jack has his hand on her back between her shoulder blades, rubbing the bare skin exposed by her backless dress. But Jack hasn't said anything yet to soothe his date. He hasn't risen out of his cabin chair and told everyone to shut up or pulled her into his arms to shield her. Instead, he is trying to think of what he should say to console her. What would he say to himself if he were in this position? He can't tell her that. He can't tell her to "Shut up. Stop crying. Don't let them see. Don't let any of them know that they can affect you. You're beyond them. Nothing can touch you." Jack knows those words are only for him and him alone, so he keeps his hand on her back while he thinks of what she wants to hear. He usually knows that almost by instinct, but this is not normal for him.

Suddenly Smashley looms over them both, Jack and his date, "You're a fuckin slut, and no one wants you on this bus." Jack's date has to career her neck to see Smashley speak, and lifting her head so high has left her no place to hide her tears. Even if Jack's date stood, she'd still need to career her neck to look up at Smashley, but sitting makes the height difference tenfold. Finally, when Smashley finishes speaking, Jack's date stands to her feet, ducks under Smashley's arm, the one that holds the seat in front of Jack, and races up toward the driver.

Jack immediately slides over to his date's seat, next to the walkway, and his right foot lands on the grooved rubber mat that runs the length of the bus. He turns slightly toward the aisle and begins to gather his weight and strength under his toes and the balls of his feet. His hand and arm pull against the headrest in front of him, lifting him from his seat. Smashley still blocks his way.

The bus is silent now except for the driver. He yells at Jack's date to move back to her seat. "Get back to your seat!" The bus slows by a degree, and Jack shifts his weight to balance against the loss of momentum. Jack sees his date standing in front of the stairway leading up from the bus doors. "Behind the yellow line!" The driver yells.

Smashley starts to laugh. Jack can hear her laughter echo in several seats from the mouths of her friends, and it bounces off the white low-lit roof of the bus to fill every available decibel on board.

"Behind the yellow line!" The driver yells again.

Smoker sarcastically yells a quote from a movie, "Over the line!"

"This isn't Nam! There are rules." Luggy joins him.

"Mark it zero!" Mutt yells as the boys laugh at the driver and any authority he tries to impose.

Jack's date takes a step down toward the doors. Jack is off his seat, ready to gather his date, when Smashley pushes him back down. Smashley's hand is on his shoulder and her knee across his lap with all of her weight. Jack can't go anywhere. Smashley has done all of that without even a glance his way.

The driver continues to yell. Finally, the bus swerves over a lane and lurches to a stop. Peering over the chair in front of him, Jack sees the bus's doors open, and his date sprint down the stairs and leave.

Bree knocks Smashley into Jack as Bree runs down the aisle and towards the door. The driver yells about everyone needing to stay in their seats or something close to that effect. Bree ignores the driver, shouldering past him, and exits through the door as well.

"Over the line!" Smoker laughs again.

Smashley and her friends chant, "slut." The bus driver grabs his handset and announces, "Everyone is to remain in their seats."

Jack sees Bree with her arm around his date standing on the sidewalk in front of a grocery store and pharmacy. They hug, and Bree spins the girl so Jack's date doesn't look at the bus. The bus's doors close. As the charter pulls away, Smashley's leg digs further into Jack's lap. Jack stares out the window. Bree still holds Jack's date, and Bree extends one arm, one hand, and then one finger as the bus pulls away. Bree stares through every tinted window flipping off each and everyone until she falls behind Jack's frame of vision.

Jack shoves Smashley's legs off of his lap. "Probably too late to change anything now," Smashley says. Jack watches light poles, stop signs, and traffic lights sail past the window to his left as the bus gathers speed, heading toward the after-party at the Hotel.

Smashley heads back to her seat. This is all Jack's fault. He should have just gone with Smashley, but they've been in a fight. And so he took the girl with whom he cheated on Smashley. He let Smashley know about it when they started arguing over some summer plan she had for them, and when bickering turned to yelling and blaming each other for not being the person they wanted the other to be, Jack let Smashley know about cheating on her. Jack shouldn't have mentioned that he and the girl, his prom date, had sex the first night they hooked up. That's the ammo Smashley needed to start rumors and drive the girl from the bus. Jack said it to hurt Smashley, and she used it to her benefit. And it ended up breaking his poor date, who had done nothing wrong. Smashley is just so much better than Jack at these games.

The murmur of disjointed conversations continues back up. Traffic pole after pole fly by, there one second and gone the next. Out of Jack's frame of vision. The bus moves faster, and everything disappears behind him quickly. Shadows continue to fan and disappear on the low-lit white roof. Jack counts the poles that slide behind him. After several minutes, and the number growing too quickly, he gives up. It is too late to change anything. Smashley's so good at capturing unintended truth, the only time she says anything worthwhile is when she isn't trying. And the truth is that it has been too late for change for a long time.

CHAPTER 38

September 10, '07

Jack wakes with his right leg lying outside of the covers. He rolls his ankle and stretches until blood pushes into all of his toes. When he relaxes, the returning blood brings a wave tingling back up his leg, and the air around him tickles his skin.

The morning light fills the room falling in around the bright red curtains against the window. Jack knows he can't go back to sleep. Still, he doesn't want to get up and leave. Bree lies asleep next to him.

Jack adjusts his pillow, lifts his body off the mattress, and rests the back of his head against the wall. And rubs sleep out of his eyes.

The room is unlike many of the rooms of high school girls Jack had seen. No posters hang on the walls. There are no bulletin boards with the chaotic pinning of pictures. Stuffed animals don't clutter the bed or the small chair in the corner. Only framed paintings hang on the walls. One photo of Bree and her brother sits on a small table. A brushed silver frame houses the black and white photograph. Bree sits on her brothers' lap, both of them looking off-camera, clearly a candid picture.

He wears a smile and has a toothpick between his lips, and she holds an innocent expression of genuine amazement. Jack wonders what keeps her so captivated. He wonders if she remembers what is not captured in that silver frame.

Bree stirs. He lies as still as can be. He is trying as hard as he can to not wake her. She pulls tighter on the covers and rolls further to the side of the bed away from Jack. The blanket pulls off of his shoulders and chest. He lays there naked. Now his entire body feels that tingle crawl up his leg through his skin—every pore of his body breathing in the clean morning ocean air. It passes through him. Surrounds him. Lifts him and carries him, and in this moment, he has escaped. Jack is free. Free from everything.

Bree rolls over toward Jack. Her eyes part slightly, and with their closing, she moves closer, resting her head on Jack's chest.

"Hi,' Jack says.

"Hi," she answers. Her ear rests just above his left nipple, her nose down into Jack's sternum, and her mouth hovers above the pronounced line of muscular division of Jack's pecks. He remains silent, and so does she.

His thundering heart lets her know what he is feeling. Words would not have been so direct or so eloquent.

"When do you come back from school?" He asks.

"I think my parents are coming out for thanksgiving, so winter break. We have more than a month off." She pulls her head back on her pillow so that she can see each other's faces.

His mind whispers thoughts where they are together, "I hope we can see each other during that time," his mouth isn't as bold.

"That would be nice. So are you planning on staying around here?"

"I don't have many options. Maybe I can come with you to Hawaii?" Jack buries his question with a smile that lets her know he is mostly joking.

"Jack…" her tone is gentle.

"I know. I know I was just kidding."

"Really, what are you going to do?"

"I don't know. I have to figure it out."

"I think you should stop selling drugs. That should be the first step."

Jack thinks about his trip later that day with Montana and immediately wishes he could cancel. "Yeah. Then I'll go with you to Hawaii." He laughs. Thankfully she smiles and rolls her eyes. "How did you know I was selling?"

"I have heard things," she is still smiling.

"You checking up on me?" The thought is titillating.

She answers with a smile.

"Stalker," Jack sarcastically deadpans.

"Don't worry, I won't be around to keep tabs on you." She probably meant to play along with the joke, but the words are just too real, and Jack's smile fades. It is too apparent. "How about this?" Bree starts, "I promise to stay in touch. We can talk all of the time. We don't need to mention who we are dating or anything if that will make you upset. And you can visit whenever you want to."

"That's fine. Whatever kook you end up dating this year won't last into the summer when you come home, and I get you all to myself."

"Yeah, what about all the girls you have been dating? What about Ashely?"

"Oh, we broke up."

"So, you'll be back together by the weekend?" She is teasing him.

"No. No. This is for good. Now about all the other girls. I'll make sure to set aside Wednesdays for you." It is his turn to tease. He doesn't mean it. In fact, he can't think of a reason to be with another girl until a good amount of time goes by, and she is living well past the western horizon.

"Don't think I haven't heard about you and the girls." She gives him a look.

"Let's just call them placeholders." He smiles. "Is that your stink eye?"

"Yeah."

"You have the worst stink eye I have ever seen."

"Is it that bad?" She asks, laughing.

"Yes, it really is."

"Well, show me yours." Jack makes a face by lowering his eyelids, pouting his lips, and raising his chin just a little. "You look constipated."

And with that, she kisses him on the cheek and puts her head back on his chest. After a fair amount of time passes, where they lay together in silence, she asks while tracing the most recent burn in his armpit, "About last night... You really looked upset. Is there anything you need to talk about?"

"Yeah, I'll be fine. It's just. It's just sometimes it can be really hard."

"I know. And you've had tougher than most. But what would life be without the hardships?"

"Fun? Happy? I really don't know. It's been so long. When I was a kid, I was only happy. Never seemed to have a bad day. And I don't remember being happy sense."

"One, you weren't happy all of the time when you were a kid. I can remember. Two, if all you had were the things that bring you joy. Then you would never even be happy."

'How so?'

"When I lost my brother at first, I thought what more can I give? What more can be taken from me. Then my parents got a divorce because they couldn't get over him. Like a lot of people, I confused hardship with self-sacrifice. But now, when I think of him, I end up wondering, and I hope it doesn't make me sound self-centered, but I wonder what I would be like if I didn't lose him. I know it sounds selfish, like shouldn't I wonder what his life should be like right now? He'd be in college. Actually, if he didn't take more than four, he would have graduated this past spring." She sighs. "But I always end up thinking about myself. I wish I didn't, but I do. How would I be without that loss in my life? Would I be more "normal?" Would I be like your girlfriend?" She smiles. He doesn't. "I think those girls are so simple. They aren't even happy. Not really. They are on some path toward happiness but never arrive. I really think that losing my brother gave me a depth they don't possess. A baseline to measure everything else off of. An appreciation for everything I get to experience that he never got to. Loss an accent to life. Because life isn't one thing, we weren't built with only one emotion. Life is a strata."

Jack kisses the top of her head. "I can see it sometimes. The spectrum you're talking about. It's like falling through the ocean. Its light green, vibrant, then a light blue, joyful, darker blue, reasonable, purple, sorrowful, then black, mournful.

As you fall, you can't see anything other than the color that surrounds you until you hit bottom, rock bottom, and lookup. Then you can see it laid out, every feeling in color, the whole spectrum of life, and it's so overwhelming that my skin jumps off my body. It's so beautiful that I can't even handle it. And at first, I am happy to get to experience it, but I am also sad because I know this is the best I feel, the best I'll ever feel, and if I could only end it there on that feeling, then I might even forget what I've become. But mostly, recently, I live in a grey of nothingness. That I can't escape."

"And what have you become?'

"Not what I was supposed to be, in the simplest of terms, a disappointment, a bad person."

"You know the ocean really isn't a color, right? The water just reflects what's around it. Sometimes it's grey, sometimes blue or green. It's muddied or cloudy, or it's clear. How many pairs of glasses, fins, or watches, or just straight cash have we found on those clear days with the simple snorkel in the shallows? Maybe you just need more vibrant color in your life."

"You know you are really smart for an 18 year-old." Then he kisses her on the cheek.

"What do you like? What makes you happy?" She asks

"I know I am happiest talking to you and being near you."

"And I love being in your life. I loved being best friends. I also like the beach at winter better than summer and swimming in the rain. But that isn't why I want to be a marine biologist. In the ocean is where I belong. I can't imagine life without it. What do you see for yourself?"

"I like being in the water. Being on the beach." He looks down at his exposed leg, his bare feet. "I know I don't like wearing shoes. I wish I could just be barefoot all of the time. I know that sounds lame."

"No, it doesn't."

"I'm tied to the ocean too. It's who I am. Maybe I can be a ship captain. The lifeguard swim is in the spring. I can captain Baywatch," the boat, the show was named after, patrols the Santa Monica Bay. Jack could save someone. He'd have to save himself first, though.

"You'd be a really good Lifeguard. I know your dad would be proud."

Jack doesn't let his mind wander, doesn't let himself drift into a fantasy, a sun soaked boat deck rushing toward those in danger to save them. He doesn't want to leave where he is at that moment. With Bree's head resting on his chest and their legs intertwined.

Jack looks around the room, clear and uncluttered, bright and vibrant, and he knows he'll never be happier than he is now.

CHAPTER 39

September 10, '07

Reluctantly Jack left Bree, with promises to see each other again soon, and headed directly to The Tards house. He has little time until he's supposed to be at Montana's, and he still needs to go home, change and pack a light bag.

He will have to be quick at the apartment. He can't linger for fear of who might come. And he has no choice but to ask The Tard to drive him and wait to give him a ride back. Somewhere along the way, he will talk to his friend.

He hurries up to the front door and rings the doorbell. Sweat gathers on his forearms and runs into the palm of his hands. The Tard's mother answers the door and invites him in.

After being offered food, which he declines, he heads downstairs to his friend's bedroom. Jack pushes open the door without knocking and immediately realizes his mistake when his friend slams shut his laptop computer.

"Crackie!" He is flustered, confused but quickly composes himself. "What's up, bro? How was last night? You totally bailed on us."

"Hey, I really don't have a lot of time. I really need you to drive me home and then over to Montana's. Cool?" Jack sputters and without concern for the standard introductory cadence of a typical conversation.

"Yeah, bro, anything you need."

"Also, I need to talk to you about the apartment. Man, it's really important that I move out of my place soon." The Tard is further confused, and it is evident with the look on his face and how he tilts his head. "Is everything okay?"

Jack wonders if The Tard hears anything other than the alarm in Jack's voice, his urgency ringing through every word. "It will be. But we can talk in the car."

They drive on mostly empty streets and make good time. Jack doesn't bring it up right away but finally says, "I can afford my own place, but I don't want to. I don't want to live alone anymore. I have been alone for three years." He stops himself at the thought. He never said anything like it before. He takes a second to make sure grief doesn't overcome him and becomes the focus of the conversation. When it's more critical, he explains what needs to happen. "And I need to move ASAP. It doesn't make sense for me to get a new pad before you're ready to move. I'd have to break a lease and probably eat a deposit. Plus, it's only four months we're talking about here. Just four months. I know your dad said no, but can you tell him that's really important to me?" His plead borders begging and makes sure to clean it up from here on out.

"What's up, bro? What is this? You okay?" Tard turns down the music that had been quietly playing.

"I can't talk about it now. I'll fill you in later, but it's important. You have never let me down, and I appreciate it. I know it was you that always made those dudes come over to my pad even though and live really far away."

"Well, it was Mutt who drove most of the time."

"Yeah, but would he have on his own?"

"Didn't he pick you up or surf class every morning even though he lives on the beach?"

"Yeah, but that was later. After you made sure I was l looped in?"

"Are you pissed at our friends or something? Is this about Smoker and Smashley?"

"You know?" Jack is stunned now and forgets the whole point of what he wanted to talk about.

"Yeah, man, sorry, I probably should have told you, but Smoker told me he was going to bring up at some point. Plus, it didn't seem like my place to get involved."

"I don't care about that at all. She can sell crazy someplace else. We're all stocked up." Sometimes movie quotes just appear without any thought. "When did Smoker tell you?"

"Right after it happened. I slapped his big fuckin dome for you. Fuckin moron. He said that he was going to tell you about it. Maybe that's why he is going with you on the trip, so you don't have to go with Montana alone. Some kind of olive branch?"

"Yeah, that's what I think too." He says gratefully, knowing that someone was standing up for him the whole time.

"Again, I'm sorry I didn't tell you."

"I get it. You hit him hard?"

"Hard enough."

Jack remembers that this isn't the reason why he needed to see him this morning. They pull up in front of Jack's apartment on an empty street with hardly even a car parked. "Thanks. But more importantly, please talk to your dad." He says the last words emphatically as if there were their own sentence.

"Yeah… Listen, you need to do whatever is best for you. Don't worry about me. You need to take care of yourself first."

"I know. Just please try."

The Tard pauses. Jack expects some kind of long speech with the amount of thought his friend gives to his following statement. "I'll always want you to be happy."

Jack is grateful for the short remark as he gets out of the car and runs into his apartment. The door is unlocked. Jack listens to any noise that someone might be inside. Sounds eerily quiet—no noise from traffic or neighbor, just the hum of the powerlines. When Jack opens the door, his breath is taken from him. Spray painted on the wall and couch are the same letters the intruder had tattooed on his stomach, in large block format.

CHAPTER 40

Christmas '06

Jack walks down the stairs feeling the carpet on his feet. It takes him a second to realize that the tree is still there, and so are the presents. And a family, one that is waiting for him to make his way to the living room. It's the winter break of his senior year, and his mom didn't come home for the past two holidays, and when The Tard found out he made Jack come over for Christmas. He holds on to the railing gripping it tightly. He locks his elbow and leans forward on that arm, resting a good portion of his weight in that hand as he slides down the stairs.

With the scene laid out before him, family, presents, tree, he grips the railing tighter. His legs seem unsteady. The lights from the tree are playing a trick on his eyes. They sparkle and shine, glowing disproportionately to any lit Christmas tree he has ever seen before. They are nice but somehow dizzying, disorientating, not in a bad way, just in a way where Jack can't trust his eyes, can't trust his legs to carry him down the stairs without giving way.

"Good morning Jack," Tard's father proclaims.

"Finally," Tard's little sister bemoans.

"Yeah, there he is," Tard celebrates.

Tard's mother promptly adds, "Jack, honey, there are coffee and cinnamon rolls, grab whatever you want, and we can start opening up presents."

Jack replies, "Go ahead and start. I'll just grab that stuff. I don't want to stop you guys from open up your presents."

"Well, we all take turns opening up our first because, after that, it becomes a madhouse." She looks at her daughter, who smiles back excitedly, wickedly, in response. "Then, we just let them go crazy."

Jack looks at the clock in the kitchen above the breakfast table adjacent to the bay windows that look over the backyard. He is surprised to see the little hand on the nine and a big hand on the three. He can't remember the last time he has slept in this late. And to think that it happened sleeping in another house, in another bed, an unfamiliar arrangement. As strange as it is to walk down the stairs and see an entire family waiting for him to open up presents.

Jack pours himself a coffee and takes a sip, then immediately dumps out half of the dark brew and pours in as much sugar as he thinks will fix the flavor. Then he notices cream next to the sugar and takes it as a suggestion, and pours a heavy dose that billows up to the top of the black coffee like a cloud. And Jack stirs it into a creamy mocha. He tries it again, and this time it is like the ice cream of its namesake. This is Jack's first cup of coffee.

"Come on, Jack, hurry up." little sister says. She is usually so kind to him, so deferring to Jack when he's around. She lets him change the television channel when she doesn't let anyone else do that. She gets him snacks and drinks when he is over without him even having to ask. Jack forgoes the rolls and heads to the couch to take a seat next to his friend.

"Come on, let's go." little sister exclaims.

The father starts to distribute presents. He has been holding his daughter's gift, so she is the first to tear into the wrapping. Before Jack can even tell what she got, he hears her celebration and her thanks before tearing off all of the paper. The Tard gets his present next, and he thanks his parents before opening it, tearing at the tape that holds the wrapping in place, and undoes the paper without ripping it.

Jack sips on his overly sweet drink and wonders what Christmas might have been like the last couple of years if things were just different. It's hard to remember, but his parents let him open a gift on Christmas Eve, and much to his complaint, they were always pajamas and never a toy. "Don't worry, Jackie, there's plenty of loot to be had," His Father reassures him. "Yes, but we're sleeping in." His mom commands. They set the alarm the night before, and Jack wasn't allowed to leave his room before it went off. And after he opened presents, they went to mass and then had dinner with Bree's family, and they exchanged gifts as well. Now that Jack thinks about it, his parents held coffee mugs too. Would he have had coffee before now if things were different? There is no way to know.

The Tard's father pulls out another present. The Tard stands and says that he is going to grab his dad one. The father walks over toward his wife and then past her, and he extends his arm and a present to Jack. Jack can't think of what to do with the coffee. There is a side table he sits next to and a coffee table in front of him, but he holds on to his drink, unable to put it down. Still reaching toward the present with the cup in hand though, totally bewildered, thankfully the father removes the coffee from his hand and gives him the gift. Jack pulls it back onto his lap. The rest of the family watches him. Waits for him to open it. Jack's eyes well from the dizzying lights. His throat is dry from the coffee. He begins to tear at the paper before he stops and remembers to say "thanks," but the words barely form. He barely has the breath to push them out. So he mumbles his appreciation and tries so hard not to let tears come out.

After he opens his gift, he holds it tightly against his chest, letting the coffee stay on the table that the father had placed it in their exchange. He didn't need another sip. He could still taste the sweet, rich, decadent flavor on his lips. He closes his eyes so that the lights will stop tricking them, making them water. His throat finally relents too. It is no longer dry with a lump. His legs, though, are still weary from the climb down the stairs, but he does not need them. He doesn't have to go anywhere. He can sit and recapture his composure while he watches a scene that didn't use to be so unfamiliar to him.

After everyone opens up the rest of their presents, Jack carries his present over to his friend with little sister doing most of the unwrapping. Then he buries himself in a hug, with his face pressed against his friend's sternum, and wraps both arms around him. He has never hugged any of his friends like that before.

"Merry Christmas, little buddy." The Tard pats Jack's head.

The lights begin to play their tricks again, so Jack closes his eyes once more.

CHAPTER 41

September 10, '07

"Hey, I am going to do a bump now. Who else wants one?" Montana asks in the living room of his small apartment. The floors and fixtures are all modern, and the furniture is nice, but none of it matches.

"Sure… I'll do one."

Smoker agrees after clearly giving it some thought, probably weighing the early hour of the day versus the command in Montana's voice. Jack already knew the proposition fell on opposite ends of an imbalanced scale. Smoker takes his shortly after Montana takes one.

"Jack take yours," Montana says, pointing to the one small line left on the old plastic CD case. Jack grabs the straw Smoker hands to him. When he lowers his head, and no one can see his eyes, he closes them and thinks of all of this behind him that he has somehow escaped. And it isn't a fantasy either. He has money, and with the amount of money he can make in the next three months will be enough for him to pay for school and pay for a life in line with old expectations.

The Tard will come through for him. He always has. It's just up to Jack to come through on his end and survive the interim.

He feels the coke go up his nose. He feels it slide down the back of his throat. He tastes its bitterness in his mouth, then the back of his throat, and he chokes on it a little. Then he feels it in his jaw as it clenches, his teeth press against one another, the top and bottom rows biting each other, Jack biting himself. He just has to accept the fact that there will be a price to pay, and he'll have to fight something buried inside of him to endure the cost.

"Alright, let's go," Montana barks. With that, Jack follows everyone outside.

Montana unlocks the car doors as the boys leave the house. Smoker opens the door on the passenger side and folds the seat forward, allowing Jack to crawl into the back. Smoker pushes the passenger seatback slamming it against Jack's knees, and when Smoker sits down, Jack can feel his weight pressing against his legs. He hasn't said anything about Smashley. If she told him that Jack knew about their tryst. There was a look on his face, though, when they saw each other, one of apprehension and regret. But he still showed up anyway, and that is all Jack needed to know.

In the back of the car, the black leather interior holds the glossy shine of a brand new car. Jack knows the car is not new, just that no one sits in the back seat. His knees see the reason why that is. The car starts up like a jet—both the speakers and the engine blare. Montana backs out of his driveway with no regard for what could have been behind them.

After a brief stop at the gas station where Montana pumps gasoline with his shirt off, and the boys took just one more small snort of cocaine, the car races down the town boulevard. Punk rock resonates through the speakers and Jack's body. As if the pistons of the engine turned not just in the car but in Jack as well. And if he and the car raced, Jack could keep up.

Montana motors up the freeway on-ramp as if he is trying to roll the car. Jack's body slides slightly across the seat toward the drivers' side. He holds onto the side of the passenger seat, and he can feel the power in his arms and the strength in his grip. All of the boys remain quietly excited, a balled fist not yet thrown as a punch. It is this excitement that causes Smoker to ask for another line. Jack quickly agrees. Montana hands Jack the baggie with the cocaine in it, an old plastic CD case, and his driver's license. Jack carefully pulls out a small amount of blow. His arm resonates with the vibrations of the speeding car, but he manages not to spill any coke in the backseat. Jack hands Smoker the case, who holds it for Montana by the gear shift with his right hand, and Smoker grabs the steering wheel with his left. Montana lets go of the wheel, and he lowers his head below the dashboard, and with the dollar bill, Jack has rolled into a straw. Montana takes his line. With Montana back at the wheel, Smoker lets go and takes his. Jack grabs the case and the rolled straw and takes his, and then licks the case clean.

Jack's mouth has no feeling. When he bites down, he can barely feel the impact in his cheekbones. Whatever piece of him that had been hesitant to go on this little trip is buried behind the vibrant numbing energy now possessing him. He pushes his tongue against the roof of his mouth and the back of his lips. His saliva has thickened into a paste. He wishes he had something to drink, a beer would be perfect, but at the speed they're driving, they will be in San Luis Obispo shortly. He just had to hold on until then.

Buildings fly by on the side of the road, and in ten minutes, the car and the boys are out of an area of Los Angeles they would never go through on a surface street. Ten minutes away on the freeway and maybe twenty on a large street like Rosecrans, the neighborhood becomes poor and dangerous. These are the areas surrounding Jack's neighborhood, which serves as a buffer between them and the nicer beach towns.

Montana asks for another line, and Smoker wants in as well, so Jack hands Smoker the case and dollar bill. The operation begins like the last time, with Smoker steering the car and Montana lowering his head to the case. Montana begins to snort, and as he finishes, a red wall of brake lights materializes from out of nowhere. Jack flinches, pressing his body against the back seat as if he is slowing the car down from its stampede.

"Break!" Smoker yells out. He is easily heard over the thundering music. Montana's hands flash from the middle of the car back to the steering wheel, and he slams on the breaks. The sound of the tires startles Jack. The high-pitched squeal probably startles everyone next to them. But the car stops a couple of feet behind the one in front of them. Eyes from all over the lanes turn toward the boys. To the dangerous stop and the noise it caused.

Before Jack felt the moving car as an island, moving too fast for others to tread upon, but now, even separated by metal, plastic, and glass, the people stuck in traffic with the boys sit right next to each other.

Smoker bends over, hiding his head from Jack's view, and when he comes up, only one line remains on the case. Jack takes it, places the case on the seat next to him, and presses his head back against the seat of the car where the metal of the car door blocks his face from the other vehicles.

"No worries, dude," Smoker tells Montana with the certainty that he says most things, "Traffic doesn't start to get bad until about three. This crap will clear up in a mile."

"Of course, man," Montana says, turning to Jack, "let's take advantage. Crackie, hook it up."

Jack grabs Montana's drivers' license and keeps his head down so that he won't have to think about the eyes of fellow travelers veering his way. If Jack doesn't see anyone looking at him, it is the same as if no one is looking at the car. Maybe even as if no one else is on the road.

It is much easier to cut up lines now that the car has come to a complete stop.

He hands the case over to the front of the car, and they take their lines and then pass it back to Jack.

He tries to snort the remaining line, but his right nostril has closed. He switches to his left, and like a miniature landslide up the straw, the white powder goes. Jack chokes on the coke that has begun to slide down the back of his dry throat. The car has not moved in five minutes.

Jack notices commuters have gotten out of their cars, presumably to try and get a better view of what is holding up the flow of vehicles. Some even stand on top of their hoods to have a higher vantage point. The freeway bends right about three miles down the road limiting all views no matter how tall the person or car, and nothing in that stretch gives any evidence as to why the traffic has stopped.

The car remains still while the pistons inside Jack continue to crank. His nose is swollen, and the air doesn't easily pass, so he opens his parched mouth to breathe. He thinks of the beer that is waiting for him. He looks around for any bottle of water that may have been left in the car. There are none in the cup holders or the pouches behind the driver and passenger seats.

His hands wear a tremor. The engine's power vibrates through the back seat, and its compressed energy pushes deep into his spine and up through his skull. Still, the car does not move, the tires will not roll, and the vehicles in front of them will not get out of the way. The strumming of the engine inside him makes Jack feel like he can stand up and jump through the metal roof. To break out and break free, but the freeway, a concrete river of rushing metal, coagulates and lays lifeless while the thunders inside.

"Bro, this fucking sucks," Montana complains.

"What the fuck is going on?" Questions Smoker. "Dude, we haven't moved in at least an hour."

"Bro, we need a line to calm down" Montana turns to the back seat and remains that way until Jack hands him the case with three small lines on it. Jack's body begs him for another line. He can feel its urges independent of reason and thought. He knows he doesn't need one. Stuck as he is, he needs room to breathe, to pace, to do anything else but feel Smokers weight pressing into his legs, or the thirst cracking his throat, or his tongue sticking to the side of his mouth.

He wants to yell, but he remains silent. He needs to get out of the car and run, but he remains still. The case quickly bounces back, and Jack holds the dollar to his nose, and again he feels the cold burn up his septum and down the back of his throat.

After an hour stuck in place, the cars in front of them begin to move without any warning. "Finally," Smoker says. No one else speaks. All of the red lights unlock, and every car aggressively speeds as fast as they can.

The speed that Jack feels in his chest is a welcomed change to the quiet pounding of his heart.

The race, though, is only a short one. After a mile or so sprint, all cars brake again. Red lights flash on and off. No one comes to a complete stop as before. Still, the odometer never rises past 30 miles an hour and mostly flicks the illuminated 20 on the dashboard. The getaway is underway, but the car crawls at a snail's pace. Montana turns off the stereo in a frustrated swipe at the center console, allowing Jack's disappointment to echo even louder. There is no doubt that this will hold the entire way, as the freeway begins to swell with the commuters' traffic the boys had tried to avoid.

Jack's legs are pinched in the back seat, and he can't move them, only flex his muscles. The rear seat feels tight like a coffin. He pushes his body into the floorboard to feel his legs. The boards, to his frustration, don't move. His body has become a self-contained blaze burning away from the inside out, leaving his mouth and throat barren.

"Hey, Dude, I need another line. I'm completely pinned up here." Smoker asks Jack. Jack goes through the process once again. Unfortunately, the CD makes its way back to him with the final stripe he doesn't want to see on top, so he makes it disappear. Jack curses it as if he isn't the one who put it there in the first place.

More time passes. Again Jack checks the cup holders for water and even reaches a hand underneath the seats. In the front, they talk to each other and thankfully ignore Jack. Their conversation is about love and heartbreak. Jack catches snippets, but always without context. He guesses that the whole discussion exists without context anyway. In what world would these two discuss love? It's only the drug that speaks. They just are compelled to listen.

Jack catches the words Smoker speaks in response to whatever Montana has said. "Dude, and am I supposed to care? I mean, we have all had our heartaches…." Their heads will turn toward each other slightly, a chin will rise, ahead bobs in agreement, and so Jack can see that they are speaking to each other, but he isn't listening.

"Crackie, load another round" he hears that command.

He reaches for the bag. Thirst burns through his chest. The seat crushes his legs. Jack wants to claw through the leather and pull out its meaty foam. He needs to disembowel the metal sprigs and rip through the vinyl door and stand on the hood, and shout until all breath had left him speechless. He wants to throw the cars in front of him, push them to the side, pick them up over his head, and throw them off of the road. His heart cries out for this. Every beat calls for his destruction or freedom.

It doesn't matter what finds him first. Jack, the prisoner, can't escape. Every thump of his heart yells to his legs' kick' and to his arms' punch,' but he can't. Jack flexes all the muscles in his body to move his blood. The case bounces back to him, and he takes his line.

The wind whistles around the car, whipping away freely, there and gone, taunting Jack, while the air inside remains stale. The red brake lights of the cars in front wink at him teasingly, goading him. He can feel the brakes grab the car just when it seems like they can get some speed going to dishearten him. The heads in front continue to move, and they continue to talk, but Jack can't hear them. They have been in the car now for four hours. Even with regular traffic, the entire trip would take, at most, three and a half. They're not even to Santa Barbara yet, the halfway point. More time passes.

"I need another line," Smokers says. His tone makes it sound urgent, like he had been repeating himself.

Has the case been in Jack's hand from the last line he took? He thought he had set it on the seat next to him, but there it was on his lap with three lines already placed on top. Jack has become a cog, unwitting, and inhuman.

Outside concrete rolls underneath the car like a slow drip, and the segmented white highway line slowly passes by. His body has given way. No longer full of explosive energy that can break through a roof or push a car off the road. Jack is inert and powerless in the back seat, a firecracker with its fuse pulled out.

Thoughts began to shorten in his mind. Smoke from the flames that are engulfing him clouds his clarity. His thoughts aren't congruent, bouncing from one issue to the next. He processes them in bits, and before he can form an opinion or insight, they disappear. And each next thought is only a search for what has gone missing, only to lose that in the same way. He has become a path walked in reverse. With each step taken backward, the picture of what lays before becomes smaller and more clouded. Fleeing the fire, he has turned and now runs. The new destination a position already possessed and then gone. Unable to keep track of how much time has passed, he is unsure of long he has been in this haze. It feels like a lifetime. And if given a lifetime, would he ever move on?

He looks outside, and traffic still clouds all of the windows, but Jack can see the sky starts to darken, and the clouds that had once floated like sheep in a dream lay stagnant and crimson as if they have been slaughtered.

Finally, Jack hears Montana say, "You guys were an awesome team. I had to play on a shitty basketball squad. I was all CIF, but we lost so many games...."

Smoker interrupts, "Dude, I wish I was playing in college..."

Their conversations run over each other.

"Luggy is playing at UCSB, right?" It is Montana's turn to interrupt. "I heard The Tard is going to Texas now."

Jack leans forward to tell Montana that he has heard wrong, that The Tard will be going to UCLA and living with Jack in Westwood, but he can't speak.

"No, he is going to UCLA." Smoker answers. Jack realizes he hasn't said anything in over an hour, at least, maybe even three.

"He told me he was going to Texas last week...." Montana says with a slight edge in his voice, and Jack can tell that he is a little annoyed.

"No. Man. Not Texas." Smoker speaks the words that Jack, more or less, expects to hear, but his left hand says something entirely else. Smoker keeps his hand horizontal an inch or two above his seat. He waves it back and forth with enthusiasm, but he controls his arm and shoulder to leave Jack no other conclusion that this is supposed to be a private and silent conversation. Smoker's hand closes its fingers, leaving the thumb exposed. He turns the thumb to point to the back seat to Jack, and it looks as if he is shaking dice, and then he goes back to waving his hand flat. "He is going to UCLA."

"Oh," Montana catches on. So does Jack. "I guess I misunderstood. Anyway, playing with all these great athletes makes everyone else look better...."

Jack slides back further in the back seat and slumps against the window, without any regard to prying eyes. He feels something paralyzing in the back of his dry throat. It's like the numbness that Jack has handled all day. There's no feeling in him, but this different. He can't place it. Like the cocaine, it is chalky. He chokes on it. Gags on it.

Coursing from his neck down, through every tendril of nerve and every fiber of muscle. He no longer pushes on the floorboards. No longer feels Smoker's weight against his legs.

No longer flexes the muscles in his body to move blood. There is no blood. It has been replaced. By what? He doesn't know. Whatever is left of him clenches his jaws and can't feel the pressure.

He hopes to get rid of it. There is no water; there is nothing with which to fill himself. So he grabs the only thing available. Jack pulls out the bag once again without anyone else calling for it and lines up three very fat and long stripes of chalk. They're in hour five of their drive, the bag of coke is almost gone, but Jack's already left.

Only an hour later, at the Camarillo grade, in the northernmost section of the Santa Monica Mountains, where LA becomes Ventura, the highway lanes constrict from five to one. Large concrete pipes as big as igloos lay across the other lanes.

A red semi-truck rests crookedly on the highway's dirt shoulder with a small blue car pillowed under the cab. Lit flares guide the merging traffic, and for each one burning, five black powdery remnants show that they have been burning all day. Fire engines and ambulances must have come and gone. Only two CHP cars remain. Clearly, the pipes will lie there, too heavy to lift, for long after the travelers pass them. Jack recognizes then what coursed through his body, what he had choked on before. The black powdery remnants, the ash of what has burned through. It no longer runs through his veins as blood has become dust. Muscles and bone have charred too and turned to ash. He is consumed by a fire he caused.

Several miles disappear in little time. The car races down the stretch of highway just south of San Luis Obispo as the 101 freeway turns inland and the road inclines.

Coming from the opposite direction, cars race downward, weaving into and out of bowed curves, testing brakes, not engines. The speed built by such an extended decline gathers like a falling rock. Still, the turns are deceptively hung, and the wrong combination of speed and diverted attention would cause damage to the automobiles careening down the hills.

Montana has such curves to deal with, and the powerful engine more than handles the incline but the steep roadway tests more than the engine or brakes. Montana shows impatience by passing cars in blind curves, along the shoulder of the freeway, and in the roadbed. Jack can tell that Smoker is nervous with the looks he gives toward the road and back toward Montana. Smoker says things that Jack can't hear, Montana seems to respond at times. It doesn't matter to Jack, he's not really there, and this isn't happening to him.

Finally, they pull up the long asphalt driveway past the overhanging oak tree with torn bark. Seven hours after Jack climbed into the back seat, Jack lifts his legs from the space between the back seat and the front. To free himself, he has to twist each leg, bringing up one foot from the floor space and then the other, and steps out of the car. His black powdery remnants move down the driveway. Clearly, he has burned all day long.

A dim porch light and empty beer cans greet the three travelers. Mumbles walks up to Montana and Smoker, with Jack standing alone toward the back.

"What's up, boys?" Mumbles says with a smile. College students stand in a circle around a keg behind him. Mumbles bro hugs Montana and then Smoker, and once Jack reaches him, he gets the same welcome. But Jack can't feel Mumbles' hand grasp his, nor can he feel their shoulders and arms touch or Mumbles' other hand pat him on the back. Jack is finally free. Free of being. Free of himself. They turn toward the keg and toward the people surrounding it. Mumbles summarily makes a general introduction, meaning he tells all of the people who Jack doesn't know the names of three travelers but not any of the names of the people already at the party. Montana quickly pulls Mumbles aside without acknowledging the introduction. Smoker immediately raises his arms out to the side, higher than his shoulders but not much. It looks like the compromise of a welcoming hug and victory arms. The strangers give a semi enthusiastic greeting in response to their arrival. Jack is spun around to see Montana's hand on his shoulder, pulling him that way, and Montana says, "We're late. Be better if I go by myself. Less to explain. Plus, I'm already vetted. Jack can tell he is nodding in response by the way his field of vision moves.

Smoker spins him back the other way handing him a beer, "Hot lap," and Jack doesn't remember grabbing the beer but now holds the drink. As they head toward the front door, Smoker continues, "Did you see the gun in the glove compartment? He said he's had to jam it into some dude's mouth before. Fucking insane."

There is roughly the same number of people in the small apartment as there are outside. They're playing flip cup, and Jack can't help but think if it were home, they'd probably be playing caps. Smoker hands Jack his beer takes a step, and falls on his face comically, rolling further than his momentum should have carried him. He uses Luggy's move. The game stops as the boys are viewed, measured, not necessarily greeted, but acknowledged, then people laugh loudly at Smoker. Some stare at Smoker, and some at Jack.

Jack usually skirts a room. Heads toward one side and cuts himself out of the center. It's a paradox. He knows he needs the attention, to be validated, to be something, but at the same time, Jack knows he doesn't deserve it, and if anyone were to look for too long, they just might notice that too. This time it's different. Instead caring about the glances of others, Jack floats freely through the room. Their eyes, and looks, don't affect. He hears some girl ask her friend, "Who's that?" But Jack matriculates past her and her friend as if he is alone in the room.

Mumbles beckons Jack over by waving his hand. Jack is pulled toward him the same way the passing wind of a waving hand moves a soap bubble. Mumbles has cocaine spread out on a mirror. He must have gotten some from Montana. Mumbles says something about the boys being the ones who drove it up for the party. They smile and thank them for coming up. Smoker says something about the drive, and genuine shock falls on their faces. Smoker says something else, and then looking right at Jack, says, "Right? Dude." Jack thinks he said something but doesn't know what, maybe a line from a movie. People laugh.

"What a roadie you boys had," Mumbles has his hand on Jack's shoulder.

"You guys get the first kicker."

Jack sees himself lower toward the mirror. To several white lines cut on top of it. Behind them, he sees his face. He sees his eyes looking back at him, back from behind the white bars he is buried underneath.

He knows he took a line, but it doesn't register. He doesn't feel it. There is no difference. Then his body moves away from him. He sees it sit on the bed next to someone whom he doesn't know. They offer him a cigarette, and he accepts. They go outside together. They stand next to the keg but off to the side.

They're not waiting in line to fill their cup, standing just on the edge of the dim porch light. Jack is fully uncoupled, entirely removed. He watches himself smoke. Watches the cherry red ember of the lit cigarette raise in hand. In such low light, the ember is grand in all that darkness. Jack is dark too. Just like the black remnants of the flares on the road. Just like the shadow, he casts on the ground. A thin image lacking depth and distinction. It doesn't seem to bother the other person. They are talking, but Jack can't hear them. They grab his cigarette and hold it behind their back. He reaches around them for it. And when he does, the other person kisses him on the cheek. Then they hand him back his cigarette. They go back into the room. Smoke hangs in the air. Not everyone who lit up went outside. Jack takes another line. They go back out for another smoke, and Jack chugs a beer and another. And then later, they take more lines and have an additional smoke. She continues to flirt, and he can see himself flirt back.

The night repeats itself several times. He is in an unbroken cycle that no one else recognizes that they follow a particular pattern. Only in his place, tucked away somewhere in the night, does he notice, but he is powerless to do anything about it, to stop it, to stop himself.

Finally, much later, he rejoined, sitting on the couch next to the girl.

"You're beautiful, you know," she says. Most of the party left, and if Jack had to guess, she stayed behind when her friends have gone. Jack says nothing in response. "When you come back from your surf trip to the Mentawais and Bali, do you think you will come back here to see your friends?"

"Yeah, I guess," Jack makes a mental note that he said he is going on a surf trip.

She places her hand on his knee. "I always wanted to date a pro surfer." Jack doesn't move when her face closes in on him. Her lips press firmly against his. He looks around her head at the house while he lets her kiss him. Red cups lay strewn on the floor throughout the living room and kitchen. The keg outside has been untapped, and the bags of ice have all melted, leaving only empty plastic on the ground. A few distant voices talk in the kitchen, and music comes from one of the bedrooms. It sounds like the door is closed, but Jack doesn't know for sure because this girl's head tilts to that side, blocking his view.

She pulls her head away, staring at Jack. "I live just across the street" she stands up to her feet but immediately bends over, placing her hand on his knee, "you don't have to sleep on this couch if you don't want to."

Jack realizes that her hand has slid up to grab his penis. He is equally surprised by her decisive move and surprised that he has a growing erection, that his body works in some order.

It is the first sign of life, and it points decidedly against the promise he made that morning. Jack curiously wonders which will win out.

CHAPTER 42

September 11, '07

Jack wakes with a gasp of air that makes a loud sucking sound, the same noise that awoke him. After he finds his breath and realizes where he is, lying on the floor of Mumbles' living room, with no blanket, just the clothes he wore the night before, his nose is stuffy and swollen. His eyes barely open, and he sits up and feels rickety. But his thirst prompts him to rise from off the floor in search of water.

He stumbles into the kitchen only to find that all of the glasses are dirty, so he grabs a pot from under the sink and fills it up with tap water. The water pouring removes the silence from the room. Jack finishes his first, then his second pot. Although he is still thirsty, he can't drink anymore due to his full stomach.

The living room has glasses and cups scattered everywhere. Some are bone dry others had full beers still in them. Others had spit from dipping tobacco in it, and the thought of drinking one of these cups almost makes Jack puke.

The linoleum floor in the kitchen has a film of oily grime covering it that Jack feels on his bare feet. He can still taste the cigarettes in the air but can't smell them through his impacted nasal cavity. The blinds have been left open, and the room faces the East, so the early morning light floods his eyes. He needs several more hours of sleep, but he won't find it there.

Jack goes to the bathroom, which stinks of urine, lifts the toilet seat with his foot, and relieves himself. Jack finds Smoker on the couch and wakes him up by turning on the TV so that there is no way he will go back to sleep. Smoker gets up with a few complaints and then uses the same pot for water and sits back on the couch to watch TV.

The boys sit quietly for a while. Only the TV makes noise, but Jack isn't paying attention. It is just a way to keep from having to talk. Jack isn't sure what happened the day before. It all seems so distant that it feels like a story about which he only heard.

"How was she?" Smoker breaks the silence.

"I don't want to talk about it."

"She was deese. Not as hot as Bree or Smashley, but then again, who is?" The words pierce Jack's eardrums, and the pain is so intolerable he almost throws up. "Speaking of fucking sluts and Smashley, I have something I need to tell you." He's casual and confident as if he has some minor tidbit to share, just a little fact that might be of interest.

Jack doesn't respond. He wants to pretend as nothing happened. The images come rushing in despite his best efforts to block them mentally. She, whatever her name was, led Jack across the street. She said the night air was cold and clung to Jack for warmth. Jack did not know if it was that cold or if she just wanted to get close. He still couldn't feel a thing. She opened her door and asked Jack to be quiet because her friends were sleeping. Jack turned on loud music to wake her roommates up. She didn't get mad enough to kick him out. He turned on the lights in her bedroom. Her roommate woke up in a bed on the other side of the room, the two girls shared. The roommate yelled a little at Jack but then pretended to go back to sleep. Still, even after all of that, he was welcomed into her bed.

Above her bed, a sparkle of light fell into Jack's eyes occupying all of his small and shallow pupils. A silver-plated picture reflected light onto the ceiling. Jack felt her body bounce into him as she was on her hands and knees. Jack was behind her in a semi-squat. He had his right leg bent with his right foot on the bed, and he rested most of his weight on his left knee, pushing into the mattress.

How many silver-plated picture frames were there? Jack thought to himself. The answer did not detour him from the image that came into his mind. No matter how much he looked at the picture, he saw only Bree and her brother looking off to the left, where Jack held his body firm to withstand the thrusts of this girl. The slapping of her butt's flesh against Jack's bony hips smacked against his ears. Her body bounced Jack backward again. He was not even moving anymore, but she kept knocking him back.

The sly grin on Bree's brother's face became a sneer, and the amazement Bree held in her face became awe and then shock. Jack could see the anger in their eyes. Under this light, he could see what the picture meant. That Jack was the thing off camera. He was the thing not captured in the frame. The disappointing and sad thing that in a gallows sense of humor finally made them laugh.

Jack felt her hand close around his. He held the thick part of her hair close to her scalp. Maybe he held it too tightly was she motioning him to release his grasp. Jack ignored her. The room smelled of sex, and the clapping of flesh continued. They had sex with the lights on, with a girl pretending to be asleep just feet away. Jack made her talk dirty. She had to ask for everything with a please. "Please, I want your cock in me," "Please fuck me." He called her names like "slut" and "bitch," but she would not kick him out of the house no matter what he did. The cocaine prolonged their sex for an hour. Her small hand reached back and cupped Jack's testicles, and he came on her sheets.

Jack stood up and left without saying a word. He was a character, playing someone who need not explain his actions, a person who didn't need anyone, but someone everyone wanted. He was a leading man.

After an hour of watching television silently, Montana steps into the room. The boys grab their shoes and gather their phones and wallets. A little more than 12 hours since they had gotten out of the car, they climb right back in and start their trip home.

The long ride home went softly. Montana left the radio off for the first half-hour. Jack closed his eyes and rested his head against the window, using a crumpled sweatshirt as a pillow.

The backseat still felt small, and Jack stretched his left leg so that his left foot dangled behind the drivers' seat, and his right foot had the entire floor space in front of him.

The area may have been tight, but this time it felt comforting. Jack felt secure by the closeness. Though Jack had closed his eyes, he didn't sleep. He stayed silent, as did Smoker and Montana. The hypnotic pure of the rubber tires brought thoughts back and sent them away again. With his head against the window, Jack felt the cool rush of air on his warm temples. The passing air, along with the soft murmur of rolling asphalt, created a white noise that filled the car until they got back home.

"You guys hungry?" Asks Montana softly. No one has spoken for almost three hours.

"Yeah, I could maul," Smoker says with a hoarse voice, and then he clears his throat and repeats himself more distinctly.

"In," Jack agrees, sending the car to get food.

"Hey, Mario, what's up?" Smoker greets the man behind the counter and then proceeds to order breakfast. Jack orders a number three combo, two eggs, two bacon pieces, two slices of sausage, two pieces of toast, hash browns, and a medium drink. Jack asks why it is not called the number two. Mario shrugs and hands Jack his cup, and greets the next customer.

Jack fills his cup up with Strawberry Fanta and sits down on the red vinyl cushions holding his ticket with his number on it. The silence of the road follows them into the restaurant. They seem like three children in trouble waiting for the Principle to call them into his office. One by one, they pick up their meals and quietly eat them.

The restaurant is empty, with only two other patrons eating. Jack hears the cooks speaking Spanish in the kitchen. He can hear the deep fryer sizzle and pop. Smoker finishes and picks up his phone. When Jack finishes, he grabs a refill and sits down.

Smoker asks Montana a question that Jack had wondered about when he first heard about the trip to San Luis Obispo. "Why SLO?"

Montana explains, "Did you know that California is the biggest agricultural producer in the world? Garlic, kiwis', almonds, lettuce, broccoli, tomatoes, you name it, we probably grow more of it than any other country. And wine, don't forget wine. All of these companies have huge transportation capabilities. And SLO and Salinas are two of the biggest hubs in the state, and from there, these products are distributed across the county, in corporate-owned trucks."

Smoker sounds perplexed, still holding his phone in hand, "Yeah, so?"

Montana continues, "Well, imagine a company like a Dole with trucks full of lettuce and coke."

"What are you saying? These companies are smuggling drugs?" Jack asks, surprised.

"No. No, they don't know. You don't have to get the CEO to sign off on something like this. You just need a director in charge of scheduling, some warehouse workers, and some drivers. It doesn't take much to co-opt their supply chain. But it's a free ride to anywhere in the country courtesy of some of the biggest brand names."

Smoker's impressed, "Fuckin genius."

"So what happened with the meeting?" Jack asks.

And Montana begins to fill them in on his night. "They weren't happy I was late, I'll tell you that. Although I only ended up being an hour late. They heard about the freeway, though. So they understood. They weren't happy I came in with a piece, either. I told them next time I won't carry one. They said that they were expecting two of us. I said with the late arrival I thought it best they only deal with the one person who had a voucher. That next time they can meet you. They were interested in learning more about you. Seems like they had already had you on the radar."

"Huh?" The statement hits Jack like smelling salts. His eyes open wide and head pushes back. "What do you mean?"

"I wish you told me earlier. None that shit would have happened." Montana isn't upset; he sounds disappointed instead.

"What happened?" Smoker puts down his phone on the white table, suddenly interested more in the conversation than he was before.

"A local syndicate was putting the heat on our boy here." They both look at Jack, Smoker's face, his eyes wide, and raised eyebrows to implore for more details. Jack doesn't respond. After a beat, Montana continues, "Really, they thought it was Taurus' people overstepping their border. Funny that we went to send him a message, but it was really us, but it's all settled now. See, these guys have a method. Every bit of the stuff they move has a landing spot. There are agreements in place on who and where people can operate. They just didn't know you were really working the beach, even from inland. Once I explained that there was no overlap in clientele and no friction resulting in it, then they were cool. Plus, we pay so much more than the other guys that a tie goes to the bigger wallets."

"We pay more?" Jack is surprised to hear.

"Fuck yeah, we do. We also make more too. What you sell a gram for, the gang from your neighborhood sells for half the cost after they cut it. We don't cut our shit, and we have access to much deeper pockets, so our clients pay more for a better product. We pay more to our suppliers and get certain strategic advantages from that, like being afforded protection. When you can offer more than the next guy, you're going to get more in return. It's all about what you can give them, and the more you can give, the more you get.

"We pay a higher price, and we move more. That's one of the reasons I let you onboard the program. Once you explained what you would bring, it came to me that we'd hit a volume threshold beneficial to our position.

"That, and we sell to rich people. Police don't care about us. Fuck I got a buddy on the force, and he could give a shit. No murder or robbery is coming back on them through us—no witnesses to worry about or snitches. We have so much more to offer. You're untouchable. Just wish you told me sooner."

"Fuck, man, what happened?" Smoker asks, concerned.

"Nothing," Jack responds as he stands. He walks back over to the soda fountain and hears himself repeating the word over and over, nothing. He isn't speaking it, just hearing it echo in his brain while silently mouthing the word as he pours root beer into his half-full strawberry Fanta. The soda reaches the top of the cup and pours over the rim into the ice collector below. Jack continues to push in the lever, and more falls, much more than the cup can hold. Nothing has to change; he thinks to himself, nothing.

CHAPTER 43

September 11, '07

After being dropped off, Jack walks into his apartment and doesn't bother to lock it behind him. He leaves the television off, and he goes to his room and crawls in bed. He has a deep sleep. A dreamless sleep cast into an impenetrable black depth that can't be seen through, and time no longer passes. When the phone wakes him, he checks the time first before looking at the number calling.

"Hello," his eyes are barely open.

"Hey, Cracked." It is The Tard.

"Oh, hey, what's up?"

"How you feel?"

"Better."

"Smoker told me about yesterday," Jack wonders what about yesterday that Smoker told him. "Crazy story, huh? Maybe one of the gnarliest roadies I have ever heard."

"It wasn't that cool."

"Yeah, well…. Maybe in a couple of years, it will make a story." There is a pause. Jack reads it as a hesitation.

Maybe he only called to check in and doesn't have anything about which to talk. "He also told me about some heat you were getting. I wish I knew. You can always stay at my parents if you need to until stuff blows over."

"Yeah… thanks. It sounds like a bigger deal than it was," Jack lies, "and anyway, Montana took care of it."

The Tard doesn't reply for some time, and Jack lets the silence fall where it may. "Dude, I am not going to be able to live with you this year," The Tard pauses, "I'm to go to Texas for school."

"Really?" Jack's voice doesn't carry the inflection of tone that would make it sound like a question. But it is present when he adds, "When did you decide that?"

"A while ago, I just did not know how to tell you. They said I could start my freshman year for the baseball team and play volley."

"Can't let it go, huh?" Jack doesn't let any hurt or anger come through his voice. After all, he knows how that feels.

"I mean, there is no cash to be made in it. But I'd still miss it. Plus, I'd rather play third, and UCLA has an all-American there already." There was another pause. "Anyway, I'm really sorry that I didn't tell you sooner, it would have been really fun to share a pad, but I got to do this. My dad said you could stay with him if you needed to."

Jack hesitates before he answers. "No worries, dude. I guess I have to make my way out to Texas then, huh?"

"Damn right. Get used to me saying Y'all a bunch. Hey, did Smoker ever say anything about Smashley?" It's a nice change of topic, which is surprising to Jack and gives him confidence that he can move on.

"No, he didn't. I think there was a time he kind of brought her up, but he didn't say anything about hooking up with her…. Honestly, I really don't care. I am sure he will tell me when he can." Jack means it. "As far as she is concerned, we're not going to do what we have been doing. I don't need the drama."

"Oh, hey, did you hear about the pier?" His energy is palpable even through the phone.

"No?"

"That new coffee house was totally demolished. John Doe went fucking crazy!"

"What?" Jack is suddenly curious and fully awake. "What happened?"

"John Doe, he's trashed, of course, starts yelling at all of the construction guys, calling them Fascists."

"What!?" Jack laughs a little.

"I don't know. Lots of 'fuck you' and 'fuck all of them' and something else. What was it? Oh yeah, he starts screaming 'sponges.' No idea why. But it's funny as hell, and you know me, I'm dying, laughing so hard. Then, and I still can't believe it, the crazy son of a bitch climbs into the crane they were using for the lampposts and drives it down the pier. The workers are yelling at him or jumping out of the way. One tries to get on it, but John had the fucking thing going fast as hell. The crane is flying all over, hitting the lamp post and bouncing off the rails. All the way down the pier. Then full throttle fuckin thing slams into the coffee house and just demos it. I mean, he fuckin crushed it. Wood and the tile roof are flyin all over. And then he goes over the end into the water takin the new rail guard and lampposts with it. The police are there now, so are the firemen. Everyone can't believe it. The pier is fucked up."

"What happened to John?"

"The lifeguards sprinted down the pier, jump in after him, and pulled him out. He was unconscious. They did some CPR and rushed him away in an ambulance. He was under for a while.

Man, it was crazy you have to go see the pier; it's fucked up."

"I'll check it out later."

"Man, it's a good thing there were no waves yesterday."

"Why is that?"

"Because if people had been in the water, someone would have died. No doubt about it."

The thought pops into Jack's head so quickly it felt more like a reflex than anything else. He had just been next to the pier only days earlier. And as quickly the thought had come, it vanishes just as fast. Jack's relief, though, lingers. "I'll check it later."

"So, is everything is cool?"

"It's fine."

"All right, little buddy."

"Late."

"Late."

Jack begins to tidy his room, putting away clothes and trash. As he busies himself with a light workload of straightening up his apartment, Jack sees the shotgun in the corner of the closet. He unloads the shells and places them in a box. He finds the handgun and does likewise. Then he tucks the guns in a storage area in the hallway closet."

For some reason, Jack thinks of Bree. Maybe it was the gun though he never mentioned it to her. Jack sits down on his white leather couch and dials her number. The leather sticks to his sweaty skin, and when he leans forward, it peels away like flesh.

The phone rings several times before someone picks it up.

"Hello?" The voice is older than expected.

"Oh… Hi," Surprised to hear Bree's mom answer her phone. He hasn't heard her voice in years. Jack hesitates before asking, "Is Bree there?"

"Hi Jack," she sounds distant, "No, she isn't. You guys spent the night together two days ago, right?"

"Umm." He doesn't know how to answer.

"I meant you were together, uh, hanging out the other night, right?"

"Yeah, we were hangin out. Can I ask why?"

"I'm glad you called. I haven't seen her since yesterday. I have called all of her friends, and they don't know where she is. Did she say she was going anywhere? Or doing something? It's not like her not to call, and the only time she leaves her phone behind is when she goes to the beach."

Jack can hear the concern in her voice, "No. Nothing."

"Last I got from her was something about finding a watch? I don't know. She was running out the door, and I missed most of it."

"Yeah. She said she was going to find my watch for me…" The last two words barely make it out of Jack's mouth. His breath dies on his tongue, and the words trip on his lips, falling to the floor.

"I'm sorry, what do you mean?" She has to repeat herself several times before he can answer.

"At the pier. I lost my watch at the pier. She was diving for it."

"Oh my… You don't think?"

CHAPTER 44

September 19, '07

Jack skates along the beginning stretch of the downtown area, on the street closest to the beach that runs parallel to it. The vibrations from the wheels bounce against the soles of his bare feet, penetrating no further. Jack registers nothing, not even the strain in his thighs from the long skate from his home. The journey has come to an end, and Jack doesn't even remember the hills he walked up or skating the descent the other side offered. Somehow he is just much closer to the beach than when he left his apartment.

Today is the day Bree would have left for college. The same day that most of his friends left too. They discovered her body not long after he spoke to her mother, found her that night. Trapped under some debris but not drowned. Her death came from a blow to the neck from a fallen lamppost.

Two white lights flash as a luxury car begins to back out of a parking spot.

Jack swerves to avoid its rear bumper. He holds his surfboard back behind him to avoid any contact, and he smacks the trunk with his free hand so that the driver knows he is there.

Jack readjusts the towel and wetsuit that hangs over his left shoulder to prevent them from falling to the ground. More cars, more people, collisions abound.

Jack skates past what was once Lamar's Hamburgers. The restaurant his dad took him to every Saturday afternoon, after a morning surf or swim at the beach. They were able to bring their boards inside and lay them next to the table. Jack still remembered the server's name that always took their order and left him with a white placemat and a box of crayons. They used to put Thousand Island dressing on their burgers, which has always remained Jack's favorite. Now it's a trendy California Cuisine restaurant with black windows, a fancy green copper sign, and a wait that stretches nears two hours on Saturday night.

Next, Jack rolls by what once was the old Ocean liquor on the corner. Generations of kids bought sodas and candy from there after junior lifeguard and volleyball classes during the summer. They kept their floor concrete and bare so that children could walk in with sand still stuck on their feet. It has since turned into a boutique shoe store that no child would venture into on their own.

Downtown Toys was no longer around either. It burnt down a couple of summers ago. Jack watched the fire, and he saw the dolls and plastic guns washed away by firemen's hose, half-burnt. Long gone were the candy stores. The Ice Box where Jack went after soccer games and bought coke bottles. Or the Cookie Post that, according to his mother, had the best pistachio ice cream. The Bijou Movie theatre was gone too, and so was his father's favorite Mexican restaurant. Jack thought to himself that it would have been easier to list the stores that still stood from his cherished youth than those that had disappeared. The ones in which he grew up.

As Jack passes an intersection, a woman with big white shopping bags walks out off the curb in front of him, crossing against a red light. He lifts his right leg off of his board and drags his barefoot on the ground to stop his momentum. She is on her phone and doesn't notice him. She crosses without an apologetic word, and he continues on down the street.

Jack maneuvers past several stopped cars. The first has its blinker on, indicating it will pull into a parking spot and is waiting for the occupying vehicle to pull out. Jack cuts in front of one of the cars to pass them on the left side so that he won't get clipped by the car pulling away from the curb. The exact same scenario is happening on the other side of the street. Five cars sit behind that lead car with nowhere to go. The city swarms congested, full of people whose stories Jack doesn't know, and they don't know Jack's either.

Jack wonders, did the crowds come because of all the changes, or did the changes come from the crowds? The large shopping area built over the old pottery complex certainly brought more people to shop at high-end boutiques and eat and drink and sophisticated restaurants. Did they know that the land lay empty for years because of lead contamination?

There are more parking lots, and some old lots added a second story to accommodate the influx. There are more parking spaces on the street and valet parking for visitors and tourists who only came there a night a week, once a year, or maybe just once in a lifetime. Obviously, those who came here only once have more of an influence on this city than Jack, who never wanted to leave.

The avenue dead ends, and Jack shifts his weight from the balls of his feet to his heels angling the board left down a minor slope and into an alley that runs behind the strand. He ollies over a curb and stops in front of the ocean. From here, Jack sees the pier and the damage done. He can hear the crew of workers and their big tools roaring through the air. They have already begun to rebuild. The incident will be completely undone, and the pier will finish otherwise.

Jack places his surfboard on a thicket of ice plant, on the plants thick dark green succulent leaves, like fingers that taper at the end to a point, and creeps down the hill toward the water. Large camping tents are set up on the sand. They usually have some type of padding underneath to keep the sand at bay. A few umbrellas are sprinkled in, but mostly they have lost ground to the canopy and tentpoles. The same thing happened to the low canvas beach chairs, which have been replaced by the higher resting camping chairs.

They are part of the new flavors to the scene that, without consent, and notice, took over from what once had been.

Jack takes off the wetsuit and towel from off his shoulder and places them onto the orange bench. He flips his skateboard onto its 'back' with the wheels pointed toward the sky so that it won't roll away. Jack takes off his shirt. He feels the sweat that had gathered on his shirt around the upper back and armpit areas in his hands. He didn't realize he has been so sweaty.

Next, Jack grabs the towel and wraps it around his waist, tucking the corner in the makeshift waistband to keep it in place. Jack slides off his board shorts undercover of the cloth and drops them on top of the shirt on the bench.

The wetsuit is inside out, so Jack flips the body of it back through the hole for the head. He sticks his arm inside and pulls out the legs first and then each sleeve for his arms. Jack steps through the neck with the suit back to normal, stretching his wetsuit with his body. First, the neck engulfs his legs until it reaches his knees. Jack stands on his left leg only with his right leg dangling in the air. He grabs the right ankle of the suit pulling the neoprene mass up his leg, and maneuvers it until the wet suit covers his right ankle with its corresponding part. He repeats the movement for the left ankle.

Next, Jack pulls the neck up over his thighs, past his waist, up to the middle of his chest. He slides his right arm into the right sleeve and then the left arm into the left sleeve. Jack zips up his suit, completing his towel change, and is now completely covered, completely insulated.

He shields his face from the sun. The hottest day in a week, not a cloud in the sky, Jack had to apply sunscreen to his face, and it begins to run into his eyes, causing them to burn and water.

Jack is so hot in his wetsuit that his throat feels dry and compressed. No amount of swallowing makes this lump disappear.

The noise makes it worse. Jack wants the workers to put down their hammers, drills, and saws. He wishes he didn't have to hear the pounding and the screeching, and now his headaches. But despite the fact, they continue, utterly unaware of the pain they are inflicting. As if the world refuses to recognize its loss and pretends to carry on as if nothing has happened. That they choose to simple to ignore it.

His feet dig into the sand. And it easily gives way. And why not? What is sand but stone-ground down to its lowest component, stripped barren and broken into its smallest piece? The leftovers, the remnants, readily giving way to all the elements that once tore it apart. All the indentation that it captures, all the activity it records, will also give way. Give way to someone else who comes to trample on it, give way to the tide as it rises and retreats, give way to the breeze that pulls from off of the water.

He reaches down to grab his surfboard from off the thicket of ice plant upon which it rests. It is the only patch on this block. The rest has been removed, replaced by rose gardens. It's part of a new ordinance for homes on the strand. If they put a garden in front of their house, where the ice plant grows, then that portion of the strand wall can't be sat upon by passerby's, that their new garden would be private to them and off-limits to everyone else.

As he grabs his board, looking down at that thicket of ice plant, he sees something that he had never seen before. It is so obvious he can't believe he has never noticed it before. The top of the ice plant is a vibrant green, and it comes off the ground to reach his knees, and the succulent leaves of the plant follow a vine, like a back bone.

But inside the plant, in its dark recess and crevasse, its hidden tendrils, the plant is an ash grey. As the ice plant grows, the newer portion ends up blocking the old. Choking it out and taking its place. Each has its own time. It lays on top of what came before it, and it gives way to what happens after. "Grows to die." The words of John Doe make perfect sense when Jack speaks them to himself.

He can see himself somewhere in there. Ash grey and buried. He can hardly breathe, and his eyes water more, fueling the dry lump in his throat. Then he thinks of Bree, and he cries. He cries ugly, with tears rolling down his face dripping onto the dry sand. He wipes the snot from his nose with the sleeve of his wetsuit. He gasps and snorts, and he makes painful faces with his eyes half-closed. People pass by, but he pays them no attention. It is as if he is alone with no one else around. And that is how he feels, entirely and utterly alone.

He is compelled to move. To try to get away. So he crosses the wide beach. The sand has been absorbing the heat of the sun all day, and it is more than Jack can handle, even with callused feet. He does what every child has learned to do, dig his feet below the sand, and drag them underneath, where the cooler sand won't burn them. He makes his way to the water, but the noise of the workers still follows. Jack falls to the sand, falls unto his knees, and languishes there. The wind pours off the water on its way to replace the air that came before it.

Jack sits there the rest of the day. Listening to the noise of the work on the pier. Hoping that it would stop, that it would offer a moment of silence, and acknowledge Jack's loss. But it doesn't. Nothing stops. There is no pause. There is only being left behind. Finally, the day begins to end. As the light gets lower, the sun shows itself. All day long, it hides behind its own blinding glow, anonymously racing overhead. Dipping toward the water, the light diminishes. Tangible the sun has shape, it has parameters.

Jack watches the sun sink into the water. It is someone else's sunrise. As the very last of the sun descends, the tip turns a bright green. Hardly a flash, more like a wink of the eye. All that is left is a horizon still glowing pink and orange.

Jack strips out of his wetsuit and stands naked on the beach. He runs into the water and feels it splashing under his feet. Jack lifts his knees out, freeing his legs, racing through the surf. Once he reaches a certain depth, he lowers his head and dives in, porpoising through the surf by jumping off the bottom, to dive again, and push again. A wave crashes over him and he dives below the broken water so that it passes above him as he digs his hands and feet into the sand so that he isn't pushed back by the waters' momentum. And when it become too deep to porpoise, he swims. His hands carve underneath his body, and his legs furiously kick frothing up the water behind him. The air bubbles his mouth release roll across his cheeks, and parachute up toward the sky. He is chasing the sun.

Hours later, he stops. Exhausted, he lifts his head out of the water looks back to a shoreline he cannot see. He is beyond them now. He puts his head back in the water with his face looking towards the heavens. In the middle of the desert night, sky Jack sees a star and makes a wish.

CHAPTER 45

August '01

Jack's father sits on the strand wall in the same spot where they check the surf in the morning. Jack is the last of the group still on the sand. His mother headed up first under the pretense of getting dinner ready. Bree's mom and dad led her away quickly, so quickly, she asked them, "What's the rush?." But Jack knew the reason why, why his father is sitting there waiting for him. Jack stayed quiet when Bree protested against her parents ushering, why, for no apparent reason, they were all of a sudden in some big hurry.

And now Jack walks up the slight incline where the sand rises to meet the strand and its wall. He moves much slower than the small incline dictates. He finds the footholes that require the most steps, the smallest strides in which hardly any progress is made. His father patiently sits there, next to a wagon carrying all of their stuff, staring off toward the horizon. Jack looks down at his feet for the next step to take, and then, regretfully, he reaches his father, who pats on the concrete next to him, begging him to sit.

Jack can feel granules of sand underneath his bathing suit, and he shifts his weight uncomfortably. His father is quiet. His jaw slightly opens and closes as if he were looking for words to pour in, words he can't seemingly conjure on his own.

"What a perfect day," He finally spurts out. He still looks toward the water, toward the horizon, and the setting sun. The cirrus clouds are golden orange and have moved further over land, joined by others from over the water. The eastern horizon, the little Jack can see of it behind the small beach cottages on the strand, has darkened purple and fills the spectrum all the way to light blue, then green, yellow, orange, and red, over the farthest reaches of the water. His dad again opens and closes his mouth, his lips part, and then press. Jack can see them purse and then flatten. So much action for someone so silent. Then Jack hears the inhale. He knows what's to come. He wishes he could stop it, turn it into a sigh, but there is no loud exhale that follows, only the beginning of words that he doesn't want to hear, "We need to talk."

Jack shifts his weight again, brushes his hand underneath his seat, and stays silent, moving his foot over the ice plant, letting it tickle his insoles.

His father puts his arm over Jack and continues. "There is something I need to tell you... I uh, uh, got some news. Some important news."

Jack asks though he already knows, "Is it bad?"

The words his father speaks, that once seemed to drag on, now came on suddenly, quickly, cuttingly. "Well, uh, um, it's not necessarily good. The doctor found something that doesn't belong, and I need to get treatment to fix it." They shoot out of his mouth like a bullet. And though Jack knows it was going to be bad news, it doesn't alleviate the pain in hearing them hitting his ears.

Jack closes his eyes. "Are you going to be okay?"

"I hope so."

Jack is quick to respond as if he is offering a counterpoint in an argument. "Mom thinks you will be." Jack's father looks back at him, confused. "I overheard your conversation earlier." He lowers his head in embarrassment. "She doesn't think God would let anything happen to you." Jack clarifies.

"You were listening to us?" He wears a confused smirk.

Jack lowers his head again. "Yes. Are you mad?"

"No, no, I'm not." His father readjusts his legs, unfolding one, and crossing the other, then he pulls Jack closer to him. "Your mom thinks that everything that happens to us happens for a reason. That there is some great plan for all of us."

"She says that you were her destiny," pride saturating every word, "sent from God to save her."

"Yeah, she does say that. But she's never given herself enough credit. She is the one who saved herself, and I was just there to help. Maybe when you're older, we can talk about what she's gone through. She's amazing. One tough lady, your mom."

"So you don't believe that everything happens for a reason?"

"I… um… It's not that simple. Probably not in the way your mom does. What's the point if everything we do doesn't change anything? I believe we can make choices, and those choices end up determining all our lives. That isn't to say random things don't happen, things beyond our control. Maybe that is the predetermined part, all the things we end up facing. The things that just fall into our lives. But how we choose to handle them is entirely up to us. What do you think?"

"I dunno. What if there isn't a good choice? If all of your options are bad. Like what choice do you have in getting sick?"

"Well, I guess, this is just one of those times there's not much to decide other than to fight. Fight to be healthy. Fight to stick around and see you grow up. Fight for your mom. You're right. It isn't much of a choice. Just have to believe things will work out, you know for the best."

"It didn't with Adam."

"I know. It doesn't always. But you have to believe that even when things get bad, that they aren't so bad that you can't overcome them."

"You sound like the Monsignor, talking about faith."

"Yeah, I guess I do."

"I'm surprised to hear you say that."

"Why would you be?'

"Just today, I overheard you talking about not going to mass anymore. Even though mom would have a heart attack. And you're the one who has always pointed out where science and the Bible conflict. And you always bring up any church misdeeds in the news."

"I know." Now his father lowers his head. "And now you don't like going to church anymore, which I didn't expect, and I feel bad if I ruined it for you. But I never wanted to force you into anything. I want you to be able to come to your own conclusions, and how can you without all the information available?" His father lifts his head and looks Jack square in the eye. "It does make sense to go to church, right? We are naturally spiritual, and we are naturally communitive, so doesn't a spiritual community make sense? But faith, right, what we are talking about, doesn't come from a church. It doesn't come from religion. It's entirely human." His father squeezes Jack's shoulders and continues, "The church just reflects it, celebrates it, let's us celebrate it together, and it gives it a landing spot, but it was in us first. Before the written word, before language.

"Maybe God gave it to us, maybe it evolved in us, or somehow both. Call it Faith. Call it the will to live. It gets us out of bed in the morning, even on bad days, and it gets through tough times. It is why we prevail even when things seem harsh and bleak. It's why we stepped onto the African plains. Why we moved over frozen seas and onto far away continents. Sailed in boats across the pacific without knowing where inhabitable islands lay. It really is the most amazing thing about us. The belief that there is home out there for us, no matter what. That's why it is a part of all religions because it is a part of all of us."

Jack begins moving sand with his feet. Smoothing over one small uneven area and stays silent. Without looking at his father, he asks, "You're 100% certain that faith is real?" His tone is clearly skeptical.

"I wouldn't lie to you. It was a part of us for millenniums, and then it found its way into the scriptures. I know that it's hard to accept things that you can't see or prove. I have a hard time accepting certain things too, which is why I think it's important you make your own decisions about this stuff. If you accept these things without any thought first, you never really truly believe in them. So I am just sharing this with you to think about, right? Here, when you consider faith, just look at the sun. You can see it now that it has started sinking below the water, but it's practically invisible all day. Hiding behind its own bright light. Only an idiot would stare at it. Otherwise, it passes overhead completely hidden, but we know it's there because we feel its warmth, and it lights our world, and we can see the shadows it creates. We know it's present even if it is so unbelievably far away.

"And then there are times in our life that are so joyful, so pronounced we can see, and it feels like life just started. I felt that way when you were born and when I married your mom. And then there are times when we need it, and we can feel it so greatly that we can see it perfectly. See its form perfectly, just like we can see it now as it sets."

"But what happens after it sets? Does it leave us?"

"I know it can feel like that at times. But no. It's just somewhere beyond the horizon, ready to circle back to us again. And the stars are out. Billions, trillions, maybe an infinity of stars all casting their own light. Shining across the universe. To remind you that you're never alone.

"Jack, if you can't believe in things bigger than yourself, how can you see the world better than it is now. To envision what can be, as opposed to what is?"

Jack leans into his father, and they wrap each other in their arms and watch the sun sink into the water.

CHAPTER 46

September 19, '07

Most people would be terrified to be out at sea. To be buried under a dark moonless night far enough away from shore where stars have escaped the lights of Los Angeles, with nothing to hold onto, nothing to stand upon, and God knows what, filling the depths below.

Underneath a great black canvas, Jack floats at the surface above the leagues of water that lay below. He feels his open wound, a torn soul, and calculates all that has poured through it, everything that he has already lost, and the feeling of fading away overwhelms him.

Jack is out in the channel, a fissure on the ocean floor, an underwater canyon created by divergent tectonic plates. One plate flees west toward open water, while the other is slowly crushed under by another coming to takes its place. Out here, in deep water, is where monsters patrol.

The ocean laps over his shoulders, climbing his neck, and splashes unto his ears. Jack is exhausted, with not much more left in him. He raises his chin and breathes through his nose as he lowers further into the black sea surrounding him. He opens his mouth and lets the water pour in, and tastes the salt. Salt is everywhere. In every drop, and every drop has gathered to form a great ocean. The largest and deepest ocean. One named after peace.

The salt gives the water its buoyancy. Salt is lift. Salt is carry. One can let the salt pick them up, hold them, and keep them. Likewise, one can choose to slip under, to sink below, and let the salt drown them. To bury themselves not only under the night sky but under the night's inky black water as well. And lay themselves to rest in the rift on the ocean floor created from being torn apart.

The water climbs over Jack's ears, and he can so clearly hear his beating heart. His breath escapes into the night in a thunderous hush, and the following inhale is quiet in comparison and feels so short of what his body needs. The hairline above his forehead dips below the surface as he floats on his back, with only his face, eyes, chin, and mouth, out of the water.

He looks up at the brightest star to cut through. Its pulsating light is ancient. The star producing it is at an unfathomable distance, and even as fast as light travels, Jack sees the light it created before the dawn of man. Still, it has arrived at that moment to shine that down onto the water that night. A message from the past only now come home. He makes a wish. He can feel the depth below and space above. He isn't scared or worried. He's finally free. Free to make his own decision. And right now, he is only thinking of where he should let the salt take him tonight.

Jack takes an inhale, gathers his strength, and resolutely turns toward shore.

About The Author

Ry C. A. lives in Austin TX with his wife, two sons, and two dogs. He was raised on a beach in Los Angeles and still has a passion for the ocean and a life lived in it. While not writing, or parenting, Ry C. A. enjoys his time outside, hiking, swimming, getting in the biggest body of water closest to him, and making his way back home. The author is interested in any adventure, especially those that he can share with his family.

Made in the USA
Las Vegas, NV
05 July 2021

25922643R00148